D1274967

SIX
MILES
TO
ROADSIDE
BUSINESS

MICHAEL DOANE

Alfred A. Knopf

New York

1990

SIX MILES TO ROADSIDE BUSINESS

THIS IS A BORZOI BOOK

PUBLISHED BY ALFRED A. KNOPF, INC.

Copyright © 1990 by R. Michael Doane
Published in the United States by Alfred A. Knopf, Inc., New York,
and simultaneously in Canada by Random House of Canada Limited, Toronto.
Distributed by Random House, Inc., New York.

Library of Congress Cataloging-in-Publication Data
Doane, Michael.
Six miles to roadside business / Michael Doane.
p.   cm.
ISBN 0-394-58106-7
I. Title.
PS3554.0143S59   1990
813'.54—dc20   89-43293   CIP

Manufactured in the United States of America
First Edition

This book is for Graham Davis, Mark Donaghue, Justin Bearne, Neil Walker, Bob Friend, Chris Foulkes, and the rest of the tribe, fellow travelers in the cities of Nunc bibendum est.

And for my mother, Margaret Louise Doane.

"He who would do good to another must do it in Minute Particulars.
General Good is the plea of the scoundrel, hypocrite & flatterer . . ."

WILLIAM BLAKE, "Jerusalem: III"

CONTENTS

ROADSIDE BUSINESS 3

0 + 2.2 43

CATHEDRAL 65

THE ER 89

RUNNING WITH GABRIEL 145

PAINTER 161

ROENTGEN EQUIVALENT MAN 207

THE BOOK OF TOM 217

ABSOLUTE LIGHT 241

WALKING INTO LIGHT 247

SIX MILES TO ROADSIDE BUSINESS

ROADSIDE
BUSINESS

COMING through the Escalante Desert, at least ten more hard miles to Paragonah, in southwest Utah, he catches himself walking eyes up, forgetting to survey the ground around his boots for scorpions. It's nearly sundown and they'll be coming out to cool in the night air. This is the first time he's crossed the desert without a map and he's been saving his energy for these last miles. Now he is surrounded by distance and a vast silence, and every word he mutters to himself takes on an exaggerated weight. If he interrupts his confession to catch his breath, the clamor of the past seems to gain on him: a tiring argument about trespassing, coveting, pride, and false idols; whom he's bled and who's bled him. Contrition isn't the half of what he's up against. He has to use words instead of a compass to stay his unsteady course.

He is walking on a flat straight road, packed dirt on the desert floor, though it's occasionally difficult to distinguish the road from the rest. The whole desert looks like an enormous road. But someone took a tractor and roller and a lot of time to flatten out a determined strip between Modena and Paragonah, eighty empty miles from nowhere to nowhere.

He is out of food and water now, and therefore out of options. To his knowledge, there are no ambulances heading this way, and if he stops right here he may never get up again. One hundred and ninety-odd miles behind him and ten, maybe nine if he's lucky, to go. He recognizes the end of desert, as he walks into a region of red sandy soil with patches of bunchgrass and greasewood. Behind him, the land was sparse and dry and less forgiving than this eastern edge.

He climbs a steep rise and scans the horizon. Roadside Business is to the northeast, and he leaves the road to head straight for it. After a few steps he comes to a gully, where he stops, bends, and picks up a stone the size of his fist, painted blue. He assumes it is one of his own from a long time ago. The point has faded to a sparrow-egg blue, and one entire side is bleached white from the sun. He had forbidden the others to use this same color, reserving for himself the privilege of a personal symbol. Ego-ridden, Gazer had called him. As if Gazer could see better than most into the shadowy hearts of men. But when Painter and the others had gone out to do his work, they had obeyed the rule and had taken various other pigments in their bags; ocher, green, scarlet, gold, white. Never blue. Blue had become the color of Ravel's signature to the desert.

He stands erect and searches the eight horizons for signs of people and is relieved to find there are none. No Painter, no Weaver, no Gazer. Wherever the Er have gone, that dispossessed tribe of his own shameless making, none of them is on his trail. There is only the painted stone to remind him that his name is indelible in these parts.

When did he paint this? he wonders. Ten years ago? Eight? Five? Madness has its own skewed chronology and he can't remember the details. At the very end of his time with the tribe, he didn't paint at all. He didn't write or speak. He barely ate. He brooded. The others carried on the work, signing themselves to the desert in the form of painted rocks. The key to the hieroglyph: colors were nouns and the shapes of stones were verbs. But since red pigment was the easiest to manufacture, most of the rocks were painted red or pink or sickly orange. The Er carried on with the tradition, this rite of self-identification, and Ravel had slipped away. Now it's been three years, and here's this ancient blue rock to greet him.

Ravel, you've changed.

Not so much. Older is all.

Don't kid yourself.

I'm thirty now.

And no longer immortal. Not even well known.

For three years he has been among strangers and has had to insist upon the proper pronunciation of his name. Ravel, as in Ra-vul. No accent, the *a* as flat as this desert, as in sad, bad, had. It's an easy enough name to remember. Rhymes with travel.

The stone goes cold in his hand and he swears it has lost some of its color, though this may be only the effect of the failing sunlight. He drops the stone and it rolls as if on its own strength down the gully and comes to rest on a patch of mesquite. It occurs to him that by moving the stone he has disturbed the scene again, has rearranged the delicate chessboard of the desert into something unnatural. He feels a sudden urge to run, but the urge is canceled by fatigue. He cannot run. Walking is chore enough.

A thousand steps later he skirts the southern edge of Little Salt Lake and can see the place in the distance, the carbon strip of highway and the outlines of the low buildings. Roadside Business. He's been walking for eight days and hasn't eaten in two, and when the sun sets like a hot knife over his shoulder blade he feels a prodding from the cosmos to get home or to perish. When the light is almost gone, dwindled to a rose-and-lavender bruise, his resolve goes with it and these are real tears he's shedding, like water from stone, nasty and stinging of salt over his parched face. He refused to ride the last leg home in the guiltless comfort of an air-conditioned Greyhound, hoping that by the time he got this far he'd have agonies other than heartbreak to distract him: blisters, bruises, thirst, hunger. That the sun and salt would wither the tree of grief into a simple burning bush; then tumbleweed, then dust. He has no one but himself to blame. But all he ever wanted was to walk into absolute light like his father before him. This is his alibi, if not his excuse, for the mayhem that's occurred. He's been wandering aimlessly for far too long, from the west to the east and back again. Roadside Business is the only place left that can bind him to the earth. Elsewhere, he's convinced, he's run plain out of gravity.

Ecological corruption; desert rot. Things die out here that never get buried. Time vaporizes them. Time and the sun.

Cassie would be waiting for him, that coal in her eyes turned to diamonds with anger. Or she would already have shrugged him off like a dying skin. Their son, Jered, four years old when Ravel left, had just turned seven. He would have things to say to Ravel, and Ravel was willing now to listen.

He rode a Greyhound from San Francisco to Las Vegas and then got out to walk. He had the money to ride the rest of the way but was counting on the desert to distract him from his thoughts, to nail down, by virtue of sun and solitude, what three years of wandering had settled for him. Inflicting pain on yourself is just another quick way of preparing to face the music and where he was headed whole symphonies awaited him. He emptied what little he wanted to keep from his suitcase and put it into a paper bag, then gave the rest to an Ursuline nun on her way to an immigrants' orphanage in Flagstaff. For the fatherless, his unwanted shirts and socks would serve a purpose. Where he was going, he might as well be naked.

It wasn't as far as it sounds, two hundred miles, and anyway he didn't walk it on his knees. The western wilderness was dotted with towns where an occasional bed and bath did him wonders. When he arrived at the left-hand edge of the Escalante Desert, he scattered the contents of that cursed shoebox to the four winds and some of the ash blew back in his face; a sacrifice rejected and an insult from whichever gods he'd failed to murder properly. But at least he was shut of the whole deal. All he had left was that desert to cross. To Roadside Business.

South of Modena, he had this vision: It was night and the sky was like blue slate, clean and pure, pocked with mother-of-pearl stars. Rising from the desert were a man and a woman, both of them naked as at birth, the man's erection blue and shining. The image was so deathly clear that Ravel nearly fell to his knees in fright until, coming over a rise, he realized that what he was seeing was a drive-in movie on a nearby plateau. Strange. He'd thought that wasn't allowed in these parts, open-screen skin flicks, but the image persisted: the woman falling to her knees and embracing the man, her mouth opening like a red flower, the man's body yellow and hers a ghostly white, the hoods of sports cars, pickup trucks, and Dodge vans at their feet. Loneliness, not Ford, created the car. Ravel could imagine all the thrashing and clutching going on in the cars along the back ridge. Some came to witness and some came to sing along.

He watched until the film ended and the screen had gone black, the cars dispersing like white-and-red fireflies into the north. Alone, he felt an itching in his breast, as though he'd been bitten by something, a desert flea, perhaps, burrowing through tissue to get to his lungs. There would be a reddish welt with a white center, but in the darkness he couldn't see clearly. He wouldn't sleep that night. The moon was at three quarters and illuminated the desert floor enough that he could make out the contour of the dirt-and-tar road. All he had to carry him were the pair of boots he'd worn while working on a highway crew in Northern California.

Roadside Business lay before him. He followed the red horizon out of the desert and back to its fields of endless wanting. He refused to think of this as the end of his penance. It was only the end of the desert.

STRAIGHT-UP noon in Roadside Business, Utah. He awakens to a void of shadowless sunlight and the boom of a semi rumbling past, the long-hauler jacking it up to sixth gear to get a good run down the flats, heading southwest out of the desert and into the Nevada-Utah corner, toward Death Valley, away.

His bad habits are uncontrollable. *Bodhicitta*, for one: the thought of awakening. Sitting up in bed, he touches fingers to his face and opens his eyes to the sun, Sūrya. The burns on his face are healing and something in his eyes no longer hurts him when he looks at himself in the mirror. His mother has smeared his face with creek-bottom clay, an ancient balm of the dispersed Indians—Hopi, Papago, or Ute—invoking the spirits of healing if not the science. She calls in from the kitchen, saying that if he's up she'll make more coffee. "All I've got is cold but maybe that's how you want it."

He tells her hot and she says fine, adding that she doesn't have any Shy Knees tea. Which he never drank anyway, but that was the image Mircea had of her son. Beard, hair in a single braid, sitting lotus and sipping tea, staring at his own navel. His beard is long gone and his hair is cut short now, but his past has its power over all of them, including his mother.

It is Sunday but he decides he can no longer lie in bed. There are fences to mend as far as the eye can see. He's been in Mircea's trailer for three days of rest after his desert walk and now he's fit. She has hung a crucifix over his bed, hoping for a miracle, that her only son will forsake his false idols and come back to the True One, the Only One. That he'll make some sense of his life. He could tell her about burning the icons but it might only give her a false hope. He can't imagine humping through life with Jesus at his side and somehow doubts that He's holding any grudges. Ravel is nevertheless certain that if he and Jesus had crisscrossed paths out in that desert, the greeting would have been cordial.

The night he arrived in Roadside Business, half crawling through the front door of the trailer and into Mircea's arms, her first words had been of love for him and only later had she thought to praise the Lord. Balance, perspective. Sweet Jesus, I have my son again. Home from the desert to put an end to my heartbreak. Here is the sanctuary of a just God.

Ravel has been prodigal these many years, greasing her rail into paradise, and she loves him for his straying. In the old days, when he'd come in from the settlement to visit her, they would even pray together silently, heads bowed to the table or upraised to the tiled ceiling. Afterwards, she would ask him to whom he'd addressed his prayers and his answers were usually unsettling. Wehntwin, Tundun, Rukat-Tundun. Udgitha, Nidhana. "Don't ask me," he'd said, "and we won't quarrel."

She brings him his coffee in a cowboy mug, the handle a wide ceramic lasso. She has already been to church, having driven to Paragonah at dawn and stayed for two services, she likes the pastor so.

"The worst of summers," she tells him. "This one. Like eight years ago, not a breath of rain. The tap water is getting yellow again and tastes like sin. My tomatoes are tiny little things, hardly even red this year. I do miss snow."

Ravel figures it's been twenty years since she's seen it, but she still brings it up every summer.

He takes his coffee out on the porch for a look around. Roadside Business is what you might expect of a place deriving its name from a highway marker six miles north on Interstate 15:

PARAGONAH   1 1

ROADSIDE BUSINESS   6

There's an eight-pump Shell station with lead-free, regular, and diesel, condom dispensers in the men's and nothing whatsoever in the ladies'; out back, a rusted aluminum garage serves as a muffler shop. To the north about ten yards is a western souvenir store where Mircea works every day but Sunday and a Tastee-Freez that's closed more often than it's open, depending upon its ownership, which changes at regular intervals. It isn't true that you make a killing selling ice cream in the desert.

Behind these buildings, on a low, unriven flat, are three

mobile homes: a sky-blue sixty-footer, the Ravels, mother and son; an eighty-foot double-wide with a low chain-link fence around it, the Beechams; and a yellowed aluminum thirty-footer surrounded by various junk that belongs to Randy, whom they called Stand-up in the old days because of the many times he couldn't. Farther down the service road is a three-bedroom ranch house owned by a retired air force major who lives alone and spends most of his time holed up in his air-conditioned living room, cursing at the television. In the rear is a satellite dish the size of a small stadium and powerful enough to pull in channels from Lima, Brussels, and Copenhagen, though small good they'd do the major, who is monolingual. Most evenings near sundown his neighbors can see him, or hear him, out back of the house, gunning down beer bottles and Campbell's soup cans with his .22.

The settlement is built on a shelf of earth hugging nothing but a creekbed that is dry almost year round. There are mountains to the east, some near, brown and ash gray, and others farther off on the horizon, powder blue most of the time, a high series of flat peaks called the Paunsaugunt Plateau. Dry grasses grow here and there, and if you look closely enough you can see that the earth is really not as flat as all that but is ridged and veined and gullied, as porous as a broken heart. Rain, when it falls, is swallowed up by those gullies and an hour later the topsoil is bone dry.

Ravel finishes his coffee and Mircea joins him on the porch. He built it for her ten years back, laying a pine-plank surface across the wide east wall of the trailer and a rail around three sides. He painted it white but time and the wind have burnished it to the color of dust, and she has installed canvas deck chairs and potted marigolds, a char grill, a footrest.

"Why so many chairs?"

She says she's not always alone. "That's something you don't have to worry about while you're migrating around the planet. I read your worry in your letters and it was wasted."

He hadn't thought of his movements over the past three years as migratory, any more than a pinball considers its bumps and falls nomadic. He was close to unconscious most of the time; damn near inanimate. "So who comes?"

"The Beechams, mostly. Or other widows from Paragonah or Parowan, though I'd prefer it if they didn't compare dead husbands like they were all saints on earth. Always the same widow talk and cookies. And Cassie comes out quite often with Jered, usually on Sundays."

"That's today."

Mircea waves a hand. "She's already been and gone. You were sleeping and she said not to waken you. She didn't know what to say. Words and all. You might at least have called ahead."

So she's seen him before he could see her. He doesn't know if this is a good omen or a bad one. His facility with signs has vanished.

"I gave her all the money you sent and she sometimes wondered why so much. The presents, too. She'd accept whatever you sent for Jered but wouldn't keep the things you sent for her. I've got everything in the trailer still, the jewelry and books, even those dried flowers. Maybe she'll take them now that you're back."

He says they'll know soon enough. "What about her old man?" Cassie's father had opposed the union, to say the least. "Why settle on this oddball?" he'd asked Cassie. "What's so special about him?"

"His heart," she'd answered. Breaking her dad's heart in the saying.

"Her father," says Mircea, "wants to burn you for firewood. Says you abandoned his daughter and should be hung out to dry. You can count your blessings he's in retirement now and gone off to Arizona."

Which one of them abandoned the other is of no consequence anymore. *She* walked out on him, initiating the marital rain dance. But the next step called for him to follow, and he had sat alone and brooded in his own corner of the settlement and kept half an eye on the spectacle of the Er's collapse. Uncivilization had settled in like a sexual disease, manifesting itself at the extremities and then heading straight for the brain. By the time he'd split that scene there seemed to be no way to get home. He couldn't have come back to her like that, just the pallid flesh of him and his moth-eaten soul. Here, Cassie, choose whatever you want from this closet of picked-over rags. If he'd come to her then he wouldn't have stayed and the going would have been much worse.

Anyway, that's his alibi. He tells Mircea it's not as though he ran away.

She makes one of those sounds, a sigh or an inhalation. This is a woman who loved one man to the end of his days and has spent a quarter century in the arms of only his memory. There's no wondering whose side she takes in this matter.

"I've been doing penance," he tells her. "Prayers and all. And all I've got to show for it are these beat-up hands from the roadwork."

"I'd rather not hear all this, Vance." The look on her face is terrible, as though he's struck her. "Who on God's green earth asked you for penance? We just wanted you to come home."

Leaving him alone on the porch, she takes her gloves and shears into the garden to prune the dying branches from her plants. There are a few green shrubs, patches of marigold and alyssum, some rosebushes, and spindly salt cedar. All around, the soil is rocky and dusted with alkali from an ancient sea. Ravel never managed to teach Mircea how to filter out the alkali with water and charcoal. She doesn't need chemistry lessons, she says, to know which way the wind blows, and whenever her roses bloom she displays them to him with a smile of triumph, as if to show her imbecilic son what's what. Hauling a bucket from under the porch, she heads toward the rosebushes and leans over the cracked earth. "Shit," she says.

"What's that?"

"Dogshit," she answers. "Randy saved up a bucket of prime dogshit to spread around the garden but I just can't touch it. Not even with gloves."

He tells her to think of the roses.

"He meant to be kind," she says.

"Good dogshit makes good neighbors." As he says this his gaze drifts over to the highway, where a struggling speck rises from the apron to the road. A sixteen-wheeler that he figures is doing ninety is heading straight for it.

"Kindness," Mircea intones, "has an aroma all its own."

"Amen," says Ravel.

And he waits, in the silence that always follows that word, for the merciless collision of machine and mammal.

Things die out on that highway. Birds, skunks, even snakes. You feel a whump and in the rearview mirror you see squashed fur and assume the worst. But there's nothing to be done about it, you can't raise the dead, so you just keep on driving.

Ravel fetches a shovel from the shed, walks out to the road, and scrapes up the pancaked remains of an unidentifiable pup. A sudden way to buy the farm, the Grim Reaper roaring across your path at 90 mph. Looking up in mortal terror, you have only time enough to read the nameplate: International Harvester.

Nothing much to bury and nothing whatsoever to eat.

He has finished burying the pup when Randy strolls out of his rusting trailer and heads across the yard to say howdy. He is tall and thin, his gray hair swept back under his black cowboy hat, and the silver buckle on his belt glints in the sunlight. Only one of his shirt snaps is fastened.

Ravel has known him all his life and they've been an odd pair, the monk and the cowpoke. His memory of Randy is ambidextrous, and though he's happy to see his face he is also relieved to see he's unarmed.

Randy stops about four paces from Ravel and looks as if he's going to hold out his hand. But the moment passes just as suddenly, as though some nagging memory has kicked in.

"So weirdo's back in town."

Still holding the shovel, Ravel extends the other hand in Randy's direction, but Randy doesn't reach for it.

"It's a gesture, Randy. Peace and all."

"Fuck you, you space cadet. What's in the hole?"

"Dead dog."

"One a mine?"

Ravel says he didn't think to ask. "He was dead on arrival."

Except for the gray of his stubble, Randy appears unchanged. When Ravel was a kid and couldn't distinguish between vulgar and flashy, Randy was his hero. He had done a stint with the Marines but had always been a cowboy at heart, even though he rode a Dodge pickup rather than a palomino. When Ravel was ten, Randy had taught him how to shoot a pistol with his head held high and his arm parallel to the ground. When Ravel was twelve, Randy had given him his first whisky and a touch on the shoulder as from father to son. Randy's wives seemed to come and go with the seasons, though no one would ever swear that he'd actually been married. The last Ravel had heard he was alone.

"Must be one a mine," Randy decides. "Trash got his end in with a collie, and the bitch had pups. This was the last of them. Gray and brown and ugly as you, you hokus bastard."

"Great to see you, Randy. How's tricks?"

"You think you might be staying awhile?"

Ravel nods. "Thinking about it." Then he adds, "They still call you Stand-up?"

"What's it to you, space cadet?"

"You already said that."

"So in hell what? The words don't wear out, do they? Anyway,

no one's seen your choirboy face in two years and no one's missed
you 'cept your mother. You or your sick friends."

"Three," Ravel tells him.

"Three what?"

"I've been gone three years."

Randy's face takes on the colors of the sunset, livid reds and
swooning golds. "Who in fuck is counting?" He turns on his
bootheels and heads back to his trailer.

Ravel waits until he's gone before saying, "I am."

His sick friends, the Er. Hippie scum, vandals, dog-eating voodoo
trash. Hoodoo, Ravel? You do. They're still out there somewhere,
pawing the desert, painting rocks, and baying at the moon, waiting for the son of light to lead them out of darkness and into the
white fury of his holocaust. Waiting for Ravel.

What he'd meant to be a simple hideaway in the desert for
Cassie and himself had certainly become unholy with passing
time. Wherever you go you take your terror with you, your own
smell, the rotten seeds of your next failure. Ravel was not a
shaman but no one knew the difference, and what became, for
all of them, a blind kind of faith in him might only have been
blindness pure and simple.

He considers the string of years that led up to his arrival there,
all the days of living in one dingy place or another: an apartment
crowded with frustrated art majors, a houseful of Mother Earth
pot smokers and revolutionaries, a Zoroastrian summer spent in
a tent, the smell of stale incense clinging to his clothes, and not
a single day of those years can be distinguished, not one. Smudges
of youth and a blur of good intentions. The first step had been
when he'd gone north to college to get away from Paragonah and
his mother's endless preaching. He had a small stipend from the
government left over from his father's years in the service, though
continuing his education was mostly a flimsy excuse to avoid

finding a job. His Paragonah friends stayed home and watched television, getting cathode ray burns and feeling cheated somehow. Ravel and his new friends struggled through courses in subjects they were suspicious of. Wars were raging, race wars, ecological wars, Vietnam, and learning French was not the balm to soothe the burning. In a short space of time he closed his textbooks and began sleeping past noon. At night he separated stems and seeds and stared into the black light, the lint and dust turning to neon while drugs of many colors rode his veins. It was his age, he could tell you. Or he could tell you that he had other ideas.

After three years of failure at the university, he returned to Paragonah and lived for six months off his mother's good graces. She spoke to him regularly about looking for a job. "Not for the money, Vance. Maybe just for the distraction. Something to occupy your thoughts."

But he had already slipped off the Christian edge of behavior and begun to sample from the Eastern basket. Shinto, Buddhism, Zoroastrianism, Tao. The trappings of humility, his robes and bare feet, were a source of humiliation for his poor mother, who finally begged him to explain himself to her.

He was preparing, he told her, for a walk into light.

"Light?" she answered. "What light?"

Randy stopped coming by and then went to great pains to avoid the Ravels altogether. He even turned his trailer around so that the front door was facing the eastern hills and not his neighbors.

"It's the robes," he told Mircea. "Those robes and that chanting. And he keeps going on about his old man. You better have a talk with him."

The other locals, with the exception of Cassie, taunted him or mocked him. Paragonah was cowboy country, far from the sacred river Ganges. So Ravel avoided Paragonah and the trailers around Roadside Business. He spent his time walking in the desert or up the hills. He chanted and he prayed. He sat among rocks and scorpions and felt no peace. So he climbed higher, to a point in the hills from where he could look out over the whole of the Escalante Desert, almost to the spot where his father had taken that walk.

Into light.

When a pair of drunken yahoos beat him up for no good reason, he knew he had to leave Paragonah. The first thing he thought of was to take Cassie with him. She didn't trust him, she said. He could pray if he felt the urge, could even burn incense in the kitchen, but the robes would have to go. "And shoes would be a pleasure, really."

San Francisco. Tribes. Hallucinations. The sounds of finger bells and the smell of patchouli oil. They went Zen for a time and were kind to animals. Ravel was respectful to his woman and to his friends. The ecology was safe for his children's children, in the night, in the rapid-fire sunup and sundown of a strobe light, a white cross in either palm.

Ravel stopped doing drugs when his internal dialogue dried up and he realized that he didn't have anything whatsoever to say to himself. To carry around a soul with which you are no longer on speaking terms is a terrifying bore. There were nouns in the cupboard, the garden variety—man, house, dog, baby, street, et al.—but the verbs had disappeared; no being, no acting, no belonging.

A. B. C. Through the middle years of the seventies Ravel had a hard time integrating into his own country. The western states. He blamed it on his father. Not his dying but the way he had died, walking into absolute light like that and not leaving behind any word of why or what he knew. Ravel always assumed his father had seen something undeniable and was heading for those curtains of light with a given purpose, a golden certitude.

And after a decade of pointless fretting, Ravel finally headed into the desert with Cassie, who followed him and was a steadying hand to help him over the rough spots.

He wonders, seven years later, what they had thought they would become out there. Cassie and himself. He remembers only that in the beginning they didn't want anything more than each other and those limitless distances that they'd thought of not as lonely, only reaching, reaching.

Searching for a place safe from snakes and flash floods, Ravel had swiftly built a two-roomer of pine and stone on a high flat forty miles west of Roadside Business. It was deep in the desert, in the direction where his father had made his walk. They imported their water in fifty-gallon tanks on the back of a pickup and plowed dust and stone into a garden patch. Ravel remembers scratching the parched earth as if to find answers beneath the dust. Cassie kissed his broken palms in the night and he kissed hers, and the gesture was healing.

"We'll need tools," he told her.

"And time."

"Years."

She suggested they get married.

He cut his hair and cultivated a beard. Two rooms became three. They built a porch that faced east and conjured corn, tomatoes, cucumbers, and green beans from the once-dead earth. In the desert, the color green was a pleasant shock. Ravel intended to live and die there. In this language, that means it was home. Cassie swept scorpions from under the bed and Ravel began to paint rocks in the desert around them. There were groups of blue stones for each week in which they lived alone there, all unnumbered. Scattered time. Time strewn. He was doing what he had always said he would do, holding his breath until he died, but his tantrum was somehow serene and the quiet of the desert worked wonders on his frayed nerves.

Later they lived with the Er and the Er with them. At first the Er came one at a time, and then they came in small groups, like survivors from a war that went unreported. Cassie never told Ravel to send them away, though in her heart she must have prayed daily that they'd move on and leave the two of them alone again. She suffered them for Ravel. She who had always lived without a cross to bear. In the beginning Ravel was devout. Later, when he couldn't even read his own handwriting, there were enough crosses to go around for everyone, even for Cassie, who loved him.

There was a lifetime of breast-beating awaiting them all, and Cassie never flinched while he nailed her to the cross with the hammer of his lunacy.

T HE AIR is hot, and the young man pauses between breaths, measuring, exhaling, inhaling. For a long time he has been atop a short mesa, where he can keep an eye on the road and the low buildings alongside it. How long a time he doesn't know. He has slept and wakened and now it is morning again, or almost the end of the morning. The sun is straight overhead and his shadow is nearly his exact size. Later it will grow away from him, as if trying to leave him altogether. If he has no shadow, he will perish. His spirit will leave him and he will be only dead flesh. Someone will find his dried bones and wonder who he was.

Reaching into the larger of two canvas bags, he pushes aside the canned goods, his thin, worn blanket, socks, pocketknife, canteen, and cap. The papers are wrapped in a plastic bag to keep the water out and he extracts them from the bag and carefully smooths them over his knee. There are two uneven sheets, from a single page torn in half. Each of them has Namer's writing on it. The paper was once white but has gone yellow with travel and the edges are worn from his own fingers touching and re-touching them. The first sheet bears his old name, beginning with the tall letter that looks like a tree or a crucifix. Namer once told him to bury this name, to leave it below the desert floor, but he had disobeyed her. He was afraid that he would bury himself with that name, the writing of it, and himself turn to paper. On the second sheet is his new name, the first tall letter a bubble at the end of a stick. This name he can write. He can scratch it into the dirt with a stick or he can chip it into sandstone with his pocketknife. For a while he had a ballpoint pen that he stole in a coffee shop up north, but the desert made the ink dry to dust. And anyway, he didn't have any paper other than these two yellow sheets. So he writes his name in the dirt or on stone. But only if he looks at the paper first, to remember.

There is a book in the large bag and he takes it out as well. It is a paperback that he lifted from a trucker who brought him the last fifty miles to this place where he has to watch the road. On the cover is a woman with a torn dress and a man who is kissing her on the neck. It is his newest book; he has three now, and, as with the other two, he scans the pages to find his names, the same letters as those on his papers. In the first book he saw his old name many times but not once his new name. He took that for a good sign. In the second book, his new name appeared twice, but the first letter wasn't a tall letter. It was small like the others, as if it was weak. So when he saw a book on the seat next to him in the long-haul truck, he slipped it into his bag while the driver wasn't looking. He has been through many of its pages now and has not found either name. Whenever the wind blows, he is afraid he is disappearing and has to hold his hands in front of him to know that he is not.

When the sun is directly overhead, he folds the papers back into the plastic bag and puts them and the book away. He stops for a moment to survey the road below him. A car pulling a trailer stops at the gas station, and a man gets out of the car and bends to look at his right front tire. A dog is barking but from his perch on the mesa he cannot see where it is. Though the day is hot, there is smoke coming from the house on the other side of the gas station. Other than the man looking at his tire, there is no one in sight and the long white road is empty from horizon to horizon.

Reaching into his bag once again, he chooses a can of fruit cocktail. He opens his pocketknife and pries forth the can opener blade, then wedges it into the top of the fruit cocktail can. He works quickly, flipping the top, and replaces the can opener blade with his cutting blade. He spears first a pineapple wedge and then a slice of peach, eats everything, and then tips the can to his lips to drink the juice. There is a cherry pit left at the bottom of the can. He takes it out, digs a small hole in the mesa floor, drops in the pit, and covers it over. When he does so, he thinks of Namer and is uneasy.

He has to figure out how long he will have to wait and watch the road. He has been waiting longer than he can remember. He has come to this spot many times and has waited without seeing him. Sometimes he has lost faith and gone away, to the cities or to the small towns not so far off, to find food or shelter or just to hide from the sun and the endless light. But he always comes back to wait again.

A few nights earlier, while stealing those canned goods from a small store in the nearby town, he was almost caught. He'd spent a long time thinking how many cans he would need. Five? Ten? The number twelve was stuck in his mind, but he didn't know well enough how to count that high to be certain. There were already two cans of tomato soup in the space below his crotch, where, if he walked slowly, they would not be noticed. He put three cans of fruit cocktail under his shirt, in the pouch at the small of his back. He would have to turn at the door— facing the old woman at the cash register, who was reading a magazine—and back out of the shop. He'd been at his limit and known it and had begun to wander, as if shopping, up the aisle farthest from the register, when his gaze had encountered a rack of paints. There were large cans and small cans and a display of colors overhead. Reaching for a pair of small cans of the brightest white, he turned his hands so that his palms were to his back, then he approached the door at a sideways angle, with his back against the wall. The old woman didn't look up from her magazine, and as he reached the door he slowly turned, keeping the bulge of his shirt out of her sight. But just as he was backing out the door another man was coming in. When they collided, he dropped the paint cans and they clattered on the sidewalk. The man wore a cowboy hat and looked half drunk.

"Hey, Norma! Take a look a this one! I've caught me a thief!"

The cowboy had held him by the arm but he'd pulled free and run clumsily across the parking lot and into the street. Crossing into darkness, he'd continued to run, the cans in the back pouch slapping his spine and driving sparks of pain as far as his eyes. He'd run until he'd gone deep into the desert and was certain the cowboy wasn't following him. He will not be able to go to the same place again. Someone might recognize him. That means the next time he needs food he will have to go farther down the road and it will be a long, long walk. So he waits on another can of fruit cocktail. He knows how to wait. He knows how to let the time pass and he has memorized the colors of the road: the dirty silver of it at dawn, the pale blue in the morning, the burning white of the afternoon, and the sulfur gold near sundown. At night that road glows gray in the moonlight, and when there is no moon it is a charred strip on a black and empty surface.

Opening the canteen, he allows himself three swallows of water and dabs a few drops on his hands to run across his forehead. It is past noon and his shadow is growing out the other side of him, his gray profile distorted on the ground. He reaches for stones to place on that shadow where the eyes should be, but each time he moves the shadow moves with him, and there is no way to lean without missing his mark. So he places two stones a short distance apart from each other and then moves his shadow until they fit where the eyes should be. Gazing blindly back at him.

He hears a dog bark, looks up from his shadow, and turns toward the road. A small dog is struggling up the side toward the highway. He can see this with one eye and with his other eye the truck roaring down the road. He knows he is too far away to do anything. He has already seen other deaths like this. He has been waiting a long time. Once at sundown a number of birds were diving and swooping at passing cars. Eventually he counted three that had been caught by a windshield, tossed high into the air, and fallen dead at the roadside. The dog is in the very middle of the road, still barking, when the truck arrives. The driver doesn't even brake and the right front tire bumps just slightly as it runs over the body. From the distance, all that he can see is a black pool on the otherwise white surface.

Minutes pass and his shadow is still the same height. A car swerves to avoid the mess on the road and then he sees a man coming out from one of the trailers. His trailer. The man is carrying a shovel and walks deliberately across the yard to the highway. Something about the way the man walks makes him forget his shadow for a moment. He stands to get a better look. The man crosses the road, drops his shovel, and scoops up the dead dog.

From his mesa hideaway, he can see clearly enough. His shadow is standing alongside him. Together they watch the man carry the shovel back to the yard and drop the dead dog to the ground. He is certain it is him. He can recognize him despite the distance and despite the time that has passed since he last saw him. He is close now. He can almost be touched.

Climbing down from his mesa, he searches the desert for all that he will need. The cacti, the stone, and the wood. He fills an empty bag with his raw materials and then returns to the mesa to work.

First he breaks the dried cactus wood into long splinters and chooses the sturdiest among them. He takes out his knife, hones the splinter into a long stick, and slices away the bumps until it is straight and the length of his arm. Then he cuts a deep notch at one end and at the other end he fastens a pair of feathers he has been saving. They are tattered and no longer stiff and he worries that they may not be sufficient. But the arrowhead is intact, a parting gift from Gazer, and it fits neatly into the notch he has cut. Wrapping twine around the sides of the notch, he pulls tight and secures the arrowhead to the shaft. Then he holds the finished arrow before him and admires it for a long time.

It is nearly sundown and he stops to eat from another of the cans. When he has eaten all the fruit and drunk the last of his water, he takes a packet of powders from his bag and, slicing open the cacti he has gathered, he mingles the juices with the various powders and mixes everything in a large wooden bowl. The paint is thick and so he adds a little water, until it takes on the consistency he requires.

White. The first of the colors they had taught him to make. The naming. He begins with the pair of stones he'd chosen for his shadow's eyes. They are smooth and oval-shaped, the appropriate verb. Dipping a brush into the bowl, he applies the paint until both stones are fully covered, gleaming in the light of the dying desert sun. As soon as they have dried, he applies another coat. The white of white. The naming and the greeting for the man he has awaited, the son of the man who walked into light.

THE SOUVENIR shop where Mircea works is called the Outpost. Trinkets by the roadside are always a hot western item: handicrafts, pottery, postcards. Belt buckles in tin, brass, or silver, personalized or inscribed with generic nicknames like Gunfighter, Dude, and Cowpoke. Turquoise rings, string ties with arrowhead clasps, velvet paintings of desert sunsets, Indians on horseback, and the inevitable crying clown. Print scarves with fake Hopi writing, scattered symbols that, if correctly deciphered, might read Rocks Travel Sun High Corn Lost Sleep Rocks Trav, but the Pennsylvanians passing through on their way to Las Vegas can't tell the difference, and does it matter? Close to the cash register and locked under glass are the Authentic Items: fossil shards, arrowhead chips, swatches of Genuine Hopi or Real Paiute blankets, and unidentifiable bits of clay pottery. Some still have their paint.

You'd need more than a shovel and a thousand years of digging to know there were ever any Indians here. The Utes, venerable root eaters of the surrounding desolation, are long gone except for these souvenirs and keepsakes. The manufacture of Authentic Items takes place in a small house north of Paragonah where half a dozen old ladies meet once or twice a month, depending upon stock levels, to press fishbone to sandstone to simulate those fossils and carve arrowheads from rock, dye old horse blankets with Real Hopi Pigment, and smash their own oven-baked pottery into a dozen salable fragments. You can lay your money down with the best of intentions, seeking to own a relic of the past that might bind you to misplaced centuries, but the purchase will be an empty one. The charm of those artifacts, when you come right down to it, is as bogus as the Day-Glo Jesus on the dash of that passing station wagon.

Twin roads lead from Roadside Business to Paragonah, the interstate and the old county road, a ruined mosaic of asphalt and gravel grudgingly maintained by Iron County to keep the locals off Interstate 15. Ravel is taking the old road and has already covered two of the five miles on foot when a battered red pickup stops to give him a lift. He climbs in and there's Randy with his dog Trash at his side. "I suppose," he says with what he takes to be a shit-eating grin, "that you're lost again."

Ravel doesn't bite. "Paragonah's still this way, isn't it?"

"Same place," he answers. "The rest of the world turns but Paragonah just sits there."

"A still point," Ravel says. "Sitting lotus."

Randy glances at him out of the corner of his eye, as if looking at Ravel straight on would leave him vulnerable to some hex. "Don't you ever," he asks, "say anything that isn't half bullshit?"

Ravel is as fond as ever of the way they talk to each other, every other word a slap in the face. They've been doing it for years, and he assumes it was Randy's idea. If he ever had brothers, they were probably of the type who beat each other up to show affection.

Ravel answers that it's a form of sincerity, saying out loud whatever's on his mind. Drool runs off Trash's lips and onto Ravel's hand and though it might be considered holy water to a madman, he doesn't say as much to Randy. He says instead, "Same truck?"

"A hundred and sixty-six thousand desert miles."

Ravel whistles to show he's impressed. "My father had a '53 Ford that gave out at seventy-five thousand. You remember that car?"

Randy cocks an eye in his direction. "You plan on talking about him just now?"

Ravel says he wouldn't mind asking a few questions.

"One more word on the subject and I'll take you back to where I found you."

"I just—"

"You get to asking questions I can't answer and then you turn into a goofball again. I should a known better and left you to walk."

There are more than a hundred houses in Paragonah, the oldest of them, dating to the late nineteenth century, clustered together in the center and the rest arranged in a broken matrix, facing not each other but some private distance. To each his horizon. Randy drives through the middle of town and turns left toward the Two Guns. The bar is closed on Sundays, but Randy has known the owner for fifty years and by now they make up their own rules. In the center of town is a gas station that does about half the business of the place out at Roadside Business, a diner with three booths and a long Formica counter, a white pine Church of the Divine Word, a combination drugstore and garden supply, and a lone dress shop that seems to do most of its business in the week before Easter. The flash and excitement—Kiwanis Club, VFW post, cinema, and bingo parlor—are farther south, in Parowan. Paragonah only looks like the end of the road. When most people get there they just keep on driving.

Randy pulls the pickup into a lot behind the Two Guns and parks it in the slim shade of a yucca that rises out of the cracked cement. He points across the windshield with a trigger-callused finger. "She lives up there, on Cimarron Street. The white house in bad need a paint."

Ravel asks how Randy knew where he was headed.

"Ever hear of common sense, Ravel? Anyway, everything else is closed and you sure as shit aren't coming to the Two Guns with me."

Word is there isn't a breath of money in Paragonah and hasn't been in a century, since the silver mine was shut down. Poverty has long since settled over the brick-shard rooftops like sulfur dust, and the color of virtually everything—lawn, street, and sky—is ocher, yellow, tan, beige. Cimarron Street is an asphalt arm flung helplessly toward the blind desert: twelve houses, or cottages, the cracker-box variety, with square plaster walls and those rooftops tilted optimistically to run off the occasional rainfall. It is the end of the summer and the lawns are white wherever weeds don't grow.

He spies the house but is not prepared to approach it. All the time he's lost has got him by the throat. Across the street there's a Joshua tree with a semblance of safety to it and he takes up his position there, half hidden by a shelled-out Chevy Bel Air, combination rust and white metal, parked on the street. Out front of the house is a bike with a flat front tire, and the lower half of the screen door is torn. The house needs more than paint, he is thinking. The way Randy needs more than his Cutty Sark or Mircea her Jesus. What he needs is unnameable but the word is on the tip of his tongue.

When she comes out of the house, everything in him kneels down. She is carrying a straw basket and her long dark hair is pulled back, fastened by a barrette, giving her a Mexican air. She wears jeans and a rainbow-colored tie-dye T-shirt. Jered trails after her, lugging a cooler, and Ravel tells himself the boy is tall for his age but admits he has no way of knowing. There have been countless times in the past three years when he has tried to imagine his son, holding an out-of-date photograph in his hands and retouching it with his own heartbreak. He is five now, in kindergarten. In the afternoon he unfurls his nap rug and lies down but does not close his eyes. Now he is five and a half and Cassie teaches him to read one-syllable words: rain, wind, sun, moon. He is six and can swim from one side of the pool to the other. And now, as Ravel looks at him for the first time in three years, he is seven and Ravel recognizes the face he has imagined.

They cross the yard and head for the street. In a panic, Ravel realizes they're coming straight for him. Flattening himself against the earth, he sees their feet approach the white Chevy. Cassie opens the back door on the street side and puts the basket and the cooler on the seat. Jered gets in the driver's side and she tells him to scoot over. "You're too short to drive."

"Too young."

"Both."

Ravel sneaks a glance at the window and the boy is looking at him. He's hardly hidden at all, except from Cassie.

"There's a man," Jered tells her.

The car starts, misfiring twice.

"Where?"

"Hiding behind that tree."

"That's a Joshua tree, Jered. It's too spindly to hide behind."
And she drives away without seeing him.

The kitchen resembles the room that is his soul.

Dirty dishes, dried ketchup on the counter, bread crumbs, blackened banana peel, a brace of dead flies. Whatever's left over from the sandwich making: open mustard jar, yellow-stained knife, a lone pickle swimming in its juice. He gets to work on the dishes first, soaking the worst of them in a sinkful of scalding water. Dipping his bare hands into that water is a rite of courage and the pain cleanses him of unkind thoughts about what a slob Cassie has become. He puts away the remaining bread, wipes down the counter, and sweeps the dead flies onto the back porch. While drying the dishes, he notices a picture taped to the door of the refrigerator. It is a picture of his own face.

So I'm not all dead.

In one of the drawers he finds a knot of wire and in another a pair of scissors. Threading the wire through the torn screen, he stitches the loose ends together and then adjusts the side boards to pull the screen tight. The night is safe. The flies will be repulsed. There follows a long moment during which he doesn't know what to do with himself. Up until now he's been running on batteries charged with guilt. The house terrifies him. Too little is familiar and he is only too aware that *he* is the anomaly, the rent in the screen. What lets the flies in. This seems too much to think about, so he goes outside to catch his breath.

Seeing the weeds in the yard reminds him of what he meant to do in the first place. Work, he once read, is love made visible. A decent enough thought. He cannot bear the way those weeds in the yard give the house a look of having been abandoned. Bending to it, he begins tearing at them with his hands, but the ground is too dry and hard and he is getting only the grasses and not the roots. He circles back to the kitchen, where the best he can find is a rusted fork with two long tines. Still, the tool is sufficient and the weeds spring up from the concrete earth when he attacks them with oblique jabs.

That's what he is up to when the Chevy reappears and Cassie gets out from behind the wheel. Scrambling to his feet, Ravel drops the fork and raises his hands as if to show he's not armed.

"The neighbors called. They said there was a man in the house. I told them, That's not a man, that's Ravel."

"I washed the dishes," he tells her. "Then I stitched the screen."

"What on earth for?"

Something to do with my hands, he's tempted to say. Gestures insteads of words. Fixing what I can't fix just by looking into your eyes. He says only, "It seemed like a good idea at the time."

"And these holes in the yard. What are you planning on burying?"

"Nothing," he answers, all too lamely. "There were weeds."

She says she prefers weeds to nothing at all. "So does Jered. Weeds instead of just dirt. Did you see any grass on this lawn?"

He says he didn't come to fight. "Where's Jered?"

"With friends at a picnic. What did you think?"

He admits that he wasn't thinking. "I just came home."

"This isn't home," she says, the anger leaving her eyes. "This is a house."

"The house needs paint," he says. "No kidding. I can help you with it if you'll let me. I'm not begging, Cassie. I just want this, to paint the house."

"This is pathetic, Vance. Go back to Mircea's. I'll see you another time."

"Day, place, and hour."

"I don't know. Just go." She turns her back on him, sees the fork lying in the weeds. Bending, she holds it in her hands for a moment and then flings it into the street. "I hate your surprises.

I knew you were back and I *wanted* to see you, but not like this.
Please go."

"Afterwards, I'll get rid of the weeds. I'll paint the house and
then kill all the weeds. Jered needs a lawn, so—"

"Don't tell me what Jered needs!"

He can feel the heat from where he stands. This isn't what
he expected. He had this vision of a repaired screen door and a
weed-free garden awaiting their return; himself sitting on the front
step with a pitcher of lemonade, and Cassie coming close to give
him a shy embrace while his son looked on with wonder.

He watches Cassie's back as she walks away. When the car
door slams, it sounds as though she's broken something.

So that's how it is.

When she's driven away he goes walking without knowing
quite where. In random circles, he supposes. In Paragonah, every
road leads into wilderness; it's only a matter of time and a few
determined strides.

The Papago Indians had a meaningful symbol that they used
more often than any other. If you're looking closely enough, if
you keep your eyes on the earth and there's nothing up your nose
but fresh air, you can still see it on hundreds of hillsides, cliff
faces, and flat rocks around the American Southwest. A spiral is
all, an ever swirling circle. But you have to look especially close
to read them. If the spiral remains open, the last line trailing off
into space, it means someone passed through, an ancient form
of *Kilroy was here.* But if the spiral closes on itself, it means that
someone stayed. The Papago weren't easily satisfied, and the
passing through spirals outnumber the *stayed put* spirals by at
least one hundred to one.

When night has fallen, Ravel finds himself on the road between Paragonah and Roadside Business. Randy's pickup is nowhere in sight. No cars pass and he doesn't see a single pair of
headlights in either direction. A dry wind has begun to blow,
coming in from across the Escalante Desert, and he takes a deep

breath and feels his fatigue. His feet haven't yet healed from the desert crossing and this trek has reopened the wounds. He decides he has come to the place he was looking for and so sits right down on the ground. He first removes his shoes and socks and examines his feet. The breeze is soothing and he massages away the stiffness. Then he takes out his penknife and scrapes a spiral onto the face of a flat rock. No one is watching but God and the sudden stars, but it matters enormously to him when he carves the last of that spiral into a closed circle and the weight in his chest, though grievous still, feels lighter and the racket in his soul subsides.

The next morning, hitching a ride to Parowan, the county seat, he heads straight for the *Sentinel* office to put in a request for access to the archives. A woman behind the desk asks if he's a journalist.

"No'm."

"A historian, then."

"Neither."

"A writer?"

He shakes his head.

"Not the police?"

"Hardly. Just Joe Blow looking for someone lost."

She nods and smiles. "It's a national pastime."

Seated in a back room, he leans over a microfilm screen and turns the pages with black knobs. Horizontal from page to page, vertical from day to day. It is 1979, a desert autumn. There was unexpected rainfall, a sense of inverted spring, and a burst of supernatural green before the dry winds came. There were weddings, overdue road construction, a power failure in Modena, football games, and off-year elections. A nearby rancher took an M-1 to his herd of sheep to protest falling prices, and a local poll in the area condemned the taking of hostages in Iran, but the rising oil prices gave a boost to local coal interests. He scans through the words, raking in whole paragraphs at a time, in search of a body.

There was a body out there, alone in the dust, and he may be the only witness. Three years have passed and there are no photographs and no headlines on the film. Only tales of a rainy season turned dry, in which even the obituaries are brief and unremarkable and not a single homicide was reported in the region through the end of the calendar year.

Changing scrolls, he unravels the local history of the following year, 1980, whirling the film across a vertical chronology of white on blue that yields nothing of the vocabulary he's after: corpse, mummy, skeleton, remains. There is no evidence.

No roads lead there anyway; that's a fact. It is a place known by snakes and wild dogs. The body may as well have been on the far side of the moon.

To be certain, he wanders through one more year, knowing all along that he won't find anything. Shadows fill the room and a lone bulb burns yellow at his back.

What if they never found her?

Copying the number from Mircea's address book, he waits until past midnight and then dials Cassie's number. She answers on the third ring. "What? Hello?" Her voice is sleep-filled and soft. Familiar.

"If it matters to you, I'm sincere as the rain," he says. "I live in a tourist trap but I'm not just passing through."

"Vance? It's late. And who said you were just passing through?"

He begins to tell her about the spiral he's carved on the rock, but she says any more hocus-pocus and she'll scream, so he changes tracks. "When can I see Jered?"

There is a silence during which he imagines her biting her

lip. Their marriage isn't recognized by the state. The ceremony was homemade and anything resembling visitation rights is entirely in her hands.

"Wednesday," she says finally. "It's Founder's Day and Jered has the afternoon off school. You can baby-sit."

"That's a funny way of putting it."

"I'll put it however I like."

"Take it easy. I'm already down to the ground."

More silence. The static of regret. Don't say anything heartfelt, he reminds himself. We might start a brushfire of new anger and she'd only hang up the phone.

Cassie says, "He likes airplanes these days. You shouldn't show up empty-handed, so why not one of those."

"Color?"

"It doesn't matter. Just so it flies."

"What time?"

"Noon."

"Will you be staying for lunch?"

"I have other plans, Vance."

"What about later? Tomorrow night, maybe?"

"Your timing's bad, Vance. I waited a long time for you and then I just stopped waiting."

"You mean I'm no longer the only man on the dance floor?"

"My life isn't a dance floor."

"I'm trying to be breezy."

"I don't want breezy. I don't want funny. I don't want serious."

A pause. "Is this any way for us to hold a conversation?"

"I'm tired, Vance. I'm going to hang up."

And when she does he holds the receiver to his ear for a long minute and listens through the electronic humming for the sound of her calling his name.

I T ' S O N E of those mobile homes that have never been else-where. Designed for a nomad, it's been sitting forever unmoving over the same patch of desert, sixty by twenty feet of aluminum walls laid on leveled cement blocks, the wheels long since removed and the space between floor and ground wrapped with corrugated tin sheeting to keep snakes from nesting underneath.

They hadn't always lived in that trailer. Going there had been Mircea's idea when Vance was barely six years old. Moving into a trailer home had been a handy excuse for throwing out eight years' worth of a marriage's fixed assets after soulful months of sitting around the old tract house in Paragonah, waiting for Jack Ravel to imitate Lazarus and walk through the front door. There was no room in a sixty-foot trailer for all the furniture: the coffee table with a cigarette burn for every year; the E-Z rocker where Jack would put up his feet and read *U.S. News & World Report* and fall asleep with a cat or two resting on his belly; those photographs on the walls, lamps and lampshades, end tables, dining table; and a bed that was suddenly too large, too wide, to allow a night's gentle sleep. None of it would fit into the trailer, which suited Mircea just fine, so it all had been burned. Mircea had carted four pickup loads out into the flats and waited until sundown to light the pyre. There was no thought to giving it all away, selling any of it, or putting it into storage. Instead, Mircea had followed this Indian ritual: send up in smoke what was Jack Ravel's, who is now smoke himself. He will be there to claim it.

"You loved him. Was the sex good?"

"Such a question, Vance. Don't ask a mother such things."

She glances toward the rosebushes, where the blossoms are fading. "I wasn't everything he wanted."

"No wife is, but did he smile before sleeping?"

"Mostly. Not every night."

So he slept with hardening seed now and then, Vance's theoretic brothers and sisters. Fit to burst.

"But mostly."

Or wetted of himself and at rest, liquid-limbed and grateful, kissing Mircea's shoulder with his lips still hot, the word *please* smudged into *peace.*

He was originally from Billings but had joined the Marines at eighteen, just when the war had started in Europe. They had met in 1950, in Salt Lake City, where he'd been stationed as a recruiting assistant, a job that had frustrated and angered him. He was already thirty and had the look of a man running short of experience. He didn't have much to say to her, but he was a smooth dancer and had done his courting patiently, moving through the steps of handshake, flowers, kiss, and bent knee with a touching, if slightly military, precision. After a year of this they were married, and then Jack had gone off to Korea, leaving Mircea pregnant with Vance. He'd thought he would make officer during the war but it hadn't happened. He'd come home a sergeant, one stripe gained for two years of heart-stopping fear and boredom.

Mircea was twenty-one when she married him, was almost Vance's age when he died, and is past fifty now. Ever since she moved into the trailer, she's made do with the souvenir shop and the twenty-year Marine pension Jack left to her. She still refers to his death as *the accident*, as though one of her angels had slipped up tragically, and still she has not gotten over the fact that he never made officer, not in more than twenty years of loyal service to his country.

"It had to be that business back in '57, when his uniform got stoled by a Communist. It was his testing uniform from when he was on that project, that bomb business. They never forgave

him that and so they wouldn't keep their promise to make him
an officer. And then he had the accident."

When Vance was old enough he'd talked to a witness who
said it was no accident, his old man's death. Minutes before zero
hour he had been seen walking into that doomed flat—*strolling,*
is how the witness put it—as though he hadn't known they were
counting down. "He even left his walkie-talkie back at the base,
like he didn't want us talking to him, you know?"

Some years before he died, Mircea found an armband in one
of his dresser drawers. Beneath his socks were his girl magazines
and beneath those magazines had been the armband. Red nu-
merals 0 + 2.2 on a white background. "What's it, Jack? This?
What is it?" He said it was for some sort of club he was in, some
men's thing at the base. Didn't mean nothing.

Vance drinks the last of his coffee and risks a glance at
his mother. She is staring at the rosebushes, lost in thought.
He'd like to ask her if she's heard of a body being found out
there. Female, Caucasian, with a punctured skull. Not the
type of question to put to his saintly mother on such a fine
morning.

"Mircea," he asks instead, "when was the last time you had
a vacation?"

"Why don't you call me Mother anymore?"

"Habit, I guess."

"Last summer. I went on a vacation last summer."

"Where'd you go?"

"I sent you a postcard."

He reminds her he hasn't had an address in three years.
"Seven if you count the settlement."

"I went to Provo to see your aunt Elizabeth."

"Why not Las Vegas? Or Reno?"

"I don't gamble, Vance. You know that."

"Lake Tahoe, then. Somewhere relaxing."

She takes the last of his morning coffee and throws it down
the drain. "I relax just fine at church."

They sit together on the porch, their chairs facing the roses. The ground around the rosebushes is strewn with petals. Mircea says, "I talked to Randy this morning."

He only nods, waiting.

"He says you're asking the same old questions."

"What questions?"

"About your father and that bomb business."

"I didn't ask anything. He wouldn't let me."

Mircea stands, then sits. Changing her mind, she stands again. Here we go, Ravel is thinking.

"I disapprove of Randy," she says. "He's a good man, despite the way he lives his life. He is a loyal neighbor and I respect his opinion. What is it you wanted to know?"

"Same old story."

Pulling her chair next to his, she sits down and takes his hands in hers. Her knotted hands are deeply tanned, and the sight of them somehow warms him.

"You're making me feel old with all of this, Vance. Where will it lead to?"

"The end?"

"Your father's dead, Vance."

"That's the long and short of it?"

Wherever Ravel had traveled, he had a habit of keeping his eyes open and looking closely at men his father's age. He would be around sixty now, with thinning hair and probably a paunch. Someone might have been mistaken. If he hadn't walked into light, then he might have walked somewhere else. The hard evidence of his death was in short supply. No body, no gravesite.

"I love you, Vance. I hate to watch you do these things to yourself."

Ravel puts on his boots.

"Where are you going?"

"Here and there. Up to the hills for a look around. Some place where you won't have to watch."

. . .

Glorious morning, endless sky. Dressed in dust-blue timeworn Levi's, new cowboy shirt, and his desert-trek stomping boots, Ravel goes forth. The desert floor is already hot under his worn soles, and whatever wildlife is in the area, bird, rat, or snake, is hidden in shadow and burrow, out of human sight. The retired major is taking potshots at backyard refuse and beer cans leap from the ground, pinged; shattered bottles leave seeds of glass in the dust.

Taking along a canteen of water, Ravel heads north where the flat rises onto a plateau overlooking the highway and into a greater expanse beyond. God, these vistas. He chooses a spot he used to know well and sits facing that distance for long hours, drinking occasionally from the canteen and waiting for the silence to enter him. It is a private ritual, neither Eastern nor Native. Knees folded beneath him, eyes straight forward, he looks into the sky just above the sunburned horizon. The sun swings a slow arc over his shoulder, on a path to Las Vegas, and Ravel shifts his weight gradually until he is staring toward the southwest, where, in the midst of that desert, his father watched bombs land, ignite, and bloom upward. In its place is a perfect stillness, a vastness that ends, even on the clearest of days, literally nowhere.

Looking down upon the highway, he sees two specks moving across it, approaching each other from opposite directions. A blue point and a black point on the blue-brown dead sea bottom of the desert. A pair of atoms converging on the same space. They seem about to collide, but when he blinks they have already passed each other, and the distance between them lengthens until they disappear, almost at the same moment, at opposite ends of the horizon.

"What did the numbers mean, Mircea?"
"What numbers, Vance?"

"Zero plus two point two."

"Ground zero. Two point two miles. I figured it out myself after he was gone. I had a lot of time to think things through that first year. It was his first watch distance, the first time he saw the bomb. He was two point two miles away."

0+2.2

EVERY YEAR for the past five years, the club has held its
annual reunion, come hell or high water, on the first of July,
amid the rhinestone and glitter of Las Vegas, Nevada. Anno
Domini 1957 has seen the club dwindle from its original thirty-
four members to a dozen, and of these, only seven have shown
up for the get-together. What once was an affair of diversified
activities, including golf and tennis tournaments and luncheon
buffets at poolside, has at last settled, as if inevitably, into the
masculine basics of drinking, gambling, whoring, and intense,
often shouted, reminiscing. The remaining seven, thinking of
themselves as The Only Ones Left, congregate at noon on the
third of July at the Last Chance Saloon for a final drunk and a
round of beery goodbyes.

Wilkins, Danzel, Gabriel, Palmer, Ravel, Hernandez, and
Sloane take up two adjacent tables in the back of the bar. Above
their heads is a mounted pair of longhorns and a neon display
of a woman pouring beer, the neon rising and falling to dress
and undress her. Hernandez, craning his neck, can't keep his
eyes off her. "Reminds me of someone," he says when Wilkins
kids him about it.

"Girlfriend or wife?"

Hernandez says he isn't married anymore. "It's down the
tubes, my marriage. Didn't I tell you?"

Wilkins wants to know what happened but Hernandez isn't

saying. "It's something private," is all he can come up with. Closing his eyes on the word *private*.

Wilkins, the only one of them other than Ravel who is still in the service, orders fourteen bottles of beer and two fifths of Wild Turkey, boilermakers still reigning as the drink of choice. An overweight woman, stuffed into a green cocktail dress, lazily carts over their order in three trips. Her blond hair is pinned and twisted into a makeshift beehive that seems on the verge of falling over. When she hands a bill to Wilkins, the obvious leader, she tells him, "No credit," and he pays up on the spot.

Danzel says he doesn't feel like drinking anymore. "Too soaked already. Waterlogged and can't see."

Palmer coaxes him into taking a glass in hand and going bottoms up. "Or you can just sit there like some cigar store Indian, staring into space. I can't say I give a rat's ass either way."

Wilkins, Ravel, and the others all stoke up, kicking back a shot or two as though to show him how it's done but Danzel doesn't bite. He just leans back in his chair, hands folded like a deck of cards, and glares at them.

"You have become," Palmer tells him, "the pain in the ass I once dreamed of being."

"Listen here, Danzel," Sloane starts in. "Have yourself a shot or two. It might grow your hair back."

But the joke is already ancient, given its two-day and two-night life span: from the rendezvous at the Golden Nugget to the floor show at Caesars, from the dim-lit cathouse in the desert to bars, to electric casinos, and back to the Last Chance for a late breakfast of sausages and tequila. Hair today, gone tomorrow. Hair's to you, Danzel. Alcoholic humor that hasn't conjured so much as a wisp on the cue-ball surface of Danzel's skull. Each of them has a superstition, a remedy, a solution: get drunk, get laid, drink a fifth of Wild Turkey while singing "Semper Fi," or stand out under the nighttime desert sky and let the moonbeams do their damnedest. They've all purchased Hawaiian shirts for the occasion and have chosen for Danzel a hula girl motif, claiming magic in those grass skirts. But Danzel is stuck with his shitfaced grin and his confusion.

"It all came out at once," he explains for the nth time. "Not gradually, you know, like with my old man. There was whole clumps of it on my comb, and I was using this real fat-needled comb my wife gave me."

Sloane is staring at the neon knockers, wondering aloud if anyone on earth has a rack quite like that.

"Like what?" Hernandez asks him.

"Like enough to drown in without gettin' hurt."

"We all lose our hair sooner or later," Wilkins offers. "With you it was just sooner."

Danzel says he's only twenty-six. "That's too damn soon."

Hernandez says he's seen a stripper with a fifty-six-inch bust. "And they stood up real nice, too."

"Her hair?" Danzel doesn't follow.

"We're onto more important subjects," Palmer tells him, "than the state of your goddamned follicles."

"My what?"

Telling everyone to stop kicking a dead horse, Ravel asks Gabriel how his gambling panned out.

Gabriel risks a shot of Wild Turkey and follows it up with a swallow of beer. Catching his breath, he announces, "The system failed."

Palmer asks what system. "You and your numbers, Gabe. Seems like if you squint enough you can believe whatever you're seeing."

"You can't take luck to the bank, Palmer." Gabriel is thin, frail, better educated than the rest of them. Ravel remembers him as the worst soldier ever to serve in one of his platoons. He was long on contemplation and short on reaction. Just what any platoon leader hates: a soldier who thinks too much.

"I suppose you think a roulette wheel is just plain chance," Gabriel tells them. "As if the ball just falls into any *random* slot."

Sloane leans across the table until his nose is a foot from

Gabriel's face. "So tell us, Gabe. Tell us what it's all about."

"It isn't just luck," he answers. "It just isn't, and stop looking at me like that. The numbers make a field of thirty-seven, including that double zero. Even and odd, red and black, rows and columns."

Wilkins says, "We know the game, Gabe. Can you speed this up a bit?"

"Well, that double zero is green, and *that's* where the odds fall to the house. And some numbers fall more often than others; don't ask me why. But it might be that some numbers have more weight than others. Something more than simple mathematical value. As though they are chosen."

"Chosen?" Palmer slaps his forehead. "Chosen, for Chrissakes."

"It isn't random," Gabriel insists. "And there's no accident involved."

"Accident meaning luck?" Ravel asks. He has this habit of pulling Gabriel out of holes. Or at least trying to.

"That's not the word I'd use," Gabriel says. "Last night I saw the same numbers coming up over and over: eighteen, twenty-six, and eleven. I watched for five hours and that's what fell. It could have been the table; I don't know. But those were heavy numbers."

"And when you put your money down," Palmer asks, "then what?"

"I already told you. The system failed."

"To the tune of?"

"Two hundred and fourteen dollars."

There is laughter all around, not all of it sympathetic. Wilkins pours another round of golden shots. "Systems *do* fail now and then. Blown fuses, frayed wires, leaky pipes. And us standing on the outside looking in on what we done."

Wilkins is still a Marine and has been assigned to Camp Pendleton for the past two years. Prior to that, he'd been at the Nevada Test Site, on maneuvers with Ravel. He was the next-to-last of the original band to be rid of the site, leaving Ravel behind with new recruits and creepy-looking science officers. It was the Plumbbob series that had driven him away. "They're getting too big for me," Wilkins had confided to Ravel. "All those kilotons. I see the bones in my hand one more time, I just know I'll have scrambled eggs for brains." The transfer had put him back two full years in his quest to be made a lieutenant but he figured the move was worth it. "When I get my bars it won't be for running around the desert in a white sweat over mushroom clouds. If you get my drift."

So of the original thirty-four members of the o + 2.2 Club, only Ravel is still at the site, still watching, still in maneuvers. Ravel, a sergeant, always had a way of getting left behind.

Palmer is saying it's really too damn bad about Collins, and maybe they should drink another round in his memory. It's been a handy excuse, Collins dying like that, to tip one back, and Palmer hasn't missed an occasion.

"I know I always treated him rough," he says, "but I didn't know any niggers before Collins. He was an all right guy, though. Minded his manners and knew his place. I just can't handle the idea of a kid like him getting cancer."

They have had the news through Ravel, who, as club secretary, had remained in close contact with Collins. After his discharge, the private had moved to northern California and a job in sanitation. His cancer had been diagnosed prior to the fourth reunion but he hadn't told anyone except Ravel. "It's my bones," he'd said. "They're just turning to powder. Everything hurts me like a toothache but worse. Don't count on me for next year, OK? Doc tells me I'll be history before the year is out."

The Only Ones Left lift their shot glasses to their chins and knock one back in Collins's memory, while Ravel wonders if this might be the last of their reunions. How many less than seven, after all, can make a go of it? This dwindling, this subtraction, is getting morbid. A year ago there were seventeen of them, the year before that twenty-four. In the interim, some have moved farther away, or gotten married, or simply lost interest. Two of them, Kelly and Whitaker, are said to be pretty sick.

Wilkins says they're all getting old before their time. "Must be from all we've seen. Like we're chosen for something, or have *been* chosen. Any of you ever get that feeling?"

Gabriel says it's not unlike a secret priesthood. That they are the only men nowadays who can truly know the state of the earth. "No one else has seen what we've seen. The shots, I mean. The mushroom and that awful light. We did see that, didn't we? Sometimes I wake up at night thinking it was only a dream. Not necessarily a nightmare, just a dream."

The others all assure him that it was no dream.

"Zero plus two point two." Hernandez reminds him of the numbers. "That's a military precision, Gabe. We couldn't have made that up all by ourselves. Not out of thin air."

In all, they witnessed half a dozen shots together, two platoons working sisterly fashion through a series of trenches dug specifically for their exercises along the flats of southeast Nevada. Wilkins's platoon was code-named Earthworm and was assigned to move from trench to trench in a forward motion, dispersing in attack bursts and then regrouping at the next line of trenches. Ravel's platoon was called Sidewinder and its mission was to approach ground zero at oblique, crisscross slants. The club was formed as a result of their first shot, code-named Rainbow, which they witnessed from a distance of 2.2 land miles. Rainbow was a simple eight-kiloton device, a cherry bomb, according to later reports, compared to what they would see in the coming months. They were at the test site for six dirty weeks prior to the shot, during which time they lived in tents and suffered the desert heat and pointless drills and routine boredom while waiting for zero hour. From day to day, there was little to be done other than the morning run-through. Earthworm and Sidewinder, thrust and slide. Reminders to direct all fire toward ground zero. Attach film badges firmly below the pocket flap. Card games and rations and not enough Lucky Strikes to use as poker chips. Those six weeks had left them all edgy and in disarray, and when the winds blew at night Ravel sometimes heard screaming or cursing from the other tents. What kind of war is this? he wondered.

The waiting had continued, a countdown of hundreds of thousands of seconds.

Ravel had come with his platoon from Camp Pendleton and had not been told what to expect. Other than briefings concerning the maneuver, his only instructions had been to ensure that his men were turned away from the site at the moment of detonation and that no one should leave the trench until orders had been radioed ahead. To better simulate combat conditions, his platoon was given C rations the preceding night and told to paint up with emery around the eyes even though the blast would be some time before daylight. At four a.m. the two platoons were loaded into trucks and driven to the trenches, which had been dug several weeks earlier and were by this time half filled with dust and sand. Ravel put his men to work deepening the trenches, not so much because they were too shallow as to give the boys something to do while waiting for further instructions.

At around four-thirty a loudspeaker commanded them to take position. This first time, only Ravel had been issued a film badge, a gamma film pack with two exposures in a flat paper sleeve. He kept the badge in his fatigues pocket and protected it with his battle jacket. After the exercise, he'd been told, he should report to the lab and turn over his badge to the technicians. No one explained to him what the badge was for. Later he would find out, and never again would he wear that badge beneath his clothing; he would wear it on the outside, where it would be fully exposed.

At five a.m., with both platoons in place, they were given the order to kneel. Everyone followed instructions to the letter. They all slipped on their gas masks and knelt low in the trenches. Ravel watched to be sure that they kept their backs to ground zero and covered their eyes with their forearms. He was the last of them to get into position. Gazing off toward ground zero, he clearly saw Rainbow suspended from a helium balloon and a scattering of trucks and tanks across the flats. Somebody's pulling a fast one, he thought. This must be just a dress rehearsal.

Before getting into the trench, he reminded Gabriel and the others to keep their heads down low and their eyes shut tight. Then he too bent to one knee and tilted his head forward.

For long minutes the loudspeaker issued static, a disquieting signal at the butt end of night, and then an electrified voice began the countdown at sixty, to fifty, to twenty, to ten, four, three, two, to kingdom come.

Danzel says he doesn't think he'll be showing up next year. "It's a hell of a ways for me to drive," he explains. "I'm still living in El Paso, and I am thinking aloud here about how it's a damn long trip just to get drunk with you guys."

Wilkins says if that's the way he feels.

"Last time I went home, my wife could smell the pussy all over me. I couldn't smell a damn thing but she swore it up and down."

"She saw it in your eyes," Palmer tells him. "That satisfied glaze."

"Well, this time I'll be straight enough and she can smell me all she wants. It's not like I been fooling around this trip. Not like you guys. All's I did was look."

Hernandez, by this time fairly drunk, confides in whispers why his wife divorced him. "She wanted kids," he says to Ravel, the only one who can hear him. "But I couldn't make any for her. We checked it out. It wasn't her; it was me. Something missing in my juices, I guess. I think it over sometimes and usually decide I'm still a man. What do you think?"

Ravel nods and keeps his eyes on his own shoes.

"I mean, I can still get it up. *That's* something to think about."

Palmer points at his watch and says it's time for him to hit the road. "The heat may kill me but I plan on making it to Fresno by nightfall."

Wilkins says surely he can stay for one more round.

"The road round. Round road. Round red road." This from Sloane, who, of all of them, can hold the least alcohol.

Palmer says not again. "Last year I found myself in the ditch two or three times and I don't feel like driving like that no more, Chinese-eyed and all. You boys have one in my name and say a Hail Mary or two over the next few hours."

Danzel asks what's a hell mary and Hernandez makes a rapid sign of the cross. Danzel still doesn't follow.

"Prayers," Ravel tells him. "Hail Marys are prayers."

Palmer stands, salutes them all, and heads out the door into daylight.

Sloane says now he lays himself down to sleep, and he puts his head in his forearms.

Wilkins reaches across the table and lifts Sloane by the hair but the man is dead asleep. "First casualty," Wilkins says to no one in particular.

There was a loud click like the sound of clapped hammers. The first thing Ravel sensed was a tremendous heat along the back of his neck and through his helmet, and the air went hot all around him, filling his eyes and mouth and nostrils. The force of the following shock wave, later estimated at two hundred miles an hour, pushed him lower down into the ditch, where even the dirt was warm to the touch. Though his eyes were closed, the flash was so intense that he saw, through his eyelids, his arm lit up like an X ray. The bones were revealed clear and white inside a red cylinder of flesh. This image stayed with him for long seconds and then he heard the roar of a stampede crossing the flats straight for him and was tossed back and forth against the walls of the trench while dust and rock fell over him. His only thought was that death had come with the wind and that later, somewhere on that film badge would be an X ray of his heart in midbeat, a clenching and a never letting go.

Danzel has a Greyhound to catch and doesn't want to be late. On Wilkins's angry insistence, he downs a last beer anyway and then heads out of the Last Chance with his duffel bag slung over one shoulder. A real misfit, Ravel is thinking while watching him go. The original square butting into eternal round spaces. After pushing open the door, Danzel stops and stands for a while with a forearm shading his eyes, trying to adjust to the afternoon light. He closes his eyes, shakes his head, opens his eyes again. The sun over Vegas appears too much for him and he finally turns back to the table, those red eyes betraying his anxiety. "Anybody got any sunglasses?" he asks. "I can't see a thing with all that sunlight."

Ravel gives him his own pair.

"I'll send them to you," Danzel promises. "In the mail."

Ravel says not to worry about it, thinking to himself that the last thing he needs is the sunglasses off a dead man's eyes. When Danzel walks out the door Ravel knows it's the last he'll ever see of him. So does Wilkins.

"You know what he took at that last shot? Three point four. I was there when they checked the film badges. Three point four rems and that badge of his was laying *under* his battle gear."

Wilkins and Ravel had learned too late but at least they had learned. Danzel never knew anything, or if he did know he kept his mouth shut. He was the fastest runner in his platoon and liked to show it off during maneuvers. Half a dozen times he had charged ground zero and twice he'd made it within a hundred yards before being pulled away by men in lead-lined suits. Now he's walking slowly across the street shouldering a duffel bag filled with dirty laundry and some cheap Vegas souvenirs. He's heading for the bus station and a long and painful ride through the desert.

The sun burns the top of his hairless head while he squints through dark glasses and wonders why all of a sudden he's lost his hair and has these headaches and now on top of everything he's getting to be as blind as a bat.

Roentgen equivalent man. Rem. This time, when he gets the news, Ravel might not even send flowers.

Everywhere there was a thick dust, and when the platoon finally made it out of the trenches Ravel needed several panicky minutes to get everyone into formation. Palmer was screaming and tearing at his hair but responded to a boot in the ass and eventually rallied to position. Ravel had been instructed to await a signal from Wilkins's platoon, five hundred yards away, but in the swirling dust he couldn't see more than ten yards into the distance. Atkins's radio had melted onto his back and the loudspeaker that relayed the countdown was blown away in the shock wave. There was a stench of electricity, of blown fuses and smoldering wires. When Ravel tried to spit there was no saliva left in his mouth.

Formation Sidewinder. Dip and swerve. Advance, retrench, open fire. Fan out and swing an arc toward the north. Regroup. Men were bumping into each other in the dark of day, falling down, running the wrong way. Twice Ravel was forced to chase after Gabriel and shepherd him back into formation. Sloane was swearing all the while and emptied his magazine of blanks before receiving an order to open fire. When they had advanced half a mile, a fine ash began to fall like snow. Ravel brushed a few flakes from his jacket and found burn marks in their place. For a full minute, the platoon was alive with fire and Ravel ordered everyone to roll in the dirt until the ashes were extinguished.

Only minutes after detonation, the mushroom had already risen three miles into the Nevada sky and it was still going. When he was only a mile from ground zero, Ravel stopped briefly and watched its ascent, feeling himself drawn to it, mesmerized by its vastness, as though it were a mountain that had thrust upward from the flat and taken off toward the heavens. Red and gray and black and gold and white, the colors kept shifting and building and churning. He heard overhead the drone of a plane and could just make out the shape of it through the falling ash. Approaching from the east, it flew directly into the mushroom cloud and a minute later it emerged from the other side and continued on.

Waving his arms over his head, Ravel gathered his platoon into another trench, waited until at last he saw Wilkins's men on the right flank, and then signaled Sidewinder back into the field. Along the route, they came upon melted-down tanks, disfigured jeeps, and various stakes with what looked like rubber suits hanging from them. When he approached one of these stakes, Ravel saw what he at first took for a human head hanging from the top of it. But it turned out to be only a mannequin reduced to nearly unrecognizable folds of plastic. On the back of that fake head was a film badge just like his own.

Hernandez is the next to leave. Dropping a few bills to the table, he merely winks and heads for the door. No adios, no hasta luego, not even goodbye. From across the room, Ravel sees him turn for a last look at the neon stripper, but the light is gone from his eyes, erased to a smudge of what Ravel assumes to be simple despair.

Wilkins orders up another round of beers and a third bottle of bourbon. There are now only Ravel, Gabriel, and himself to carry on. Sloane is still passed out and the others have left.

"Nothing for me," Gabriel tells him. "I've had enough."

"You always start out saying no," Wilkins tells him. "And then you wind up saying yes."

But Gabriel stands and reaches for his hat. "There's a plane to L.A. at five. I don't want to miss it."

Wilkins tries one more time. "This may be the last time we get together, friend. Sit your ass down and say something memorable."

As though on second thought, Gabriel does sit but he leaves the full shot glass in front of him untouched. "Something memorable? You mean so you won't forget me?"

Wilkins says he's ready to listen. "I always liked to hear you talk, Gabe. We're maybe not from the same planet but I usually get at least a rise out of your particular brand of bullshit."

Gabriel says how about he tells them what he's been reading lately.

"Nothing in books," Wilkins says, "can change piddly about the way I see things."

Gabriel ignores him. "I've been reading about the bombs we saw. All the bombs. About the radioactivity and the . . ." He stops and looks across the bar to the neon woman, stripping, dressing, stripping.

"What?" Ravel asks him.

"The dangers."

Wilkins tips his shot glass, draining it in one go, then sets the glass on the table with emphasis. "You took an oath, Gabe. A special vow of silence."

Gabriel says he hasn't forgotten. "I don't miss much. I have a steel-trap memory and that's a fine thing most of the time. Then I come across something I'd rather forget and can't. Like that vow."

"I don't know what you're talking about."

"Those safety levels. They told us that point five rems was safe enough and I believed them. I believed *you*, Ravel. You relayed the information and we listened. And then one time this science officer told me I'd gotten dirty. I didn't know then what dirty meant and none of you had anything *memorable* to say on the subject."

Wilkins conjures a fake laugh, a ripping sound that doesn't pan out. "So they hosed you down, burned your uniform, gave you a new set of fatigues."

"But I never had a film badge except for that last shot. Ravel had one and so did you, but none of the others."

" 'My safety depends upon my silence.' I memorized that much, Gabe. Ten thousand dollars and ten years in prison if you talk about all this stuff out loud."

"How long have you known, Wilkins?"

"I never knew. I never knew anything. I did my job."

"But you had a film badge."

"I didn't know how to read it. I turned it in after every shot. They did the readings somewhere else. Some lab somewhere."

"And they never told you what the readings were?"

"That's right, soldier."

"I'm not a soldier anymore. I didn't know about those readings then but I think I know now. I can't decipher a film badge but I can read my doctor's diagnosis. He says it's called leukemia. Do you think we can believe him?"

Sloane lets out a snore. Lifts his head for a moment and then drops it back down to his arms. Wilkins reaches for the bottle, decides against it, and lets his hand drop like a heavy wing back to his side. Ravel says, "I'm sorry, Gabe."

But Gabriel waves his hand as though to brush the sentiment aside. "I'm not the only one, Ravel. It's the numbers that get to me. There were thirty-four of us in the club. Eight of us are either sick or dead. That's a lot to ask of your statistics, isn't it? Almost twenty-five percent of us are all used up after just six short years. Did Hernandez tell you he can't have any children? Is that sick or is that dying? Which is it, Wilkins?"

"It's radioactivity. It's an excess of roentgen intake. If he took it in the balls it could have been just about anything. Plutonium, barium, cobalt. It depends on what he swallowed or what got in his ears. Or maybe he just stopped to take a leak around ground zero and took it externally."

Gabriel is silent for a moment. He stares at the shot glass in front of him as though trying to read the words that are floating there. Finally he says, "I thought you didn't know."

"You're not the only one who can read. I didn't know *then*. Now I do."

"What about you, Ravel?"

Ravel says, "Same thing."

Wilkins adds, "I got out in '55, when the loads started getting monstrous."

"And no illness? No anything?"

"Nothing. All systems go. Green lights and smooth sailing."

"And you, Ravel?"

Ravel says he's still intact. "Mircea, too. My boy, Vance."

"How old is he now?"

"Just turned five."

Gabriel finally reaches for the courage in front of him and drinks it down. "Ever wonder why you've never had any more children?"

Ravel wants to know if it's really any of Gabe's business. "Or do I have to draw a line in the dirt?"

"What worries me," Gabriel says, "is that you're still there, at the test site."

"Nowadays I wear a suit."

"What kind of suit?"

"Asbestos, canvas. A lead lining. Same kind of suit we used to see those guys in when we'd get to ground zero."

"And you still watch the shots?"

Ravel says he's seen a few and then some.

"How many?"

"I don't count anymore. Numbers don't impress me all that much. Some here and some in Micronesia. Eniwetok, mostly. I once saw two in a single day, Gabriel. But we don't get as close as two miles anymore. Not with the new kiloton counts."

Gabriel gazes across the table to his old platoon sergeant, his blue eyes tranquil, if slightly bloodshot. "You're insane, Ravel."

Ravel, taking the glass from Wilkins's hand, finds the whiskey to his taste and drinks it down.

.   .   .

They came within three hundred yards of ground zero, when Ravel suddenly pulled his men up short. The dust cleared a bit and they could see molten sand, like glass, bubbling around the edge of a crater. The ground was hot beneath their boots and although the shock wave had long since passed there were little swirls of wind, dust devils, all around them. They didn't know they had come too far. The gale force of the shock wave had obliterated the markers they'd used to guide them during mock-ups. Coming out of the smoke was what appeared at first to be a phantom in white, and Ravel stepped back in a reflex of fear before realizing there was a man inside the suit. The man approached to within ten yards and frantically pointed at a box strapped to his side. Waving his arms, he signaled to them to clear out. Ravel assumed there was a fire burning somewhere nearby or there was the threat of yet another shock wave. It was enough. He ordered his men to get the hell out of the area. Maneuvers were over.

When they arrived back at the camp a technician was waiting for Ravel to report and to turn in his film badge. The men lined up in single file and were brushed down with brooms, but the dust still hung thick on their sleeves and shoulders. There were only three showers available and since no one had eaten that day Ravel gave the order to fall out. Both platoons headed straight for the mess tent. The showers came much, much later.

Ravel never saw the reading from his first film badge, but a few years after his first bomb watch he assisted in a radiological film survey. The equipment he was given was the AN/PDR 27, used for taking rem readings throughout a given sector. The maximum rem count considered safe by the Army was point five rems, and the AN/PDR 27 was supposed to measure rem counts in sectors where platoons had done exercises. For over fifteen hours the needle was buried at the highest possible reading on the scale. For the AN/PDR 27, that was point five rems.

. . .

Gabriel is gone and Wilkins has called a taxi to come and haul Sloane away. That leaves the two soldiers at the Last Chance Saloon. They are suddenly feeling conspicuously out of uniform, but the bottle is only half gone and Wilkins says it would be a waste if they were to leave now. "Anyway, it appears we're the last of the Zero Plus Two Point Two. Is this a wake or what?"

"Don't mention last rites to a man in my position," Ravel answers.

They are both willing so Wilkins pours. As they drink, each of them is thinking the same thing. They are quite a pair of liars. Wilkins with his respiratory troubles and Ravel feeling pain in all the wrong places. Growing pains, the shotgun wedding of rampant cells.

Ravel totes it up. "Danzel is no surprise. Add Hernandez and Gabriel to the list, even though we don't know how serious it is for Hernandez. You and me along with them, that makes ten, and the two of us are the only ones past thirty. Ten out of thirty-four? How long is the life span, Wilk? Yours, I mean."

"Damned if I know. Doc says I got five years if I stay south. You?"

"One, two at the most."

"You got another shot coming up?"

"In two days."

"How many k's?"

"They're all pretty hairy, Wilk. I don't count much anymore. This one's another prototype. The general says it's clean."

"They're all clean, Ravel. Clean as a damn whistle; just ask Teller. Why don't you get out now?"

"I'm going to make officer first. That's the deal. I finish Plumbbob and I get my bars. That's why I stayed."

"You told Mircea yet?"

"About the cancer? Christ no. She'd just pray and cry all the time."

"At least they give you a suit," Wilkins muses. "That's more than they gave us in the old days."

"With a bow tie," Ravel tells him. "And spats."

F OR THE first year the family lived in St. George, a two-hour drive from Frenchman Flats, where the tests were held. But as the kilotonnage was gradually raised from the teens to the thirties, Mircea was spooked and insisted that he find some place for them away from the noise and the winds. "It's getting hellish, Jack. Even from this distance. I can't believe you'd leave us in such danger." So he located a ranch-style house in Paragonah, a few hours northeast of St. George, and moved the family there in 1954.

Given his duties at the site, he often has to spend nights away from home, unable to make the long drive to and from the camp at his leisure. Mircea doesn't mind, as long as she doesn't have to put up with the visions of those rising mushroom clouds, that sense of the sun rising in the west, of great balls of helium fire turning her religion on its head. Even from Paragonah, when she scans the horizon, sometimes she can see a shaft of cloud and a gray-violet haze across the desert. So she has developed a habit of always looking east or north or south, and if ever she forgets and casts her gaze toward the west, she remembers to cross herself on the forehead, the lips, the heart.

At one point, he'd been sent to the Pacific for a six-month stretch. There, far from the public scrutiny that had begun to gather around the Nevada Test Site, the shots had been more frequent and even more terrifying. When he'd returned home, having seen twenty-one more detonations, he and Mircea had at first suffered days and nights without speaking or touching. "I saw an island vanish," he'd told her. "For weeks I awoke to the sight of that island across the bay. Then it was gone. There was only the ocean."

Time has passed like a continuous countdown, but they have settled back into the rhythms of man and wife. Mircea's disapproval cannot undo her love for him. Vance is getting older and looking out more for his father. When Jack is away at a shot, it's as though the boy knows what is happening. As if by instinct, on nights when shots are scheduled, he comes to his mother's room and insists on sleeping there.

More and more, Mircea asks why they can't get a transfer to somewhere else, North Carolina maybe, or back to Camp Pendleton. Jack tells her that after five years on the project he doesn't want to throw away what's coming to him, his promised commission. "I'm thirty-five years old and the only way I'll ever move up is to see combat. The only combat to be found is at this site. Look at what happened to Wilkins. When he walked off he lost it all. Just one more year, Mircea. Plumbbob will be finished and we'll be moving on. One more year, that's all I'm asking."

He has never told her anything about the tests. That's the rule, both hard and fast. Your safety depends upon your silence, wives and confessors included. She knows only that he takes tests and files reports and that he doesn't have to participate in maneuvers anymore. On the odd occasion when he brings another soldier home for dinner or just a visit, they talk only about baseball or boxing or hunting or army things that have nothing to do with giant mushroom clouds and flashes of unbelievable heat on the other side of the desert. Once, on Mircea's insistence, he'd invited the staff chaplain for Sunday dinner. Over coffee, she'd asked a few questions about the project, simply idle chatter about military matters that a chaplain might now and then have to tend to. "I once read," she remarked, "that during the last war the chaplains would bless the tanks and planes and rifles before a battle. Is that true?"

The chaplain said it was.

"And that there were special prayers for each of them. 'Lord bless this tank that it may shoot straight and true.' Things like that."

The chaplain admitted that, yes, there had been special prayers for various armaments.

"Then tell me, Reverend. Is there a special prayer for the hydrogen bomb?"

To buy time, the chaplain stirred a lump of sugar into his coffee, lifted the cup to his lips, and drank. Setting the cup back to the saucer, he said he wasn't at liberty to discuss it. His eyes, crossing the table, rested on Jack Ravel.

"If there is a prayer," Mircea continued, "it must be a very powerful one."

"As a matter of fact," replied the chaplain, "what might be required is a prayer of thanksgiving."

Mircea said she didn't follow.

"That the apocalyptic power of God has been given to those deemed worthy of it."

"The power of God?"

"The bomb, Mrs. Ravel. The unchaining of the absolute power of the universe."

Thereafter, each night, Ravel found Mircea on her knees, attempting to outpray that chaplain with all her heart, to overwhelm his prayers of thanksgiving with her prayers of mercy, mercy, mercy on us all. Always the lamb of God or the meek inheriting the earth. The humble and despairing works.

CATHEDRAL

Nashua Coe's Auto Body and Salvage is just north of town, between the highway and the railroad tracks, and looks, from a distance, like nothing less than the ruin of an old silver boom town. Three misshapen buildings face in varying directions: the garage, the body shop, and Nashua's unpainted stucco house, with cardboard over one of the windows. The jagged vertical shapes of stacked wreckage rise from a low horizon and reach into desert sky.

Wheeling the pickup into the front lot, Randy tells Ravel to jump and then reaches to slam the door behind him. Not a single word for the wise or even a goodbye. Ravel waves to him anyway as Randy fishtails out of the lot and speeds away.

The auto body shop is closed up tight and both garage doors are double-locked. A blue bulb burns in the front office to show that the alarms are set. The car salvage is back another hundred yards, lit only with a pair of white neon lamps burning like tired angels atop makeshift poles. Ravel has a small office near the front gate, a five-by-eight shack of corrugated aluminum, a low ceiling, a workbench, a lamp, a chair, and a 1976 calendar showing off a faded Miss March. A single window looks out into the yard, but Ravel hasn't taken the time to wash it and the dust is months thick, each day adding a layer, the window itself a calendar, closing him in.

Two new wrecks have arrived during the day, a white '67 Impala with an accordioned front end and a red MG so mangled it is almost unrecognizable. They have died, these two, in a violent embrace on Interstate 15, some inebriate yahoo having no doubt skidded across the divider separating his path from another's. Ravel never knows for sure if anyone was hurt, or how badly hurt, or killed. There is no news of torn arteries, bruised flesh, hemorrhaging, or splintered bones. He sees only the haphazard anatomies of the cars, their severed cables, cracked blocks, mangled tires, and ruptured gas tanks. Now and then there are traces of blood that no one thought to wash away, and he is reminded of Injun hoodoo, sacrifice, and whatever spirits those bloodstains may possess. There won't be much to salvage from these two wrecks. Nashua was probably paid pennies for the two and has put them in the seventh lot, the Dunes, where there are mostly long-dead chassis, carcasses gone to rust and caressed by dry weeds, nothing left to strip.

Ravel's been working here three weeks now, eighteen soulful working nights of gainful employment, and tomorrow, knock on wood, is payday.

The entire yard is divided into nine lots organized in rows of three, with alleys running between. Six-plus acres altogether, a regular empire of loss and ruin. The alleys are less than straight and, closest to the Heap, almost unnavigable. Nearer the highway, cars that might run, that might, with a wrench and some automotive affection, be resuscitated, end up parked side by side as in a used car lot. Whenever he has the time, Nashua comes out to pretty them up. He hammers dents from fenders, Windexes all the glass, wipes away the desert dust, and makes sure the windows are closed tight and that passing derelicts haven't destroyed the interior upholstery. These two lots are Limbo, to Ravel's way of thinking, and he spends little time beyond the necessary minimum in the environs. The third and fourth lots make up the Heap, where the cars are almost whole but serve only as corpses from which required organs might be removed. All the others, lots five through nine, are the Dunes: imposing mounds of disjunct bodies, engines, interiors, refrigerators, ovens, pipes and plumbing, porcelain and steel sinks, copper tubing, doors and doorknobs, all piled together and halfheartedly sorted into shapeless pyramids of waste. Broken glass is everywhere. It piles up here and there and glitters in the moonlight among the other detritus of the yard: the blackened bolts, chrome stripping, mashed fenders, and numberless disfigured hands of steel. Empty motor mounts sit with hoods torn open and the moonlight slips through to the dry earth beneath.

Though Ravel is working the graveyard shift, nine p.m. to dawn, it seems as though he is never entirely alone. The kids from Paragonah or Parowan, bored out of their adolescent skulls, drive up at odd hours, scale the chain-link fence, and set themselves up for a haunting. They gather trash and light campfires, smoke weed, pound down brand-name beer, then throw the empty cans at the cars or into the brush or at each other. Desert town fun stuff that Ravel himself took part in years and years ago. On a few occasions things have gotten out of hand, with the kids becoming too drunk and rowdy and taking hammers to a wreck or two. They seem to go for the windshields, dashboards, headlights, dangling mirrors. There are other objects to vandalize—the upholstery, for example, or those rare canvas-topped coupes. But the glass is what attracts them, the hard transparency that makes that satisfying sound of bells when it shatters.

Ravel *has* been hired to watch over the yard, so a couple of times he has gone into his cop routine. But he is already bankrupt of much of his authority, hemming and hawing as he does before finally reading the riot act and mentioning the real police. It's a cheap trick, counting on the law to do his dirty work, but Nashua wants a tight ship and Ravel is nothing if not obedient. The more difficult part of the job is keeping an eye on the transients, the rail people who take advantage of the deceleration of a train when it passes near Paragonah to jump off a few hundred yards from the salvage and spend their nights, if Ravel lets them, in the alleys of Limbo. There are Mexicans without green cards heading north to Denver or Butte or anyplace clear of the Sonora border patrols; destitute Navajos riding back and forth on the line, gliding desultorily between the parentheses of Bakersfield and Salt Lake City; certified rail bums, aware that they are the last of a sainted American breed, who look upon Ravel as just another innkeeper and don't take much notice of his unconvincing ranting. Whenever he comes upon any of them, he reads out the house rules: "Don't break anything. Don't shit or piss in the cars. Leave the glass alone. Don't steal anything." Usually he is answered with a dumb, almost respectful, nodding of heads, an assent if not an understanding. But once, while making his predawn rounds, he had come upon Sol in a just-trashed Fairlane. Cracked glass, shit in the backseat and garbage in the front, torn upholstery sprouting black springs. There was a definite stink of Thunderbird in the air, two dollars a bottle.

"This your doing, Sol?"

He looked around himself with pride. "You bet."

"Must have taken you half the night."

"And then some."

A pause. A pregnant pause. Then Sol asked Ravel what he intended to do about it.

"It's hard to decide. Cross you off my Christmas card list?"

"Can't do that." Sol shook his head. "You never liked me anyway."

Ravel assured him that his affection was universal.

"This a speech you're making? I mean, do I have to listen to this?"

Ravel asked him what he really wanted, what the kick had been.

"Bringing this snotty car down to my level. Makes it homier, you know. Cozy."

That made just enough sense to Ravel to distract him for a long moment, but he had to remind Sol that he was Nashua's hired hand. "You'll notice this tire iron I'm hauling with me. Nashua says I'm to put it to good use. When the occasion presents itself."

Sol couldn't believe it any more than Ravel meant it. "*You,* Ravel? You're a peacenik."

After more hesitation, during which he felt obliged to suppress years of religious training and conscientious objection, Ravel invited Sol to call his bluff. Sol took a deep breath and then said, "Jesus H. Christ, you sure are a changed man, Vance Ravel. Once you was a holy roller and *now* look at you with that goddamned weapon that you'd just love to use on a old fart like me." All this time he was sweeping the garbage off the front seat and brushing glass shards from the dash, cutting himself badly with his panicky gestures of salvage and contrition. When Ravel became aware of his panic, he held out a hand to stop him. Ravel meant to calm him but Sol almost jumped out of his skin. He slid from the open door on the other side, cast Ravel a look that said Judas, then bolted down the alley and away.

It was the first time Ravel had ever, *ever* exiled a man into homelessness, and it was no consolation to him whatsoever to know that to Sol's way of thinking he was merely the victim of a clash of opinions over the finer points of interior decorating.

Just past sundown he takes his flashlight and a pair of extra batteries and heads out of the shack for the first round of the night. Turning his beam from ruin to ruin, Ford to Chevrolet to Toyota, he keeps a lookout for feet hanging from windows, wisps of smoke rising from the alleys, the sounds of breaking glass. Up and down the Heap there is only the usual chaos of scattered wrecks. When he touches the hood of the '67 Impala he finds it is still warm; tomorrow it will be as cold as any other shell in that yard, and as useless. The Dunes, those far-flung reaches of rubble and tire mounds, are vacant. No sign of Sol in more than a week now and Ravel feels, again, remorse. If Sol comes back, he's decided, he can always set up in some green glen within the Heap. There must be a station wagon with leather upholstery that will shelter him, a Grande Rancho

Deluxe Master with chrome ashtrays and vinyl floor covers, tinted glass, a stray mattress from the Dunes for the wide backseat and maybe even a not-dead battery to light the night for him and fill it with a samba or a cha-cha or Mozart from an L.A. radio station.

One way or another, he hasn't seen the last of Sol.

The far side of Limbo is Nashua Coe's Royalty Row: three Lincoln Continentals, a '65 Thunderbird, a Fleetwood, and a string of garden variety Cadillacs lining the fence closest to the highway. It pays to show them off, that's what Nashua says, but it costs, too, because those are the first cars the rummies see when they come around the yard looking for a way in. All that glitter, that fine metallic paint, the shiny chrome, and those enormous, cushy backseats like queen-size motel beds. While making his rounds, Ravel is supposed to look inside each of these cars and ensure that the locks are jammed tight and that nothing wild, man or beast, has gotten inside. As he cruises down the row, he swings his light inward, passing the beam over steering wheels, sparkling dashes, radio panels that glow back at him in green or in blue, into backseats of creamy leather, buttoned upholstery, upturned ashtrays emptied of butts and gum wads. Nothing is in the T-Bird or in the Continentals. The Fleetwood is inhabited by a nest of snakes coiled on the floor beneath the steering wheel. They come and go through a hole in the steering column, and Ravel doesn't bother sweeping them out anymore. They follow the rules better than the local high school kids do, and anyway, they'd only come back the next day.

Near the row of Caddies, Ravel slows down, wondering which one of them it will be tonight. There are seven altogether and any one of them could be harboring Sandy. She has been in the yard nearly every night, bringing along various friends with twenty-dollar bills. During Ravel's first night out, he made the mistake of passing his beam into the front seat, where he caught undulating flesh in that halo of light and, as Sandy furiously put it, "ruined a Hollywood moment." She leapt from behind the wheel without bothering to cover so much as her breasts, to ask just what *was* the story. "You the law?"

He told her he was the night watchman.

"Then back off. Didn't Smithy give you the word?"

He looked her up and down and was unable to manage a blush. She was only seventeen but had that look of thirty about her. Hell-bent and ravishing and careless with her dress, but her makeup was just so. "What word?"

"This row is *mine*. It's all staked out. I get run of the Caddies and Smithy sees me once a month for some never-you-mind."

Smithy preceded Ravel at the job. An acne-riven stutterer who'd spent most of his lifetime sweeping floors and feeding himself on the small change. Nashua had found him other employment once he'd known that Ravel was available. Smithy had taken the time to show Ravel the office, the flashlight, the drawer with extra batteries, and the tire iron. But he'd failed to mention Sandy or any of their nocturnal arrangements.

But that's the setup, and Ravel wouldn't be surprised if even Nashua knows about it. Sandy goes barefoot in the Caddies and makes her tiny fortune, while Ravel, the eye of night, is supposed to blink in passing. He's noticed, gratefully, that at least she's meticulous and brings along her own Kleenex.

He stands at the edge of Royalty Row and is trying to guess which of the Caddies she's chosen for the night, when Sandy steps from beside the driver's seat of the powder-blue number. She is wearing denim cutoffs and a halter that looks to be in full sail. "You're late," she tells him.

He answers that he doesn't have any schedule. "I'm paid to wander aimlessly." Ducking his head, he checks out the Caddy, but there's no one there.

Sandy says it's the end of the month. "The rent's due. You ready to get your ashes hauled?"

"I have this feeling," Ravel tells her, "that you're barking up the wrong tree."

"Can't be. You're the night watchman and I'm a dream come true."

"Right bark, wrong tree."

"I got tricks to make your heart stop on a dime."

He tells her he's married.

"Yeah, I know. Cassie. Too bad about what happened. Hey, didn't you use to be a priest or something?"

"That's the word for it. I was something."

Her disappointment is palpable, a burst balloon. "So you don't want to cash your check? I must be out of my mind trying to talk you into this. Everyone else has to pay."

He tells her he's beyond temptation. "Not that I've never strayed before. Let's just say I'm distracted."

"By what?"

"By a loving wife I abandoned."

"Yeah," she says, looking off toward the Heap. "That's rough. Sad as all get-out."

Then as a last gesture she unravels the ribbon at her neck and pulls down the halter to show him her breasts. Perfect, he is thinking, heft and symmetry. Sweet fruit for the blur of his eyes.

"I'm speechless, Sandy."

"Time's a-wastin'."

"Time's just time."

With that crack she lifts the halter and ties it fast around her neck. "So what am I supposed to do? It's too late to go back to the Two Guns."

"There's always television. Late-night black-and-white."

"Don't make me laugh."

At that moment, facing her across a crippled Cadillac, he considers turning his morality wheel a full 180. Bite this, she might say to him, chew that, sip, suck, swallow. But he can't make the necessary move or say the word that will unroot him from the spot.

She is finally fed up with him. "No one cares for you, Vance

Ravel. I asked around. You leave your wife and kid to the wolves and then you come back here. You, with your college education, working at a job that any moron is up to. Everyone in town always said you were a sicko and about now I'm beginning to see their point."

Before he can answer her she has already turned on her naked heel and headed for the front gate, double-timing it out of his sight, unhad.

This cherry-red Trans Am, notorious muscle car of the biceps-flexing seventies, was owned by a black prince of real estate in his mid-forties who made a fast living selling desert land to sucker couples in L.A. in search of peaceful retirement lots. Shoving it up to fifth gear to meet a deadline with white-collar crime, he left the road at 126 mph and found eternity in a stony ditch. The dash is both a monument and an obituary. The speedometer is frozen, showing off that speed through a net of crushed glass. Oil gauge close to empty, fuel at ¼ tank, temp past hot, radio turned to KTLA. When Ravel flicks the switch there is still reception, faint as the battery provides, Jimi Hendrix, zzz, all along the watch towah . . . The chassis is at rest next to a dust-brown Fairlane with ancient french fries and blackened ketchup stains in the backseat. The car belonged to a divorced mother of two from Provo who strapped her brats into the back and during pauses at red lights turned to slap their faces to shut up their yowling. She was on her way to get her hair done and was running late. She turned once just before an intersection to slap the boy into silence and lost sight of the color of the lights. There came a jeep from the left blind side, and all in the backseat was peace thereafter.

Ravel's junkyard mythology. He's been making up these stories while on his nocturnal rounds. A Cutlass, a Falcon, an Austin-Healey. Evidence of carelessness and collision, of growing old and finding fingers of rust where once was the shimmer of chrome. The south wind singing through those cracks in the back window.

This black Ford station wagon, circa 1962, spit fatal steam and then stopped dead on Interstate 15. The Navajo couple, headed for Denver, just left it by the side of the road. Taking up their belongings in cardboard boxes tied with string, they hitched a ride into Cedar City and spent their last cash on a bus ride north. They shoot horses but they don't shoot cars.

Ravel ruminates over shattered windshields and countless bashed mirrors. Mosaic of crystal, missing teeth, diamonds, and a pattern like starlight across the yard, an astrology of shining splinters that decipher into chaos if he looks on them askance.

When he goes to visit Cassie her arms are hardly opened wide. Like that door that won't close because some interloper has put his foot into the gap.

Jered kicks up his heels at the sight of the airplane and then grows almost somber seeing the man at the other end of it. There is a long moment of silence made stupid by Ravel's not being able to take his eyes off his son, and then Cassie says she has to get back to work. She seems on the verge of saying something else, curse or blessing, but then just bows her head and flees to the rusting car. Ravel is alone with a seven-year-old stranger.

"You're on the fridge," Jered says.

Ravel blinks, not getting it.

"The picture."

"Oh, that." Handing him the airplane, Ravel asks him if he knows who he is.

"Sure. You're Dad." Before Ravel can utter his hallelujah, Jered adds, "But Mom calls you That Man."

"I'd rather *you* keep calling me Dad."

Jered only shrugs.

They take the airplane into the backyard. In Jered's hands it seems enormous. Having hitched all the way to Parowan to buy it at a Sears outlet, Ravel frets that it is too small. But he knows well enough that no gift, whether plastic Piper Cub or full-size 747, will be sufficient to pay the freight on his sense of guilt.

"It's a Cessna," he explains. "Two-seater. You here and me there."

Jered says, "What about Mom?"

"She can sit in my lap."

There was in his eyes an unreadable reply, suspicion or anger or simple disappointment. What do I know about little boys' hearts? I should have brought a three-seater, or a four, for future dog, cat, or guinea pig.

"How's this work?" Jered wants to know.

Ravel shows him the remote-control panel, steering arc, ascent and descent stick. Setting the plane in the center of the yard, Jered tries ignition but nothing happens. "You said . . ."

"Try it again."

Still nothing. "Shit!" Jered crosses back to the plane and opens a hatch underneath the cockpit. "You forgot the damn batteries!"

They go for a walk around Paragonah and Jered points out his school and the window of his classroom. "That's my desk, up front because I talk too much." Then the park where a year ago he sprained his ankle when he fell from a tree. "I *told* Mom that Terry pushed me, but I don't think she believed me." As they circle toward the center of town, Jered shows him houses of friends, some empty lots where he has dug holes or built forts, and the high rock he sometimes climbs to see the lights.

"What lights?"

"The city," Jered says, a bit contemptuously. It takes Ravel a long moment to realize he means Paragonah. Those hundred houses, three traffic lights, streetlamps at irregular intervals, and a single row of neon over the Two Guns. His city.

"Ever been to Reno, Jered?"

"No, sir."

"I'm not sir. How about Las Vegas?"

"Too far."

Ravel tells him you can see the lights in the desert distance. "Blue and red and gold. All that electricity."

"Neon," Jered corrects him. "It's a gas." Putting Ravel deftly in his place.

Back at the house, Ravel locates an air pump but no patches for the bike. There is black asbestos tape in a kitchen drawer and he cuts swatches of it and wraps them around the punctures in the inner tube, then pumps furiously until the tires swell. Jered sits on the front steps and watches, telling him to quit pumping after six pounds. Ravel answers that there is no gauge and they'll have to guess. Jered just shrugs.

When the tires are repaired, Ravel notices that the chain has gone slack. "You know where there's a set of pliers?"

"What for?"

"Chain needs to be tightened."

Jered sighs. "God, I don't know. This is a lot of work, don't you think?"

"Won't you be glad to have your bike back?"

"Don't need it. I use a skateboard now."

Ravel leans the bike against the house and stares at his son with hot eyes. "You know, Jered, I'm just trying to be friendly. Don't you want to be friends?"

"I said I'd call you Dad. What else do you want?"

Ravel's idiocy returns to him in a hopeless moment of wanting to reel back the years with a single tug. "Do you remember me, Jered? Anything about me?"

"You had a beard."

"What else?"

"We used to paint rocks. That was dumb."

Ravel nodded. "And?"

"You're on the fridge. You and Spider-Man."

Feeling he is getting somewhere, Ravel goes too far. "Any connection?"

"Spider-Man isn't real."

Desert evening; shadows leap eastward and lose form; the lizards come out and show their gullets to the sky. When Cassie gets home, Ravel and Jered are sitting in the living room, watching television.

"It's five-thirty, Jered. Time for *Star Trek*."

"Thanks," he says, standing and adjusting the dial, "for the hot tip."

"Jered, you shouldn't talk like that to your mother."

Cassie just rolls her eyes and Jered says, "Look who's talking."

Ravel follows Cassie into the kitchen. "So how'd it go?" she asks.

"He's got a dirty mouth."

"*You* say. He's fine with me. He defends himself."

"Can I stay for dinner?"

"Certainly not."

He moves closer to her, within touching distance. There follows a brief tussle of thwarted hands, a side-stepped embrace, hands reaching without landing. "To begin with," he says, "I've missed you like mad."

"Three years of madness," she answers. "And what I miss most now is hoping." Then she nudges him away with her fingertips and he is, for a moment, lighter than air.

"If I can't talk to you," he says, "how am I going to tell you?"

"Tell me what?"

"Where I've been and why I'm back."

She is putting groceries away and keeps her back to him so that he can't see her face. "Come talk to me some other time. It's too much to get used to all at once."

At the front door, he says he'll be back.

"Call first. I'll need warning. Time to load my gun."

Jered looks up from the television and, mirabile dictu, waves goodbye.

Mircea wants to know what is in the bag.

"A present for Cassie. A peace offering."

"Wouldn't it be simpler to tell her you're sorry? That you've been a genuine fool and twelve-karat jackass and you'd like to make amends for the past?"

He is astounded to learn that this much isn't already written in granite letters on his face.

"The world turns not on high-held heads bearing crowns but on the points of knees bent in prayer."

"Is this a quote? She wants words?"

"Not the flowers, Vance. The message on the card."

On his first night off from work at the car salvage, she agrees to a ride in her car. "Not for too long or too far. I don't like to leave Jered to the wolves."

"What wolves?" he asks, but Cassie isn't saying.

She takes the interstate north toward Roadside Business, then turns west onto a dirt road leading toward Little Salt Lake. It is a moonless night and the orphaned sky is hot with stars, the desert floor a shade of black and blue, dark as loneliness. A rat or rabbit leaps across the headlight, showing off, and Cassie drives slowly, peering into the near distance, defining the road as it reveals itself ten yards at a time. When they come to the lake, she swings a sudden right, tipping him across the front seat, and for a moment his cheek brushes her bare shoulder and they both feel the electricity. He hopes for a moment that it will last, that the shock will turn into a current, her to him and back again. But once she's stopped the car and cut the lights, there is only silence and darkness and he realizes he is holding his breath.

"So," Cassie says. "Talk."

Ravel figures, Here's where the river bends. "Why didn't you answer my letters?"

"I never read them. I left it to Mircea to give me the news I felt up to hearing. All I saw of those letters were the postmarks."

"Never? You never read a word?"

"Don't make me lie again. I'll say whatever comes to mind and if you don't like it I can always drive myself home."

"It's your car," he admits.

"Darn right."

He reaches for that loose thread of where he's been. Tell her the story and she might be moved to listen to the moral. "I went east," he begins. "It seemed like the only direction to go. If I'd gone west I'd have come upon the coast in no time and would have had to double back. Anyway, New York seemed like a place to be crazy in and I took my time getting there."

"About a year, according to the postmarks."

"And I was right. No one noticed me there. I didn't even stir a breeze." He is looking at her as he speaks. She is watching the dash as though she is alone. "I sold encyclopedias. Wore a tie and pants with a crease. I lived in a tiny studio in a run-down part of town but I had a window to myself. I shaved my beard."

"It's an improvement."

"I felt naked and silly at first. Diminished. And the discipline of shaving every morning was somehow humbling. That and living in the big city."

"But you stayed." She is still refusing to turn toward him. She lifts her eyes and looks out the window.

"I stayed," he agrees. "But my salesmanship only lasted six months. For one thing, I didn't make my quota. Then I got beat up one night coming home from work. I got a broken tooth and cracked ribs over a five-dollar bill and the only picture I had of you and Jered."

Despite the darkness he swears he sees her smile. "Mircea sent you another one. I couldn't believe it. A whole year gone by, and you should have come home if you wanted to see our faces. Instead you write and ask for a picture. Grabbing at the obvious straws."

Leaning against the door, he realizes he is talking to a silhouette that has been altered in his absence. Memory, the charlatan, has rearranged something in his mind's eye.

Cassie notices his staring and tells him to cut it out. "Keep talking."

"The words?" he says. "Just one after another?"

"In whatever order you like."

"After New York," he says. "That's where I can pick it up. After New York, I zagged. The southern states intimidated me but I never knew why. Maybe I'm afraid of Baptists. There are snake handlers in this town in West Virginia. I thought of looking them up but didn't have the courage. Don't look at me like that. I told you I don't do these things anymore. No more hocus and no more pocus. I'm clean. Really."

"The story," she says. "Just the story, Vance."

"I headed slowly west again, moving always from city to city. I seldom lived in the smaller towns, because there never seemed to be any work available for transient types like myself. In Chicago I was a delivery boy for a bank. There were four of us and I was by far the youngest, but we all, even a sixty-year-old man, were called boys. I took letters and packages in a leather pouch and carried them from branch office to branch office like a postman. I made friends with my landlord, who kept referring to me as that Mormon. He thinks we're all the offspring of Brigham Young, everyone in Utah. He kept asking me how many wives I had."

"And you said?"

"One, Cassie. Only one."

"I believe you."

"He thought I was a fool. Why choose a cow when you can have the whole herd? That was his logic and I never bothered to argue with him."

Suddenly she starts the engine and switches on the lights. The desiccated lakefront is white before them.

"Are we leaving?"

"I just thought of something."

"Those undefined wolves?"

"No," she says. "The Mingling."

Stark silence. He wants to stone himself in atonement for this ancient sin. "Because I said something about having the whole herd?"

"Because you did. You *had* the whole herd."

There is nothing to say to her in return. He knows well enough he is guilty as charged. Feeling out of joint, he gets out of the car and stands by the shore of the lake. Nothing lives there because of the salt: no fish and no fruit and, consequently, no birds. Their own Dead Sea without the scrolls. Unless he counts various painted stones in the vicinity. He wonders for a moment if Cassie will just drive away and leave him there. He is surprised when she joins him and stands looking off into the same distance.

"That's not what hurt me the most," she tells him. "The Mingling. I could bear that much after all the rest. It was Jered I was worried about. I thought you should have worried more with me."

He can only nod. And nod again. Three years he'd been nodding to these words, these accusations. Beating his breast so hard there should be bruises for a lifetime.

"You'll have to give Jered some time," she tells him. "He still cares about you but he's more than a little pissed off. Maybe he gets it from me; I don't know."

"He says you refer to me as That Man."

"Not always, Vance. I've told him good things, too. He's just a little boy."

"I was sick, Cassie. I'm sorry. First it was me and then it was grief. Now I need to come home."

Suddenly she faces him directly. Those are not unknowable

stars he is seeing, those are her eyes, and now he is bathed in their light. "It should be easy, but it isn't," she says. "I don't cry anymore and that's a fact. If you want me, I'll be watching for the signs. You were my first love but not my last. Don't crowd me, Vance."

"Not your last?"

But she is already climbing behind the wheel and revving the engine. He jumps in beside her and she drives recklessly back to the interstate, raising cirrus clouds of dust in her wake. All the way back to her house he is yakking at her, trying to get to the meaning of what she said. Is there someone else? Still around or long gone? Love or lust or lonesomeness? "Tell me, Cassie."

All she says is, "You'll see. I have this feeling."

When they arrive at Cimarron Street there is a car parked out front and the glow of a cigarette behind the wheel. Cassie parks on the other side of the street, removes the key, and turns to Ravel. "You'll have to go now, Vance."

"I suppose he has a name."

"Nothing for you to know. Just go home."

"I'll only come back again."

"Do. Do come back. But for now, just go."

He gets out of the car, heads to the end of Cimarron Street, and then stops. Moments later a man gets out of the parked car and crosses the street to Cassie's house. There is no light at the door but Ravel can see clearly enough that she's come to open to him. But Ravel's spirits rise when he sees her lift a hand to wave him off. And the man, still a shadow in the moonless night, spins on his heel, gets back into his car, and drives away.

No one wants to believe that his wife has been elsewhere, in the caves of other men. Wanted, yes. Wanting, never. And wherever he turns there are signs and symbols that can hardly be trusted. Can he believe what he sees? What evidence is required? In a cheap motel both faucets are marked C. One of them is a lie and the other, identical, is the truth. All we can do is test the water and see what gives.

He burns, and when he's walked past the point where he can feel his legs again, the ache in them, the throbbing, he heads resolutely back to Cimarron Street and stands for a long while next to that Joshua tree that won't hide him. The choice is to go in or to go home: go back to Mircea's trailer five long miles away to stew in a simmering juice of self-inflicted pain or head inland and see what gives in the ramshackle house of reconciliation.

Jered's bike is where he left it, leaning at an angle against the front wall. Ravel skirts it and goes to the back door, which gives with a brief whine, and he is standing in the kitchen, blinded now by an interior darkness. Creeping forward with his hands before him like antennae, he comes into a shallow hallway with three doors, bathroom and two bedrooms. Behind the first door he tries he can see a toilet and the second is Jered's room.

A mirror in the hallway looks back at him in terror but he pushes forward and is standing at the foot of a narrow bed, his knees butting the mattress. The sounds of his undressing are like wind through dried brush, a whispering of another language, *please*, and when he lies down next to Cassie her hands leap to his face but he catches them and her curse goes all the way down his throat. When she sees it's only him she relaxes and he feels the unexpected miracle of her arms around his neck, pulling him down. There is a moment of hesitation, a silent measuring of before and after, and then her legs part and she leads him to her. Then memory takes over, a remembered rhythm and the woven fit of husband and wife. When she comes she screams once, not entirely from pleasure, and then, already in tears, tells him to please, please get off of her.

The crying lasts a long time, becomes an outpouring, a deluge of grief that he cannot fathom. When at last the wails turn to sniffling, he asks her what's the matter and she tells him, "I'm pregnant."

He laughs aloud, relieved. "Not so fast, Cassie. We just finished."

"You ass," she says, her voice like steam in the black bed. "I already was. Did you think you were the only one who could be so careless?"

C ASSIE casts him out of her still-warm bed.

"Where am I supposed to end up?"

She tells him to walk circles if he wants to, walk squares, but walk away.

"If I walk circles I'll be back in no time."

"Like hell."

"Tomorrow night."

"No, Vance. No more fucking."

"Don't say that."

"A mercy fuck, that's what we'll call it. Since it has to have a *name*."

The ever moonless night is abuzz with confusion. The story could end right here, he figures, with himself sitting like ashes alongside the highway and watching a sunrise the color of the flu. But he doesn't expire of heartache; he merely has the wind knocked out of him.

It might be rain, Mircea tells him back at the trailer, or it might not be. "It's all in the hands of—"

"Don't tell me."

"I was going to say the cloud patterns."

"Of course. Forgive me."

That evening, on his way out to the car salvage, he finds another of those painted rocks on the shoulder of the highway. This one is white and almost perfectly round. There is a lamina of fresh dust across the face. Although it may have been painted months before, or even years, it is clear that the rock hasn't been sitting there for very long. Stones don't roll, despite the poetry, and the wind won't move them. This rock was *placed*, like a host upon a tongue, and its proximity to the road is unnerving. The Er never come this way; the settlement is too far to the west, too isolated. The color white signifies greetings, an Er version of how-do. The rounder the rock, the more sincere the message is, and the rock he has come upon is almost a perfect orb.

The gospel according to Ravel told them that since irregular rocks could be found anywhere, these round rocks had to be sought out if the word was to be purely *spoken*. The irregularities of the rocks would reveal their meaning. If there were sharp edges, the noun of the color would be sharpened like a cry. If there were cracks or fissures, that word would be stammered and uncertain. Smooth round stones would signify clarity. In the searching for such stones, time would add its inevitable weight to the gesture. That had been the single point to everything: the gesture. And as time passed, even the colors took on significance. Blue, the original color reserved for Ravel, was female and stood for the evening. Orange and yellow were signs of having been there, of having passed through, like that Papago swirl. Red, a moment of mourning or morbid reflection. Green, a private wish for renewal: birth, rain, love. They were writing letters to the universe across the desert floor, and if in retrospect it all seems like an elaborate but silly bit of nursery rhyme, Ravel is not nowadays so corrupt as to deny the charm of that desert dotted with their gestures. It went a long way toward breaking the monotony of wind and dust and scorpions.

A few hundred yards farther on, he finds another, also white, propped on a low mound of smaller stones so that only a blind man could miss it. Bending to retrieve it, he realizes he wouldn't be surprised to see his name written upon it; the surface, however, is smooth and polished and blank. He stands straight up and scans the horizon but can see only the bronze desert floor and a white unpeopled vastness. Walking faster now, he finds another stone, also white, a mile ahead, and he begins to wonder if he's crazy or if these might not really be road markers of some kind, all of them white and placed just so. Intervals, boundary markers, or even the tombstones of animals killed like Randy's pup, some good Samaritan giving burial rites to furry messes along the highway.

He turns off that road and arrives at the car salvage; unlocking the front gate, he heads for his office. In that hut of plywood and corrugated aluminum, there is another stone awaiting him. Sitting squarely on his desk: the whitest of them all, the roundest, as large as the head of a man.

So they know where to find me.

It is only later, after he's made his first rounds, up the Heap and around the Dunes, through Limbo and past the row of Cadillacs, that he remembers the truer significance of a white rock. It is not really a greeting, one thing given to another, but a declaration. Not how-do, not hello, but a confession to the desert of what one has become. Put to words, the stone best means *One of us*.

THE
ER

TIME, we are told, diminishes everything. Archaeologists confirm our worst suspicions about our mortal frailty and the inevitable futility of good exercise, a balanced diet, and state-of-the-art pacemakers. But in those dusty tombs we're prone to paw through, in those burial mounds and pyramids and grottoes and pueblos, there are still the hieroglyphs and petroglyphs, long-winded assessments of a pharaoh's deathless glory or a chieftain's unsurpassable courage or the goodness or evil of the myriad gods, but also the blow-by-blow of ancient real estate transactions, the price of maize, goat and bird counts, occasional pornography, neighborhood gossip, a reckoning of the stars, and narratives of who bedded whom for whatever purpose under the ageless sun.

And most of what the past contains is written in stone. Ink stains may barely survive a millennium but stone, either chiseled or sculpted, has at least the look of permanence. Idle graffiti can be erased or whitewashed; books can and will and do burn at Fahrenheit 451. Films dry out in stages, from smudge to husk to dust, and oil painting has proved to be the most transient of arts, those stained canvases so utterly susceptible to decay and ruin as to resist the most arduous restorations. The data on a computer disk will, in a surprisingly short time, disappear with its oxide coating. Name, date, place of birth, height, weight, mother's maiden name, and home phone number, everything we have written on countless forms and index cards, every last trace of us and our specifics, our journals, our diaries, our love letters, and our laundry lists, all of our evidence has a life span roughly comparable to a moth's.

But the Er painted those stones. As if the stone and the paint would last forever. And if ever some crackpot archaeologist comes along, before or after the apocalypse, to kick over the rocks of the vanished Er, will he conclude, as Ravel has, that they were only a band of local crazies, burnouts, and dime-store pagans? Or will he read in those rocks a brilliant simplicity, a purity and depth of language that overcame the despair of the era, and, in his misplaced nostalgia for the noble savage of the late twentieth century, dub the civilization enlightened?

There were those among the Er who truly believed they were paving a private back road to the Garden of Original Intent, to the city of the wide-eyed and the pacific, where they would live far from the continual outrages of network television or Monsanto or Exxon, IBM or ICBM, snowmobiles, aerosol sprays, and magnum .44s. They believed that they would live their lives forever with only flint and wood and the green fruit of the brown earth. Their story and Ravel's own are written in that rock. And whatever Ravel has to say now, three years later, will have to suffice as the only surviving lexicon.

For Cassie and for Vance, the choice of the desert was based on its proximity to home. Had they come from Florida, the Er might have been a swamp people, or they might never have existed. Or if Ravel had moved east, to the Paunsaugunt Range, the Er might have been a mountain tribe and painted wood instead of stone. Their prayer sticks would have been more easily fashioned and irrigation would have been less of a problem. Ravel figures their rituals and way of living would certainly have been less austere.

The Escalante is not the most forbidding of deserts; it is merely one of the least known. It is named for Father Silvestre Valez de Escalante, who in 1776 set off from Santa Fe in search of a direct route to Monterey. But he got a bit lost along the way and stumbled from Colorado into Utah and in the years since had rivers, deserts, and various streets and boulevards christened in his name. There were miners in the desert a hundred years ago, uneasy truces between Mormon and silver seeker, and not a few small Indian wars that ended like all the others, with the Utes and Navajo of the region shoved into hellholes like the Escalante, where nothing much would grow without irrigation canals and the blessings of ever more silent gods. Ravel and Cassie had grown up on its eastern edge. When they needed a place to retreat to, after years of going elsewhere and not getting right with themselves, the choice was obvious.

They picked out a small canyon forty miles straight west of Paragonah, where the topsoil was less windblown than elsewhere and the bubble of a spring promised more water to come. The canyon was a hundred feet down, with patches of greasewood and a few salt cedar growing along the flat floor. The south and east walls rose straight upward, revealing the varicolored strata of lime and sandstone, pink and red and white and brown, the colors changing throughout the day and the roving cycle of sunlight and shadow. The north and west walls afforded natural footpaths and switchbacks leading down those hundred feet. Midway down the north wall was a hundred-foot-wide shelf that provided a natural haven from the wind, and that was where they pitched their tent. When Ravel dug an exploratory well and found that the water below the spring bubble was potable if not abundant, they decided to stop right there rather than continue west toward Modena.

They planned on staying only a year or two. If the others hadn't shown up, they might later have remembered that time as a taking of marital breath, a comma, and not an extended ellipsis leading to nothing very special. They still thought of themselves as a nomad couple, drifters, and had no special thoughts of settling down for the rest of their lives in the middle of that desert. Even the house they built was made from wood, three truckloads of secondhand lumber delivered from Cedar City, and not stone. They had a fireplace instead of an altar, and the icons ranged in tight rows across the mantel were more art than idol: souvenirs, to Ravel's way of thinking.

They lived alone there for six months, raising the newborn Jered and living partly off the charity of Mircea, partly off the odd pension Ravel was getting for being his father's survivor and dependent. It was enough. There was nothing in the desert to spend their money on anyway. The only cash requirements were for food and some medicine, building supplies, tools, and seed for the garden. They had books and time, the sun and the moon, Jered and each other, and no taxes to pay. They never did buy that land. It was government property but there was no government in the neighborhood. Just mesquite and creosote and salt cedar and the occasional Cessna buzzing overhead.

The house they put up was a modified A-frame built into the north wall at the level of that shelf. It was high enough above the canyon floor to be safe from flooding and just low enough within the canyon to be protected from the wind. The roof jutted out at a forty-five-degree slant and overhung the front wall by a good eight feet to keep out the sun. Ten steps from the front door was a free-fall of twenty feet to the next canyon shelf, so Ravel built a low pine fence for the time when Jered would begin to crawl. In a month they had two rooms, a combination kitchen-den and a small bedroom, its window overlooking the canyon floor. They left the north wall bare in some spots, which made the main room resemble a half cave, with three walls of pine and plaster and a fourth of ribbed sandstone. Ravel was not a good carpenter and often had to go back to faulty surfaces and spend nails like small change on loosened planks. His T-joints held but the V-joints were maddeningly inaccurate. He sometimes wondered whether the earth had shifted under the foundation. But after a few months of fussing and amending, he found that the place had settled and he no longer awoke in the night imagining that the roof was coming down on his head. The roof or the sky or whatever was beyond the sky.

Once they had moved from their tent into those two rooms, a pleasant kind of boredom set in. The passing of time was measured by a shifting of the sun's arc or the slow growth of vegetables in their yellow patch or the diminution of their water supply or Jered's rising up from all fours and walking erect from crib to hearth.

Having completed the house, Ravel helped Cassie with the garden. She had already scratched out a quarter acre at the bottom of the canyon where the earth was least desiccated and benefited from the occasional rainfall that trickled down the canyon walls. The well Ravel had dug led to a reservoir, a shallow shelf of water, rather than to an underground stream, and the water that they pumped upward would last only a month or so after each good rainfall. To measure the supply, they sank a wooden rod to the bottom. It isn't true that deserts see no rain. But the water drains down through the sand and rock and hard earth and is lost to the underworld. It takes more than outstretched hands to catch it. The roots of cactus and other desert plants either grow to incredible depths or fan out in all directions to create a net. In those first winter months, when the wind came from the north and northwest, they had four different days of broken rainfall, the sun shining the entire time, and the trick was to trap that water before it could drain away.

"My seeds won't take, Vance. The ground is too hard."

"What are we planting?"

"Vegetables. Some white corn, carrots, beets. I wouldn't mind seeing a few marigolds survive."

They shoveled pale soil into a wheelbarrow and emptied it through an aluminum basket into a natural stone reservoir. The basket trapped the larger stones and bits of cactus wood, and these they set aside to use for walls around the reservoir and the well. They then mixed fertilizer and water into the reservoir and turned the soil with shovels before loading it back into the wheelbarrow and scattering it over the garden surface. Cassie dug narrow irrigation ditches in the midst of the garden and they observed the first rainfalls to figure out where the water would gather once it made its way into the canyon and down the steep east and south walls. There were natural gullies that ran down those walls and they cut and shaped other gullies to lead the water toward the well and the field. They saved table scraps and fireplace ash for a compost heap and Ravel built an outhouse with a removable tub, the contents of which he poured and scratched into the canyon floor. After four months they managed to cultivate one stretch of earth no larger than their bedroom which yielded edible tomatoes. The rest of the winter harvest was disappointing: corn with tiny white kernels, the carrots frail and the size of Cassie's fingers, potatoes like small stones, and beans that grew without seeds in their pods.

So in the beginning they lived mostly on canned goods and made occasional trips into Parowan or Paragonah to buy what they needed. In the mornings they worked the garden and in the afternoons Ravel made improvements to the house, fashioning a bed frame, a kitchen table, cupboards, and bookshelves. His carpentry was still faulty and the bed tilted slightly, so that Cassie would drift slowly across the mattress each night and they would wake entwined on his side of the bed. Would embrace, shift, and separate, and the drifting would begin again. When it was apparent that he could not construct with his own hands everything they needed, they drove into Paragonah and scavenged through Nashua Coe's salvage, where they found an armoire, a mahogany table missing one leg, an oval mirror with the glass miraculously still intact, and a worm-eaten cedar chest. Cassie sanded everything bare and rubbed stain into the wood; Ravel replaced the rusty hinges on the armoire and fashioned a fourth table leg, then dismantled the clumsy table he'd built himself. They used the wood to shore up gaps in the roof, but kept the tilted bed and continued their nocturnal ebb and flow.

One evening, while Ravel was outside the house painting Jered's crib, he tripped over a full can of paint; the color blue flowed across a patch of sand and dripped down the canyon wall. The effect reminded Ravel of Navajo sand paintings, the way the colors of the stone undulated and the blue flow matched those undulations. Bending to retrieve a partially painted stone, he idly swept his brush around its curves until it was sealed in blue. Lifting another, he then repeated the gesture. Again and again, until about twenty rocks of various sizes were covered in blue. When they were dry, he arranged them haphazardly along the canyon shelf and covered over the blue spills in the dust. Cassie was pleased enough to encourage him to continue. The more stones he painted, the greater the effect. So he carried on painting the stones of that canyon shelf and later would go into the desert with a fresh can of blue and search for round stones with smooth surfaces. He would baptize them with the brush and set them back where he found them, assuming that the desert's own arrangements would, in the scheme of things, be the most suitable.

He didn't choose blue. It was the only color he had in excess; everything else in the house was painted white or yellow, and he had two gallons of leftover Du Pont Blue 103. He would later learn from Gazer that to the Navajos, blue was the color of the south, was female, and was the true color of the shadow of humans. But when he began to paint those stones, he didn't know that he was painting shadows or that he was writing woman, south, place of peace, and invocations of the bundle wands of the Navajo Night Chant. "Arts and crafts" was all he was thinking. And he was noting the passing of time.

He must have painted a thousand of those stones, in every direction, before learning that he had created the first rune of the tribal alphabet.

The night before the end of it all was warm and there was very little breeze. Cassie laid Jered in his crib and rocked him until he was sleeping easily. Then she led Ravel outside to where they could see the stars pressing through the mounting darkness and a quarter-moon hanging low in the horizon, between a pair of distant bluffs. She led him down the footpath to the canyon floor. The well spring was brimming and they filled a tall barrel with water, then shed their clothing and left it on a nearby rock. First Ravel bathed Cassie, lathering her with white soap and caressing her breasts, her waist, her sloping shoulders. She descended low in the barrel and rinsed away the soap, lifted her arms for him to help her, and stepped out of the barrel. Her kiss was cool in the warm air and she held her still-wet body close to his for a long time. Then he took her place in the water and she washed him with her fingers.

When they were clean and dry, they took up their clothes in their hands and crossed the garden to examine the new shoots, the corn and carrots, beets, melon, cucumbers, peas, potatoes, onions, radishes, and lettuce. The sliver of moon rose high overhead and threw long shadows across the canyon walls. They heard the first rumble of thunder in the west and wondered aloud whether the rainfall would reach them. They were on the floor of the canyon and couldn't gauge from the wind. Ravel had lived most of his life on the edge of that desert and never had he thought so much of rain as he did in those days. Cassie and the rain, Jered and the rain. The mosaic of the rain on the canyon walls. The smell of rain. The idea of rain. It was no matter that for twenty dollars he could fill a half-dozen barrels in Paragonah and truck it all back to his home. That was water and not rain.

Cassie walked ahead of him and bent to the earth, then straightened with a flat, round turquoise in her hand. She turned toward the north wall and headed up the footpath. Ravel stayed in the garden and watched her as she rose in the dark night until she stood thirty feet above him. Her black hair was blue in the moonlight and in the shadows her breasts were enlarged and full. Her nakedness from that distance thrilled him and he grew hard all at once. And followed her up the hillside with a gift of painted stone.

She was talking in her sleep and her words were their names, his and Jered's. Ravel thought for a moment that she was calling out to him but when she repeated the names he realized she was only murmuring. "Vance?" like a question unto itself. As in, What is Vance? "Jered," like an answer to the original question. He pressed his ear close to her lips and heard her again: "Vance? . . . Jered . . ." A silence. Then that tilt of the bed led her to him and he pulled back the blanket, bent over her, breathed upon her thighs, and awakened her with his tongue. After a long moment, she opened her eyes. "Jered," she whispered, but the boy was fast asleep in his crib on the other side of the room. Reaching for Vance, she held the small of his back with one hand and with the other led him into her. They rocked together for a long while, neither of them coming, and then separated. Moments later, she drifted toward him again and they started over. He lifted himself on his elbows and looked into her eyes, then they tipped to their sides and moved their hips against each other until she came with a short cry. "You?" she said, and he said, "Yes," and came too. Then she moved away from him to the other side of the bed and slept in a slow drift back in his direction.

He didn't sleep. He lay awake until the window grew light and he could hear the rain begin to fall. It was a light rain that wouldn't last the hour. Already it was April and the desert spring-time was ending. A warm breeze brought the smell of that rain into the room. Cassie slept with her back to him, her knees lifted upward toward her chin so that her backside curved toward his belly. He reached his fingers between her thighs and felt the warmth and knew she would not mind being awakened once more. But then he heard Jered stir and begin to cry, so he rose naked from the bed, got his milk, and pressed the bottle into his hands. The child drank with his eyes opened wide, watching Ravel. He had his mother's lazy eyelids and his father's wary eyes. When the bottle was empty, Jered lifted it in Ravel's direction and then closed his eyes and fell back to sleep.

Ravel pulled on a pair of torn jeans and went to the window. The rain had turned the earth a dull bronze and left a mist across the western horizon. A flat roll of thunder drifted from east to west. Omen, augury, *harbinger*. Ravel noticed a man at the top of the west canyon wall. The man tossed a pack ahead of him, then began to climb down. When he reached the floor, he retrieved his pack, stepped over the irrigation ditches, and crossed to the garden.

From the distance Ravel couldn't see the man's face but assumed that he was young. The ease with which he'd slipped down the canyon wall gave that impression. He wore blue jeans, hiking boots, and a short-sleeved khaki shirt and had the air of a man used to walking. He stepped lightly over the foot-high rows of new corn toward the carrots. He then bent down and reached a hand to the earth. Ravel thought he was about to pluck a carrot from the ground, but he withdrew his hand and it was empty except for a bit of earth, which he tossed into the air. It scattered in the breeze. The man stood and lifted his eyes toward the north.

Then he was looking at Ravel.

Ravel went out of the house and down the stone pathway to the canyon floor. The rain was falling again but it was more mist than raindrops and Ravel felt the cool, rich mud beneath his bare feet. The man stepped out of the garden and onto a footpath around its edge. His first words to Ravel were to call him brother and to apologize for trespassing.

Ravel told him the land belonged to no one. "We're squatters here." He wondered fleetingly if the man knew who they were. Had he been observing them the previous night? If he had been at the top of the canyon he'd have seen them in the garden, walking naked among the greening rows.

Ravel asked, "What are you looking for?"

"A few nights ago I slept in Beryl. They told me how much for the bus and I thought I'd do better to walk. I was lost most of yesterday. Where am I?"

"Still in the Escalante Desert. It's forty miles to Parowan, farther than that to Cedar City."

He had a boy's face but the body of a man. Piercing blue eyes and a scant blond beard that would never fill in. That morning Ravel took the look of hunger in his eyes as something natural, a hunger for food despite the fact that he had not disturbed the garden. Ravel noticed that his backpack was worn and there were holes in the rolled-up blanket tied to it. The man said he was on his way to Parowan to see the Anasazi exhibits there. He granted that he could use some water.

"Got plenty." Ravel gestured to the well spring. "And a place to sleep if you're in the mood."

The man admitted that he was feeling tired. "I was sleeping in the open air, and then the rain came. I never thought to haul a tent across the desert." He said his name was J.D. and he was thankful to have found some angels in the middle of nowhere.

"This isn't nowhere," Ravel corrected him. "We live here."

"No disrespect intended," he said, "but what's the attraction?"

"Solitude," Ravel answered. "A vacation from the planet. Nothing to last forever, but maybe for a long time. I suppose I could ask you what's the deal in crossing a desert on foot?"

"You could ask me," he said, and for the first time Ravel saw that smile, half mirth and half menace. "And I'd have a thousand different versions of the answer."

Ravel didn't know why they took him in just then. They were thankful for the company but not by much. J.D. was polite to

Cassie and a load of fun for Jered; he was tidy and didn't make any particular noise. But his presence was a distraction, an interruption of what had become a very quiet and not unpleasant tedium. After he'd spent a few days sleeping and eating and getting his walking strength back, Ravel expected him to move on. Another surprise rainfall put the skids to that idea and J.D. spent a day in the house, sitting quietly by the unlit fireplace and reading one of Ravel's books of the Upaniṣads. The next day the weather was clear but J.D. was still there, skulking about the garden. That night Cassie refused to make love with Ravel. "He's right there," she said, "on the other side of that wall. I've gotten used to our privacy, Vance. I keep wanting to touch you and then I remember he's here. I even have to get dressed to go down to the garden. Let's wait till he's gone."

The following day, when Ravel awoke just past dawn he could see out the window to the garden, where J.D. was bent over some new tomato plants. Ravel put on his pants, leaving Cassie to sleep, and walked barefoot down the slope to find out what was up.

"Mornin', J.D."

"Mornin', Vance. You got a bad lack of nitrogen here." He gestured to a pair of tomato buds so yellow as to seem white and as small as cherries.

Ravel told him they were a bit short on cowshit in these parts.

"What's in the water?"

Ravel shrugged. "Just water."

The sun was rising over the canyon rim and the shadows receded, changing color from blue to brown to yellow. Ravel noticed that J.D. still hadn't shaved and his beard was getting long and straggly. There was a long silence between them that he meant to fill with a query as to when J.D.'d be heading out.

"We'd better get to work," J.D. said. When Ravel didn't answer, J.D. added, "Time to treat that water with something holy."

They traced the drying rivulets from the ditches back to the canyon wall and then up that wall to where Ravel had carved furrows to catch the flow. Here and there J.D. pointed out puddles where the furrows had collapsed or where the water had run off into fissures.

"These catchalls won't work like this," he said. "You can't get enough water off these walls to create a constant flow."

His idea was to carve a series of smaller reservoirs at various levels of the canyon wall and let the overflow from one fall downward to the next. They would avoid the faults and crannies along the way where the runoff would otherwise be lost. "We'll lose a bit to evaporation but less than we'd lose along those cracks. *Then* we feed these pools with some minerals," he added. "And I don't mean just cowshit, though I gather you were only making conversation. If we mine these pools with some nutrient, when the water hits the canyon floor it won't look so much like chlorine. You follow?"

They started work right after breakfast and kept it up through to nightfall. The new gullies needed to be carved in hard stone rather than the sandstone, which absorbed too much of the flow, and it appeared to Ravel that they had weeks of labor ahead of them before the job would be finished. Though he could do it alone, he wasn't sure he had the heart. But when J.D. continued to show no signs whatsoever of heading east as advertised, Cassie began to get edgy and even began to wonder aloud if he might be a criminal of some sort, and she reminded Ravel of their intentions to be alone. "It was good to be naked with you when we didn't have to worry if we were *covered* or not. I was always thinking of the three of us. Now I catch myself hiding again, staying indoors for no other reason than to be alone. When it was just us I was never alone. I was with you at all times."

It was true that J.D. spent long hours on a high rock, looking west as though in search of the dust wake of a modern-day posse, four-wheel-drive instead of palomino, but Ravel saw in his restlessness a kindred spirit and didn't mind in the least all the help J.D. was giving him on the irrigation network.

The only thing J.D. asked of them, directly and in clear words, was writing paper. Settling near to the fire each evening, he filled page after page, but never mentioned what it was he was putting to words. In bed at night, Cassie and Ravel would wonder at it, those reams of paper, guessing at various times that it was a journal, or poetry, or simply written prayers. He was filling a dozen pages a day; they never knew where he kept them once they were finished.

J.D. slept on a mattress in the wide big room and washed his own clothing with soap and stone and water, leaving these near rags to dry on various rocks outside the house. All of his clothing lost its color, as had Cassie's and Ravel's. They were dressed in the shades of the desert, muted browns and beige and coral and powder blue. Cassie got out her old blouses and frayed blue jeans and would spend her evenings mending clothing they hadn't worn in weeks. J.D. rode into Cedar City with them and they fitted him out with new jeans, sandals, and some secondhand shirts from the Salvation Army. To show them his gratitude he worked in the garden late into the evening and they delighted in having a few hours to themselves.

J.D.'s only possessions were a turquoise ring, a ballpoint pen, a wooden comb, a number of books, which turned out to be religious in nature, and a hunting knife with a broken blade, which he had carried, he said, since a long-ago visit to Africa. Whenever J.D. spoke of himself, which was rarely and usually in answer to a question, he made references to faraway places: Africa, Indonesia, South America, the Middle East.

"He's only telling stories," Cassie insisted to Ravel in their bedroom one night. "He can't have been in all those places. He isn't that old."

The next day, when Ravel asked his age, J.D. said he was older than Jered and younger than the stone in his hand. It was an answer Ravel didn't repeat to Cassie, knowing well enough what she'd have to say in return.

After two weeks of hard labor, they had finished three elaborate skeins of rivulet and pool. There had been no more rainfall and so the network hadn't been tested. They turned their attention to the garden. Already it was May and the days were longer and the desert heating up. The corn that Cassie had planted in March was knee high but the leaves were a pale green and J.D.'s point about nitrogen starvation was well taken. He suggested they dig a second garden, closer to the west canyon wall, where the afternoon shadows would protect the plants. The men raked out the stone and dried brush while Cassie chopped at the topsoil with a hoe and fork. Then, on J.D.'s insistence, they invested in a pickup load of crushed coal, nitrogen pellets, and another two hundred pounds of fertilizer. The coal, he said, would retain water and release it gradually into the surrounding soil. They could reduce the runoff by about 30 percent.

"There's other stuff around'll do the same work but coal's cheap." That's what Ravel said to Mircea while she wrote the check. Her only answer was to remind him that he was in the Escalante Desert and not the Sacramento Valley. She had an endless supply of cold water to throw on his face.

Laboring shirtless in that desert field, J.D. and Ravel kept up a continuous conversation, finding that their common ground was the wealth of credo and superstition that existed out there, beyond them. Ravel admitted to having dabbled in everything from Catholic communion to voodoo to tantra to the Navajo Night Chants, but nothing had possessed him and he'd come to the desert as an act of abandonment. J.D. had been to Africa and to Asia, he said, to see the pagan practices firsthand in the hopes of sorting out the truth beyond what he read in *National*

Geographic. He had spent three months in a kibbutz on the West Bank, where he'd been circumcised. In a rage of pain, he'd crossed the sea into Jordan to see how the other half lived. Moving farther on, he had begged in the streets of Bombay and bathed his feet in the Ganges River. Had studied Sanskrit and struggled toward a tantric state in a remote Kashmiri village. "For a while my legs didn't work and I was under the illusion that I was being transported. As though my soul were leaving my body and reaching upward. An English archaeologist took one look at me and said 'Rickets,' and I spent three months in a beggars' hospital in New Delhi, where they fed me rice and warm water and an evil-tasting paste meant to kill the parasites."

When he was healthy again, he had fled to Tehran, but in a short time his health had failed him again and, worse, he had begun to grow lonesome for women. Western women. So after what he described as years of travel, he had washed his hands of it all and gone back to San Francisco to give in to his most persistent longings. And after a few months of northern California affection-taking—"hot tubs, oil, and candlelight, Quaaludes and long-haired women"—he'd again grown restless and angry with himself and had headed east. He'd been on his way to see the Anasazi petroglyphs near Kanab when he'd come upon Cassie and Vance. The Anasazi were pueblo-dwelling Indians. "At Johnson Canyon," he said, "there are some petroglyphs worth seeing. And I hear there's some artifacts in Parowan."

Ravel told him Parowan was a waste of time. "There's a public museum there, in Anasazi State Park. Most of what's there dates to 1050 or thereabouts but you can't get really close to it. The feeling is gone. The better places for petroglyphs are farther on, near Vernal, on this private ranch. One wall there goes on for about two miles. Or way over in the southeast corner of the state there's the Trail of the Ancients."

J.D. asked about the stone painting and Ravel related the accident of spilling the paint. He admitted that it was simply a pastime, that he had no specific intentions other than to mark time by the proliferation of those painted stones. J.D. didn't believe him and pointed out that the Navajos had left their traces in the desert in a similar fashion with sand paintings and petroglyphs. In months to come Ravel would learn that J.D. had sufficient background in Navajo myth and lore to twist everything that Ravel said and did into a variant on their ancient religion. J.D. began by explaining the signification of the colors. Blue, the south, female, evening. The purest of blues was turquoise, and Du Pont Blue 103, a baby blue, came close to turquoise after drying in that hot sun. Black, the north, both danger and protection; invisibility. White, the differentiation of the sacred from the profane. Yellow, the west, fructification, also female. Woman originated from a yellow ear of corn. Red, the color of sorcery, blood, and war. When Ravel asked about green, J.D. told him that the Navajo made no great distinction between green and yellow and blue. Green could be a more mature blue or an aging version of yellow. He insisted that Ravel's painting of the stones had to come from a calling. "In the desert," he said cryptically, "there are no accidents."

They agreed that they were living in a neglected holy land and Ravel trusted J.D. enough to tell him more about his own travels, which were far less extravagant. One day he confided to J.D. the story of his father and the walk into light. Though it was only midmorning and still in the month of May, the heat was already intense, and as they stood in the field, leaning on their shovels, the sweat ran down their tanned shoulders like a fine rain. J.D. listened all the way through to the end and then asked Ravel to tell him again. The second go-round, J.D. interrupted him from time to time to ask questions.

"You said there were witnesses. Have you ever talked to any of them?"

"A few," Ravel told him. "By the time I was old enough to ask about what happened, most of them were long gone."

"And there's no mistake. He walked into that?"

Ravel nodded. "And certain of where he was headed."

Lifting his shovel, J.D. pushed the blade into the earth and left it there. "What do you suppose he saw?"

Ravel didn't know. He had never known. So he said nothing. But in the years that followed, he wondered if he hadn't embellished something in the telling. He might have added drama to the narrative or been slipshod with his theological adjectives. He was often certain that the two-bit heresy that followed was based as much upon his loose lip as on the story. He said that his father had walked into light. He said that it was deliberate and that witnesses had brought him the narrative. *My father walked into light and there was nothing of him to be found thereafter.*

And J.D., who believed that nothing in the desert happened by accident, just took it from there.

The next day, J.D. didn't show up for work in the garden and Ravel planted ten long rows of corn without his help. Cassie climbed to the top of the canyon and saw J.D. in the desert distance but wasn't able to make out what he was up to. He was absent a second day and Ravel began to grow angry. He had a way of inspiring projects that required Ravel's aid and then leaving him to complete them alone. And on the third day, in the middle of a blazing afternoon, J.D. came to fetch Ravel in the field to say he was finished.

"Finished with what?"

"With the first sand painting," he said. "And I've fashioned some prayer sticks for the journey."

This didn't make any sense to Ravel but he followed J.D. up the north wall of the canyon and into the open desert. They walked toward the west, in the direction of twin bluffs that rose like the spires of a ruined cathedral, and every hundred yards or so J.D. would bend to retrieve an ornamented stick. These sticks were about a foot long, wrapped in yarn and string and feathers of various colors, though mostly white and black. "Sky," he said of the first, and of the second, "Earth." "Moon" and "Sun" for the next two. And then "Shooting Chant." They arrived at a high ridge halfway between the two bluffs and J.D. stopped, handed Ravel the prayer sticks, and told him to go ahead without him. Ravel obeyed and ten yards farther on, he came to the sand painting. J.D. had carved out a flat depression in the earth and filled it with sundry colors of sand to make an earth mosaic of roughly four feet by six feet.

The upper part of the painting was primarily turquoise in color and had been made from a stain of plants in white sand. The heavens. Below this was a black circle with pure whitestone flakes inside, and in the midst of this circle, which Ravel recognized as his canyon, was a yellow rectangle. This he assumed to be his house. Yellow columns rose unevenly around that rectangle—the corn—and amid those columns was a single finger of blue, which J.D. later told him represented Cassie. The sand painting had obviously been painstaking work. Colored stones had been sought out and ground into sand. Each of the varicolored sands had been poured with precision and the arrangements of color did not blur or meld. And above the yellow field, above the circle of the canyon, was a final set of symbols, a rising wall of whitestone, the purest of all that J.D. had crushed into sand. Looking upon that wall of white, Ravel was nearly blinded by the reflections of the sun that shone from it. So blinded that he nearly missed the symbol in the center, made of ocher, the symbol of a man, a walking man. The man who walked into light.

That night J.D. asked again for paper and he began to write swiftly, filling page after page until his pen went dry. Then he asked whether Ravel had another somewhere nearby. They didn't learn until it was too late that all the time he'd been with them he'd been writing to scattered friends and half-disciples, telling them he'd found something he'd been looking for in every corner of the earth and urging them now to join him. The story of Ravel's father apparently iced the deal, because a few weeks later two of them showed up. Then another. A week after that there were another three.

Ravel forgets the way they referred to themselves then. Their former names were never carved into those stones and almost at once there was a reinvention of what they called each other. Though he is guilty of multiple sins, this business of nomenclature wasn't his idea. The Indians thought of it long before the Er did and Ravel didn't have the presence of mind, in the beginning, to put a stop to it. He kept his own name, Ravel, but the others became what they were or what they did, a wrinkle in their culture that Ravel could have done without. Every new named ended in -er. Painter, Gazer, Rainer, Rocker. The dumbness of it all was the first omen Ravel failed to read. Sander, Walker, Seeder, Dreamer. Had they continued to grow, their theocracy flourishing in that desert emptiness, there would undoubtedly have later been a Shoeser, a Hatter, and, perhaps, a Burier. For the whole of it, the name of the emerging tribe, they settled soon enough on the Er.

All of them were coming from the west, never from the east. Gazer, formerly J.D., was from Oakland, Sander from Portland, and Painter from various slag heaps in and around Orange County. Palo Alto, Seattle, San Bernardino, Monterey, Tucson, and Flagstaff: J.D., now Gazer, had captured them like that rainfall, only this time his skein of rivulets was thrown to the west and brought everything to the east. And in times to come, those few who moved on went farther east, a reversal of the instinct otherwise known as Manifest Destiny, an inland searching as for a lost shoe instead of a hidden path.

To shelter the new arrivals, they built a second house on the canyon floor, using leftover lumber from the house Ravel had built for himself. Then they added two other houses, made from mud and stone and a crude version of adobe brick.

Most of them wanted only what a desert implies: distance, solitude, privation, and cleansing. They fed on bread and salt and white corn and boredom and their memorized or made-up prayers to known or invented gods. In no time Gazer had them fashioning prayer sticks after the Navajo model. They tore colored strips from their own poor clothing and knotted those sticks with yellow fire, blue water, white air, and brown earth. Around the campfires Ravel heard Hindu, Bantu, voodoo, and a smattering of San Marino County Spanish; Moses, Abraham, Martin Luther, and Jesus Christ, yogi and yaya, Wakon, Yahweh; path, order, light. Here a tent, there a sacred flame, and every evening the retelling of the story of the man who walked into absolute light.

And a gazing up the hillside to the house of his son.

Ravel declined to pray with them. On his own time he continued to paint rocks blue. He kept at it because Cassie once said that she never felt lost if she came across one of those rocks while wandering the emptiness that surrounded them. He was aware of what was happening in the settlement that had sprung up and he could see clearly enough in the glazed expressions of his fellow agrarians that he was looked upon as something more than just one of their number. Gazer had done his spadework and in no time the theocracy was literally fixed in stone. And if Ravel shrugged or looked askance on the whole business, his gestures were taken as signs of humility rather than a rejection of idolatry. They were manufacturing their own hellfire, he told himself, and he thought it was for them and not for himself.

All the while the garden on the canyon floor was expanding. Eight rows of corn became twelve, then twenty, then thirty. The well spring held up despite a lack of rainfall and some of those who joined the settlement brought real currency with which to buy real canned goods, seed, fertilizer, charcoal, red wine, and the usual drugs of choice. When there were twenty of them, Gazer held the first mass. Leading the initiates from campfire to campfire, he distributed prayer sticks and orchestrated the chanting. Then he showed them the path up the north slope to the house. At the moment of their arrival, Ravel was moving his wetted body away from a still-churning Cassie. Holding his weight on his elbows, he reached to extinguish the lamp, when he noticed them at the window. They stood silently with bowed heads, only Gazer looking upward and into his eyes.

The following day, Ravel climbed to the top of the canyon, where he found a circle of stones that he had not painted. Farther on he saw Gazer, bowl in hand, laminating a boulder in blue pigment that he had mixed from plants and sand. The color was a perfect turquoise with the barest suggestion of white.

"That's my color, J.D. Where are your manners?"

The next day Gazer was painting yellow, red, and white. His exercise caught on and the others began to paint as well, searching out flat and round stones and coloring them like icons. "Lunacy," Ravel muttered to his wife.

With the stroke of a brush, he was confirmed as a prophet.

Painter had been among the first of them to arrive. He was fourteen years old and dressed in clothes that were barely more than rags. Approaching Ravel, he had stammered a request for asylum.

"For what crime?" Ravel asked him, but he didn't say.

Of all the Er, it was Painter who most gave Ravel the willies. For days at a time, Painter would remain speechless, avoiding the eyes of those around him, and then, as though bitten, he would begin to jabber in an imitation of god talk. He threw words around like handfuls of sand: light, way, path, free, truth, cosmic, o stone, o sun, o shadow of man, in your own name is the song of bliss and who knows what and who knows when, the stone speaks and the shadows weep with joy, and the sun and the moon and the sun and the moon.

And the sun and the moon.

And the moon and the sun.

And so on.

And he had a way of using words that was unique. He said allbody instead of everybody. For the ever instead of forever. Ravel avoided him because there was in his mindless manner a mockery of his own speech from times gone by; the mockery was unintended, but it echoed deep within him. Painter was equally slavish to Gazer and to Ravel and would follow either of them like a dog into the expanding desert fields. He would accede to any request, however ridiculous, to exhibit his gratitude for having been taken in.

One of the women, Namer, had known him in Los Angeles. She told Ravel he'd been abandoned at birth, "Left by the side of the highway in a plastic bag with his twin brother. The brother didn't make it and Painter here got left to the state's limitless mercy." In his short lifetime he had lived in a dozen foster homes but recently he had fallen through the frail net of the Great Society. Namer had found him living off the street and she'd taken him with her to a commune in Bakersfield. He had seldom been to school, could neither read nor write, and, somewhere along the dotted line of his life, had lost the instinct to retreat from pain. A short time after his arrival, Ravel saw Painter reach a bare hand into a fire to retrieve a fallen potato and the emerging blisters on his hands didn't prompt so much as a whimper. He seemed merely surprised, as though tricked somehow. Another time, climbing to a high rock overlooking the settlement, he had simply stepped into thin air and fallen twenty feet to a patch of mesquite. The scratches on his body must have stung painfully but all he said was that he'd meant to walk higher up and what a dumb thing to do after all.

"I thought you were with me, Vance. I forgot I was on my alone."

Namer was the oldest of the Er. Ravel knew as much without having proof. He never asked her her age and only assumed by the lines in her face and her near-perpetual dolefulness that she was pushing fifty. Her face seemed to have been fashioned from worn rope and her dirty clothes did little to hide her shapelessness. All she told him of her pre-Er existence was that she'd had four children who'd never loved her with three men who'd never loved her either. She admitted that she didn't much buy the story of the man who walked into absolute light but was willing to play along if that was the ticket to stay in the environs.

"No admission required," he told her.

"That's what they always say," she responded. "But this isn't my first commune, Ravel. In the beginning, when everyone is still giddy and stoned, you hear this rap about freedom and ecstasy and nobody mentions who washes or dries the dishes or digs the outhouse. We always start out pretending like nature's gonna pay the rent. Then the rain falls or the outhouse begins to stink and we're on a kind of mass O.D. and there's no Red Cross within a thousand miles." She bent and lifted a palmful of dust from the canyon floor. When she opened her palm the breeze blew all of it away. "Hellacious soil," she said, with a smile that showed the unfortunate gaps between her teeth. "Mercy mercy me. I wouldn't build a parking lot here, let alone a farm. You are in deep, deep shit, Saint Ravel. It's gonna be a trip just watching how well you toe the sacred line."

Weaver came to the house with a basketful of coral-colored sand that she'd gathered from the west. Ravel figured she was sixteen or seventeen years old. Gazer said he'd met her after he returned from his Asian missions. When Ravel answered the door, she bowed her head to the dust and reached the basket in his direction. "For the next sand painting," she said.

"What sand painting might that be?" Cassie asked her.

"The prophet's painting," she answered. "The incarnation of his vision."

"And which prophet are we speaking of?"

Weaver's gaze rose from the dust at her feet and came to rest on Ravel.

He stepped forward and put the basket back into her hands. "About this pointless bowing, Weaver. It has to stop."

She answered placidly that Gazer had instructed her and that she would obey. "He's told me that the son is a modest man. A denier, he calls you. Why don't I just leave the basket by the door? The sand is from stone found between the two bluffs, in the place of the first sand painting. Someone will make use of it in the by-and-by."

"Tell them, Vance. Tell them there's been a mistake. The man they're looking for passed through but he isn't here anymore."

"Which man?"

"The walking-into-light man. Can't you see what's happening?"

He told her they should bide their time. "These people just got the wrong end of the stick. When they get hungry enough they'll move on."

Soon there were six houses with, altogether, fifteen rooms; a tent, a toolshed, three outhouses, a grain bin, a potato cellar, a rock pool for bathing; and an outdoor kiva, a holy circle of painted stones where prayer sticks were fashioned, pigments were ground and mixed, and the story was chanted of the man who walked into absolute light. By the end of the first summer, there were also three goats, twenty chickens, four roosters, three then eight then twelve cats—Ravel stopped counting after that.

Jered's hair grew long and tangled and with his deep tan he began to look like some wild Tasmanian child. Ravel hadn't meant for his family to become cave people, and so Cassie cut Jered's hair to schoolboy length and went to great pains to keep him dressed in boy clothes, shorts and T-shirts and tennis shoes, even while the Er were beginning to wear loose robes and some of the women chose to bare their breasts to that unforgiving sun.

At the same time, what for the rest of them was a river of language was to Jered a delta. He insisted on creating his own words for things. Anxious for him, Ravel would often sit with a book propped between them to instruct him, but more often than not it was Ravel who was instructed.

"These are animals, Jered. Some of them live in the desert and some don't. Horse, cow, lamb, bird. Can you say bird?"

"Bud."

"Horse?"

"Orz."

"Cow?"

"Coo."

It was not, Cassie assured him, an impediment but a creative act of defiance. Whole sentences spilled from him that only his mother could translate. Man de ho tho. There's a man on the hill. Wo gada di wo. Water the garden with water. It was, like any language, an evolved baby talk. At least half the time he spoke English but his private language progressed just as quickly.

Ravel asked Jered why he spoke like that.

"So ta neva me hoot."

Cassie translated. "So they never will hurt me."

"So who won't hurt you?"

"Wo fa. Bu han. Et ta."

"Waterface. Bluehands. The others."

Ravel didn't understand and Cassie explained that Waterface was Gazer and Bluehands was Namer. So even Jered had his own nomenclature.

Then Jered looked up at Ravel, his addled father, and said, "Ta cricri me woot."

This Ravel could translate by himself. "They're afraid of my words."

. . .

Ravel knew that words failed him, that Jesus Himself was tragically misquoted every second of every A.D. What his father had done had obsessed him since childhood and he had spoken too much of it, and here were the results: exile from Paragonah, Randy's loathing, his mother's painful silences. He had long since given up solving the mysteries of his father's last day on earth and had come to the desert with a simple enough task: a blind grab at a sane way of life which might, with luck, settle into a ritual of love, loving, loved. But then those deadbeats came along and saw a flickering of resolve in his blue eyes, and maybe because he was in the desert and wore a beard like a chasuble and spoke often to the sky, to the rocks, to the dust, they took him for a holy man. There you have it, Ravel concluded, the popular American confusion between derelict and deity.

Though he couldn't admit as much to Cassie, Ravel was a trifle giddy having disciples in the canyon. There was always someone to wash the dishes and pour the tea and, like any performing art, preaching offered immediate feedback, instant gratification, that satisfying reflection of nodding heads. No singing required, no music, no soft shoe. He seldom spoke to the Er for any length of time, usually just a word or two as follow-up to good morning. But whatever was sincere in him was gradually being reduced to rote and recitation, while he played to the Er and the Er played back. In the beginning, the Word; in the end, show biz.

All the same, he stayed far away from the rituals and the chanting. He stayed in the house with wife and child and a good book whenever the Er played at finger painting in the vast rumpus room of the Escalante Desert. What he preferred was to observe them as they redeemed the desert with water and excrement, overcoming dead centuries of alkali with their own sweat and saliva. They were not, he supposed, unlike any other vegetarian/

agrarian sect. I grow this so that I may eat it; I build this so that it will house me. They cultivated a common garden, spread water over seedlings with their fingers, and smiled to each other across the rising rows of green. The sand paintings were often stunning in their beauty and a number of the chants evolved into sweet music from the mouths of Weaver or Dreamer. And even Namer, with her tragic face and countless blisters, had a dulcet singing voice, which echoed pleasantly across the floor of the canyon. And in this she was no longer ugly or cynical or mean-spirited.

Late one night, watching from his window, Ravel observed the goings-on on the canyon floor below and could see in the light of the kiva campfire the pairings of male and female.

"Cassie, come watch."

"What is it?"

"A mass marriage."

"A group grope, you mean."

He had to admit that that was about the size of it. He watched until the fires burned low and there was nothing more to see.

"At least they're having fun," he told Cassie.

She turned her back to him and through the night she failed to drift to his side.

A second year went by, both a winter and a summer harvest. Their clothing faded to no color at all and the rains fell less frequently. A corn crop failed and three of the Er moved on. From the house high up, Ravel heard less chanting and more bickering. And with the passing of time came the final fruit of an empty desert: a yawning boredom that ached to be filled. As the food diminished and garbage began to pile up, the Er were gradually reduced to sunup, sundown, communism in all its drear and drabness, and somebody please pass the potatoes.

He's GETTING ahead of himself, he knows, outrunning his own intentions to stay calm and let time pass, to leave his family some breathing space while they get used to the idea that he's back, that he's shorn his beard, and that the barking has long since ended. He senses that if he is ever to make peace with Cassie and Jered he will first have to make peace with the rest of the universe.

Randy's seems as good a place as any to start, so on his third night off from the car salvage Ravel totes a case of Coors across the lot that separates the two trailers and lays his fist against the aluminum door. Trash emerges from the shade under the trailer's porch, sniffs, barks once, then goes back to the shadows. There is no answer. Putting his ear to that door, Ravel listens for a few seconds before deciding that Randy must be out, but as he turns his back the door scrapes open and there's Randy in jeans and cowboy boots, his chest bare. It's been years since Ravel's seen him without a shirt and he's surprised to see that the hair on his chest has gone gray.

"What have I done to deserve this?" Randy wants to know.

"Just paying a visit."

"I don't want to hear about Jesus and Hare Krishna."

"That makes two of us."

"And I won't buy the least stick of whatever you're selling."

"In that case." Ravel leaves the beer on the ground in front of the trailer and walks away. Randy calls after him but Ravel takes three more steps before turning around.

"This for me?"

Ravel nods.

"Well fuck me dead for bad manners, Ravel. Come on in."

He bends to retrieve the beer and Ravel follows him inside.

The trailer is like a fuselage or space capsule, tiny but amazingly well organized. Ten feet by thirty, with a seven-foot ceiling and with every inch of wall space bearing Randy's hung possessions: shirts, tools, kitchen utensils, keys, cutting board, pistols, a few jutting bookcases piled high with skin and car magazines, and a surprising number of novels—Dos Passos, Faulkner, Twain, Steinbeck, and Zane Grey. There is another shelf for toaster, coffeepot, and telephone. On the narrow bed is a coverlet of Papago design and in the corner a pull-down tabletop next to a folding chair. Clean laundry is stacked at the foot of the bed, faded jeans and shirts with mother-of-pearl snaps, and hanging from a nail are a half-dozen string ties, with clasps made from turquoise, agate, and jet.

Ravel sits on the bed while Randy cracks open the door of the saddest refrigerator in creation, a yellowed box of cold space, empty except for an open can of pork and beans, a spoon seeming to grow from its center. On the bottom shelf is a black flake of what might once have been lettuce or celery, God knows. Randy lines his beer cans like chess pieces across the top shelf and tells Ravel he shouldn't be so touchy. "What you need, Vance, is something to loosen you up a little. Get the trigger finger out of your asshole." He holds an unopened can in his large fist. "Any of these cold?"

"I wasn't thinking ahead."

"No big deal. Warm's fine when it's all there is. Join me?" He snaps open a pair of cans and hands one to Ravel. Foam rises from the can and flows over his brown fingers. "Just so you know," he says, "you're the first man to step in here in about ten years. All's I ever let in this way is women."

Ravel tells him he didn't mean to intrude. "I was in the neighborhood and thought I'd say how-do."

"Christ, Ravel. You almost sound normal."

"What was I supposed to sound like?"

"I don't know. Hokey, out of left field, off the deep end. When you got back from college it looked like you had stars

where your eyes were supposed to be. You still fiddle around
with dope and such?"

"Not for a while."

"Weeks? Months?"

"Years."

"What about your weird friends?"

Ravel makes a gesture, palms up. "Can't say." In his mind,
the boat is burning again, that desert ark of plasterboard and pine
where he lived with Cassie and Jered. The walls evaporate in
flame, revealing a two-by-four skeleton, the furniture smoldering
into bright ash. The day he closed up shop and the Er gaped
after him, their vanishing prophet. "It's been a long time," he
tells Randy. "We haven't been in touch."

Randy says he hasn't seen them either. "They sure as hell
don't come around here."

Ravel says that the Er were never much for Saturday night
at the Two Guns.

"I been in the desert, Ravel. I still got my truck. Used to see
one or the other of them from time to time but it's been months
now."

This doesn't jibe with the rocks Ravel's been finding, but he
doesn't say so to Randy. "They might have moved farther on.
Maybe the well went dry. I don't know anymore. I've been
elsewhere."

"Like where?" He flips open another can and extends it, even
though Ravel's barely touched his first.

"East. Mostly in cities."

"I've been to some of those places. Salt Lake, Denver, St.
Louis. Seems like there's no earth left when you get there, like
you climbed up some kind a stairway without knowing it. Nauga-
hyde, plastic, Formica, fiberglass. Mile after mile of cement and
blacktop. When I pound my fist I can't feel the resonance of
wood."

"Resonance?"

"I know the word, Ravel. I just play dumb most times to fit

in with the company I keep. I got a private vocabulary you wouldn't believe."

There is a pause. Each drinks to the other's shadow. Randy lights a Winston after tearing off the filter.

"So what'd you come to tell me?"

Ravel shrugs. "The heat's on and I'm casting about. We used to be sort of friends."

"Not friends, Ravel. A man and a boy. There's a world of difference there."

"Then I felt you hating me. Every look was a new hurt."

"You started it. You called me names. Worse."

Ravel doesn't remember.

"Maybe it was the drugs talking. You tell me. We just all up and disappeared for you when none of us got saintly and sprouted wings like you did. Don't look at me like that. I got my own version of events."

"It was a two-way street, Randy. When I was wearing robes and going barefoot, you always made shit of it."

"Your god stuff, yeah. Making a myth out a your old man." He blows a perfect smoke ring, which hangs in the trailer like a word.

"You wanted me to become a modern cowpoke just like you," Ravel argues, "and I was more inclined to the cloth."

"Bullroar. You were just a garden-variety snotnose, Ravel. Holier than thou and giving everybody the shakes. I remember now what you called me."

"So do I. The week I came home from school."

"Then you tell me, 'cause all I remember is scrambled words."

"A pagan ape with cowboy boots. A drunken jerk-off with piss stains on your soul. Things on that order, spoken from the heart."

"That's about the size of it."

Ravel can't stop himself from smiling. "You're getting old, Randy. You must have heard worse."

"Not from a so-called friend."

"You just said we weren't friends. Man and boy, you said."

"I taught you things. How to shoot a gun and read the sky. How to squeeze the water from a cholla and to find roots in the desert so you'd never starve. I gave you my *time*."

Ravel finishes the first beer and starts in on the second. "I didn't come to fight, Randy."

"You sure as shit did. You threw the first punch."

"Let's just get drunk and talk baseball till the sun comes up."

"Not so fast with this buddy-buddy stuff. I got bones to pick with you it might take years to get buried. Like how you fucked life for your old lady, who's worth twenty a you lined up left to right. And how you disappeared on your wife and kid for three whole years. A real blue-ribbon fuck-up, that's what you are. Now you come here with a case a beer and I'm supposed to shake your hand and say quits? Lame. That's what I call it. Just plain lame."

All Ravel can do is peer into his can of beer and wait for the wind to die down.

"Anyhow, I got a date," Randy tells him. "Saturday nights I don't have to jerk off."

"I take it back, Randy. All of it. We'll write down the words and I'll eat the paper."

"Too late. And anyway, you were right about some things. Not that being right ever got anybody off the hook."

Ravel sets down his beer, walks to the door, and opens it. Randy tells him it's good he's come, then adds, "Still and all, don't crowd me. I've got this way of holding grudges that won't quit."

Crossing the flat to Mircea's trailer, Ravel hears pistol shots and turns, stunned, before realizing it's only the major. There are two more reports and the sounds of breaking glass and he knows for sure he's still in the here and now. Every night at sundown the major's out there shooting for all he's worth.

·   ·   ·

A telephone call from a man whose voice he doesn't recognize. First of all he'd like to talk business.

Ravel says he doesn't know what he's talking about.

"Don't play dumb with me, Ravel. I'm talking about dog eat dog, with cash as the kicker."

Ravel answers that he wouldn't know. That he's been dealing in spiritual currency, for which no change is ever given.

"Cassie told me you were a head case."

"What else did Cassie tell you?"

"Faster, harder, deeper."

That one fairly takes the wind out of Ravel and his return is weak. "We've got a bad connection, whoever you are. Maybe you'd better call again some other time."

"Never mind about some other time. I'm talking cash, Ravel. Three thousand dollars and all you gotta do is blow town."

Ravel says he's having a hard time hearing.

"You have to admit that's generous," the man tells him. "A heel would have cut corners, but I figure Cassie's peace of mind is worth plenty."

"To see me disappear."

"You got it."

"And leave her to you?"

"This is what I call progress, Ravel. I talk and you listen. And I'm not gonna split hairs about who's the father here. I got a heart, and anyways, as I figure it, there's a fair chance it's mine."

Ravel guesses it's a good thing the man can't see him tearing at his hair. "Leave Cassie to you? You?"

"I'm a pillar of society and you're an unemployed fruitcake. When are you gonna learn the ropes?"

Ravel reminds him he's employed at Nashua Coe's as a night watchman.

"Don't say? But I can take *real* care of her. And Jered too. I can show them affection and keep a roof over their heads, not to mention furnishing a car with all the razzmatazz and putting a color TV in the living room. What's your counter-offer?"

"I can yearn for her," Ravel answers. "Till it hurts."

"What's the angle in that?"

"Beats me. Let's just say I'm rowing for the answer and I've settled on the fact that it's somewhere in the vicinity of Cassie and Jered. I'm rowing hard, whoever you are. It hurts like mad but I keep rowing. Now you figure out your next move."

Locate the itch behind the knee, at the base of the throat, in the muscles that circle the heart. Define the itch as want or need or the anxiety of losing love. Define it as impossible to scratch.

Whenever Ravel is with Mircea there is something there of his father as well. A space on the table where a third plate might be or the vacant chair over which his mother has draped a nylon stocking. There are three of everything in the trailer, trinities of objects and symbols, his mother's quarter century of remembering, remembering. And in this Jack Ravel has a presence; is manifest. And who said that no one is truly dead until the last of those who knew him are also dead? Count on half the world to lay even money on the necessity of memory. A written name may reside in some archive or bank vault or on magnetic tape, but this last, despite the wild claims of computer scientists, is not memory. It is only a flashy modern orthography.

Ravel is reminded of an ongoing Mormon project of baptizing the dead. It's a sticky point of their faith: that the dead are still innocent and can be salvaged like any of Nashua Coe's abandoned automobiles. They are feeding names like grains of sand into a Sperry Univac mainframe and the lists of those names, printed out on continuous perforated paper, provide the basis for a quarterly mass anointing. The names of the dead are gathered from the four corners of the flat earth, out of town halls, cantons, arrondissements, and rural routes, and are coded into octal bits on disk drives spinning like frenzied LPs, a monotone whispered hmm. Ravel can only assume that the sons of Joe Smith, intent upon an orderly entry into paradise, have created separate files of Saved and To Be Saved, before and after, the still very dead and the celestials.

The consent of the dead is not required. To have dared having a name is crime enough to require a second christening, one that will not have a chance of being sullied by a lifetime (you're already dead, hey) of uninterrupted evil.

When Sandy's nocturnal business is consummated, her man zipped up and gone home, she invites Ravel to join her for a smoke in the Cadillac. One of the cars has recently been sold and she's down to six rooms where at one time her motel had seven.

"It was the powder-blue job," she tells him. "The one with all that sexy chrome like silver stitching. I saw a fat man driving it down the interstate and it was like seeing someone scary in my bedroom. I wanted to scream."

Ravel tells her it's only a status symbol, a Cadillac. "Any of the other cars would do as well."

She shakes her head. "These cars are magic, Ravel. Whenever I do my thing in a Cadillac I feel so special. Dignified. If I get it on in the backseat of a Chevy, I feel just like Kleenex and the whole business is a low-rent hassle."

They are facing a chain-link fence, beyond which is a stretch of flat leading to the interstate. It is well past midnight and the highway is an untraveled band of blue with a dot-dash set of stripes. Ravel is sitting in the driver's seat with the wheel like a threat beneath his hands. He figures he could hot-wire the ignition, tear through the fence and onto the highway, and hightail it with Sandy into a lifetime of satisfying his want and his lust in some Mexican border town. Another kind of priesthood, with its own gestures and rites. Another capricious disaster at the end of which he could say, "It seemed like a good idea at the time."

Sandy flips on the radio and punches buttons until she finds a rock station from Flagstaff. Music fills the car like hot smoke.

"Would you do it?" he asks her.

"Do what?"

"Follow me to Mexico and set up house somewhere?"

Her smile hurts him, bespeaking pity. "You're nice," she says. "But you're also weird. I asked around and people told me about your friends. Was it fun running around naked in the desert?"

"We didn't run much and mostly we wore clothes."

"And I'll bet you prayed a lot and did ghost chants and stuff."

"From time to time. Sundays and holidays."

"No wonder Cassie took off."

"What do you know about Cassie?"

The music stops and a voice drones news. Ravel could not swear that it isn't the same voice as the man who called him. Sandy pushes buttons until she finds more of her music. She says, "I know Cassie's been around the block."

"Tell me about it. I'm looking for a name. A pillar of society, maybe."

"Ask her yourself. I can't do your dirty work."

"I can't. She hurts too much."

"Well if it's any consolation, she's hardly competition."

"That's not what I meant."

"If what you're wondering is how many men, I'd say three or four, though it's none of my business."

Double-timing through the register, he adds up his own digressions from the past three years. He has not suffered the quiet insanity of going celibate, nor has he slipped into a feeding frenzy. But these things happen, he reasons, and the blade of jealous pain grows dull as he remembers that whatever Cassie has done has been to herself and not to him.

"I'm not as weird as all that, Sandy. I'm just trying to get a second wind."

She lights a cigarette and blows the smoke out the window. "Some of us women love more than one man, Ravel."

"Is that wisdom or instinct?" he wonders aloud.

She says she wouldn't know. "I never think in words."

There are telltale signs that Sol's come back, traces of his coming and going, but the man still avoids Ravel, keeping to the distant reaches of the Dunes, where the wrecks date from the fifties and are now only rusty husks stripped of their buttons and dials. Bolts and springs and steering wheels and tires have all been sorted and stacked into sagging pyramids, and there is so much rust powder that the earth itself is like volcanic ground, red as crushed brick. Beneath a lean-to of propped Oldsmobile, Ravel finds a mattress pitted and ringed with sinister stains, the dead coal of a recent fire, a waterlogged comic book, and, like a signature, a still-humid bottle of Southern Comfort.

Sol. Come back, come home. I am neither cop nor innkeeper and I owe you one. Here is your bed of feathers and springs and I've put a pillow in place of the rock. Sleep wherever you like. And if the dogs come to chew you in the night, I will scatter them with my flashlight.

"It isn't true that moths love light. Are you listening, Randy? It's bullshit, what people say about moths, all based on reckless observation. I'm trying out a figure of speech, you understand: The only way I can talk to you face-to-face."

In lieu of answering, Randy cracks another bottle of beer.

"The moths can't help themselves," Ravel continues. "It's their nature to throw their brains at hundred-watt bulbs and lampshades, windows of diners, hot streetlamps, and nitelites. The brightness conjures them out of the darkness and they buy it in a flurry of wing dust, blinded from head wounds, never feeling the flame."

Randy takes a long pull from a green bottle.

"That's all I was doing, Randy. Acting out the useless life of a moth. Because my father got there, *he* felt the flame."

Sitting on the hood of a dented MG, Ravel watches for falling stars and Randy answers him from his perch on the hood of a Cutlass, his tongue thick with beer: "Well, if it kept you busy."

The daybreak is a sand painting of coral and whitestone, abalone and redstone, rising into a field of turquoise. To Ravel, it is a lazy sunrise, more tired even than he. Or maybe it's the season, or his mood. Everything he sees this morning resembles a post-card, the colors tinged and falsified with chemicals. He starts out on foot toward home and notices how his cowboy boots have lost their luster from a year of kicking rocks, then stops to observe a black bluff in the eastern distance where a Ute family is said to have been massacred. Beyond that bluff is the blue-black outline of mountains where the streams are turning the color of sulfur because of toxic waste from the mining camps and where the birds that feed on the fish in those streams will later fall like stones from the sky.

He is a mile from Roadside Business when her car overtakes him. Cassie swings open the door on the passenger side and tells him to please get in. Just like that he is sitting beside her and the ugly postcard dawn transforms into radiance. She is wearing jeans and sandals and he looks at her for a long time before noticing that her pink cotton blouse is really a pajama top.

"Where are you coming from?" he asks her.

"From town, where else?"

"Then this isn't an accident?"

"Like Gazer used to say, 'In the desert there are no accidents.' I didn't believe you about your job until just now. I thought you were making it up to impress me."

"If it's about child support . . ."

"Vance, we were never married."

"Of course we were."

"It was real but it wasn't legal. Jered didn't even have a birth certificate until he was six years old. Under 'Name of Father' I wrote 'Unknown.' "

"That's what you got out of bed to tell me? That I don't exist?"

The car is still parked by the roadside and she reaches to put it in gear. "No. I wanted to see what your intentions are."

He looks straight at her. "Bridge building," is all he can say.

She drives north by northeast on Interstate 15. They breeze past Roadside Business without saying another word and then they are in the clear, heading for the hills. Five full minutes pass before he says, "Putting things behind me. Starting over."

"What's that?"

"You asked about my intentions."

"I was expecting to hear something more detailed. One of your pronouncements. Maybe a quote or two."

"That's a dry lake nowadays. I'm retired, just another citizen with the rent to pay. All I want is a lifetime with my woman and my boy."

She tilts her head toward him and rolls her eyes. "Why does that sound memorized?"

"Because it's true. Because I've said it to myself a few hundred times."

"Then why did you take so long? After you ran away, that is."

"Let's keep the facts straight. I *stayed* away. I was trying to spare you from what I'd become."

Cassie says, "And I was right here, expecting you. For the first few months I thought you'd show up at any time. I planned to forgive you just like that."

"I had to get the Er out of my head and do something socially. Become a humble member of the insignificant masses. Otherwise, you wouldn't have been able to bear my presence."

"You could have gotten a job in Paragonah or Cedar City. Wouldn't that have done the trick?"

He shakes his head. "Too near to you. Too close to the burning. So I went as far east as I could without crossing oceans. After New York I spent six months collecting trash in Toledo, Ohio. I could never get over seeing the treasures people throw away. I picked corn by hand and I was a kind of mailman once in Chicago. The last job I had was helping build a road north of Palo Alto. Commuters can now cut half an hour's travel each way."

"No lie."

"I was hoping you'd be impressed."

"I am. I can't deny it. But don't think too much about this little visit. I still fly off the handle sometimes and do things without thinking. And about now I've got to get back to Jered."

"It's early. Let's have breakfast."

"School won't wait."

In the light of the sun, the pajama top is almost diaphanous and he can see the silhouette of a bare breast, the outline of a nipple agonizing. From behind them, a silver Mercury leaps out of the distance, going 120 at the least, and the driver hits the horn to warn them over before blowing past like a hurricane. Ravel swears and Cassie laughs aloud.

"Am I pathetic?" he asks her.

"Only a little. You're trying far too hard."

"What about this other guy?" he asks. "Is he trying too hard?"

"Mind your own business," she answers. There is a long silence and Cassie slows the car to the minimum speed. A long-hauler jackhammers past them. "Nothing in me is sorry, Vance, so lay off."

The moment is a ruin and he looks forlornly out the window to measure his inanity.

"Maybe you've forgotten *your* trespasses," she adds.

She's got him there. The Mingling was her obvious last straw and he had laid it on her frail back with a vengeance.

"Why," she asks, pulling sharply into Roadside Business, "did I think I could talk to you now? Why this morning?"

She is waiting for him to get out of the car but he takes his sweet time. When he was younger, Cassie was the only one who could speak to him in tones that weren't somehow inspired by Hallmark cards or speeches delivered at beauty pageants. And after three years of scraping the film of sanctity from his bloodshot eyes he is looking on that same woman, who has become for him a mass of right angles, jagged edges, and broken glass. But he senses there is a limit to her heartache and there may be forgiveness as well.

"There's still one thing I want to know," she says.

"Shoot."

"When you left them, how'd you do it?"

"With fire."

"That isn't like you. Earth and water were more your style."

"I was a changed man. Am. After you left, I grew spiteful and mean. So I burned the granary and the chicken coop first. Then I spread gasoline in a circle around the garden and lit it. You wouldn't believe how black the smoke was, as though the alkali and carbon of the soil were burning instead of just the weeds and corn rows and gasoline. Then I burned our house—"

"You didn't!"

"And that's when they knew I meant business."

"I'm surprised they didn't kill you."

"They might have. At least Gazer was all for it. But in the long run they didn't have the heart. I was their prophet, after all."

"I've spent sleepless nights trying to forget that part of it."

"Where there's insomnia there's hope."

"There's no audience here, Vance. Only me."

"I'm not preaching, Cassie. I'm not even confessing. I just want to sort out what's left for us. You, me, Jered, and now this baby."

Cassie says she's hoping for a girl. "Jered needs a little sister around to smooth out his rough edges."

"How far along are you now?"

"Two months. So you see, you're too late again. But it's really none of your business, Vance. Don't ask anything more."

Without skipping a beat he tells her that Saturday is his night off. "We can catch up on lost time."

"Fat chance of that. I wouldn't know where to start."

He says they could always go dancing. "Give ourselves something to do with our hands during those embarrassing moments of shy silence."

She cocks an eye in his direction. "Everything you say is half a joke, isn't it? Are you making fun of me or of yourself?"

"If I knew."

She is looking at him now and the distance is measurable as something less than an arm's length and something more than light-years.

"Penny for your thoughts," he says.

She tells him not to waste his money.

WHILE observing the Er, he came to the conclusion that most useful theologies are inevitably handmade and personal, a sorting out of what is offered and what is accepted. He figured that only a fanatic, reading the Bible or the Koran or Aesop's Fables, will swallow the story whole, while hypocrites like Gazer and himself would chew and spit according to their wants or needs. *Hypocrite*, he knows, could also mean adapter or critic.

Stripped of clothing and in open spaces, without trees or furnishings or venetian blinds to frame them or to give them shade, the Er began to look frail and somewhat clumsy; diminished and mortal and humble and sad. Though Ravel wasn't a participant, he grew alarmed at what he was seeing and tried to reel back the story of his father walking into light. Gazer, the scribe, had botched the interpretation in his letters to his friends and had made it appear to them that some legacy was involved in that walk, that the light had shone on Ravel as well. But whenever Ravel tried to set the story straight, he found he didn't have the words. The sense of his father's disappearance had always been a mystery to him and his feelings about it were jumbled and obscure, inducing an aphasia that had momentarily dispersed when he'd told the story to Gazer. But the equation of walking into light had nothing to do with the operands of paradise or sanctuary or any such sweetness. There was terror as well but Gazer had abridged it from his canon. Betrayed, therefore, by his ghostwriter and increasingly uncomfortable with his public, Ravel stayed up the hill with his wife and son and there were days at a time when he saw no one else, when he lived out the solitude he'd originally come for. He could see them on the canyon floor below but their meanderings were of less and less interest to him.

In Ravel's absence, Gazer organized the Er into a cult of his own making. And when the joys of the harvest and the chanting and the rock painting and the fashioning of prayer sticks began to wear thin, he opted for the creation of the Mingling, which soon enough became the communal obsession. Ravel didn't know what superstition was at the root of it. There were sufficient precedents in the wealth of his anthropological background: incest within various of the pueblo tribes, Mormon polygamy, Nootka wife-swapping. For the Mingling, it was decided that each of the women would lie with each of the men at least once. For every mother, the whole of the Er would be the father. The Mingling required a naked day-long walk into the desert. The man carried corn and the woman a jug of water from the spring. The walk had to last until sunset, and after eating and drinking, the couple would get down to business and could only return to the canyon at daybreak. In such a way would the bonds of the family be eternally webbed.

Namer brought Ravel the news. "It's turning nasty, Ravel. Touchy-feely and not very original. Maybe it's time for you to crawl out from under your rock."

But Ravel was mute. He shrugged and laid his head between Cassie's breasts and listened to the drum chant of her heartbeat. The sun rose and crossed the sky in an ever slower arc. The days were endless and the nights incredibly brief. Jered said "All ta og la," and Cassie translated, "They are all ugly now." When the rain fell he smelled dead animals in the air.

The Mingling commenced. Weaver went with Dreamer and Rainer went with Gazer. Then Sander with Painter and Calmer with Digger. And on, in a chain of walking days and sprinting nights. Namer held out until the end and then was taken by Gazer. When they returned her feet were bleeding and she had to stay in bed for a full week.

After a few months of this, Gazer invited Ravel into the open desert for a powwow. Gazer was wearing a loincloth cut from an old blanket and his face was covered with the dust of redstone. "Does Ravel still love us?" he wanted to know.

"I'm here in the first person, J.D. No need to speak to me in the third."

"The Mingling needs you," he continued. "To complete the circle."

Seven women awaited him, heads bowed and hands folded demurely. Whatever Gazer had tossed up for them—failed translations from Tibetan texts, hackneyed Upaniṣad fables, the gospel according to Cool Hand Luke, Leviticus, or mangled Kamasutra—they were swallowing it all down and Ravel was made to understand that he, the prophet, was gumming up the spiritual works.

"Without you," Gazer added, "this whole affair could come to a bad end."

When Ravel asked him to say it straight, Gazer answered with a question: What happens when no one on earth believes in a given god?

"Legends have it," Ravel answered, "that the god ceases to exist."

Gazer's eyes rested on a series of stones between them. He had arranged them into a small circle and was now taking that circle apart. "They believe in you," he said. "Today."

For a few uneasy days, Ravel hedged his bets. It was evident that Gazer intended to be rid of him. As scribe, Gazer would be the obvious choice to replace the prophet. And from the look in his eyes, it was apparent he didn't have any qualms as to how Ravel should disappear: death or subtraction, whichever happened first. Ravel came to the conclusion that there were only two options left to him: flee or call his bluff.

"Cassie, there's this thing I have to do."

"The Er again."

"They were getting restless and Gazer got them riled. I have to play along for a while. To keep Gazer in check."

"So far so good."

"They're like children, Cassie. They're just as dangerous."

"They're lunatic fringe, Vance. The kind of people we came here to avoid. But why bother asking me if you've already made up your mind?"

So he went with Weaver to complete her circle. She was waiting for him at the top of the canyon. "Your clothes," she said, and he removed his jeans and T-shirt and left them on a rock. "And the sandals." He took those off as well. "Have you brought the corn?" He showed her the sackful of cakes made from ground corn. She nodded and they started out. The walking was painful and he moved slowly across the desert floor. Weaver led him westward, to a spot where she'd been with the others, and when the sun had set she bathed his bleeding feet with her water. Her own flesh remained unbroken, her hands and soles like polished leather. She had made this walk before. They shared the corn until the sack was emptied and then she stretched out on her back, stared upward at the stars, and opened her legs like silver curtains.

He was the last of her men and her circle was completed. He was to complete the circle for each of them. Weaver, Namer, Harper, Calmer, and three trembling others. Each of them coiled beneath him in the dirt, the full moon flush upon their upturned faces, and he remembered only Namer among them having wept with shame.

One definition of God is Fat Boy Eats the Whole Thing. Another is He Who Is Forsaken. The applause of scorpions resounded in Ravel's ears and he rose wearily from his skinned knees and headed home to the new hell in Cassie's eyes.

"They call it the Mingling," he told her afterwards.

"Why you instead of snakes?"

"Gazer mentioned my pending extinction. I had to keep the upper hand."

"And you hated every minute of your sacred duties."

The morning after he returned with Harper, Cassie left him. She packed the jeep with books, clothes, canned food, and four-year-old Jered. There was no note and he didn't have the presence of mind to stop what he was doing. The day before they left, Jered had asked, "No tu wi ta?" You're not with them? Songer, and the next day Booker, dragged him into the wilderness and fell upon his body before he realized that Cassie wasn't coming home to save him.

As he followed in the footsteps of his own elongated shadow, he saw that shadow encompassed by another. Turning around, he saw no one. Sage grass, stone, a mound of dust.

Alone in the house, he stirred his thin soup with a steel spoon and waited for it to cool. A cloud passed over the moon and the dark room grew darker.

None of them could tell him where Cassie had gone and

none of them really cared. She'd been exempt from the Mingling because she'd never been part of the Er. She had been the prophet's concubine and nothing more. He had driven the truck into Roadside Business and all that Mircea had to tell him was that he could look high and low but if a woman doesn't want to be found it's no use. "Anyway, if she sees you too soon she just might claw your eyes out. Keep your distance, Vance. I'll let you know when the storm blows over."

He swallowed the soup and it tasted only of water. Weaver had left a basket of small, round potatoes at his doorstep but he left the basket where it sat. Still hungry, he rose from the table and wandered through the two rooms, to touch each of the objects: bed, crib, dresser, hearth. From new moon to new moon he had maintained his silence. Not a word had crossed his lips in a month. We'll see what they make of that, the blessed Er. From his bedroom window he could hear a new chant from below, a calling to the prophet to come down to the canyon floor, to speak, to join in. There was nothing to eat but the potatoes in that basket. He reached for one and held it in his palm. It had a surprising weight and felt more like a stone than a potato. A white stone. A basketful of white stones: the stones in a chorus, each saying *One of us*. He placed the stone back in the basket and went into his room to sleep. After a long hour or only a single moment, he slept and dreamed that he was watched over by wolves. He awoke late in the night and saw him at the window. Not a wolf but a man. Not a man but a boy. "Jered?" he said aloud, breaking his silence. "Where is your mother?" His wild eyes were circled with redstone and his blond hair, stiffened with dust and grease, was scattered in all directions. He raised a hand to show Ravel the stone he had painted, but in the darkness Ravel couldn't see the color.

My illiterate disciple.

My guardian angel.

My warden.

Painter.

Namer climbed the hill to the house and didn't even bother to knock. She was wearing jeans and a faded cotton shirt and Ravel noticed that there were shoes on her feet. He hadn't seen any of the Er dressed like that in a long time.

"There's a new and ugly rumor in the air," she said. "I thought you should know about it."

He nodded to show that he was listening.

"And you can stow the hand signals, Ravel. We've altered the chant, or maybe you haven't been listening. It's generally accepted now that you've been struck dumb and will not speak to us again until the next harvest. We're in a new phase of beseeching, if you get the drift."

"What's the rumor, Namer?"

"That no one ever leaves again. Till death do us part. The door is closed forever, now that the Mingling has been consummated."

He offered her a tiny tomato but she refused it. "You'll have to make a declaration. Say a few pointed words to get that door open again."

"Why's that?"

"Because I want out. And when I hit the road I don't want a pack of mad dogs on my trail."

He smiled and the surprise of the smile made him laugh. "But you never believed in any of it, Namer. Why come to me now?"

"I'm hedging my bets. You're the only one who can handle Gazer."

The tomato burst in his mouth and he swallowed the juice before the pulp. "Can't help you, Namer. You don't need my help anyway. If you want to go, go."

"You think that's all it takes? Just walk away? There was a time I thought it might work out but all I ever feel these days is tired and dirty. And just look at what poor Painter's turned into."

That night she packed up her rags and books in a cloth sack and stopped by to tell him she was taking to the road. "I'm counting on you to keep them off my trail."

He didn't have to watch her go to know which way she was headed. They all went east.

Gazer climbed the hill to tell Ravel that Namer was missing.

"I know. I watched her leave."

"You'll have to call her back. Her absence will undo the Mingling."

Ravel looked at Gazer the way he might a rabid dog. "Cut the crap, J.D. Can't you see the handwriting on the wall?"

"She can't leave," he said evenly.

"She can and has. It's over anyway, J.D. The rock painting, the chanting, the Mingling, and the walking into light. I'll be making the announcement tomorrow morning."

There was a silence, during which Gazer fidgeted with a pair of prayer sticks topped with red feathers. Ravel knew that red feathers signified bleeding. And bleeding could mean a number of things, from sorcery and rainstorms to menstruation and copulation. Gazer said, "I don't believe you."

Ravel told him to read the sky, the winds, the colors of the west wall. "And if that's not sufficient, read my lips."

The next morning, when he descended to the canyon floor to put an end to civilization, they were gone. The huts and tents were empty and there was no one in the cornfield. In the kiva circle were new prayer sticks. The yarn around them was black crossed with yellow and all were topped with red feathers.

He hurried to the house for his keys and then climbed to the top of the canyon and got behind the wheel of the pickup. But when he turned the key, nothing. Opening the hood, he found there was no motor.

Back in the house, he loaded a pack with food and water and laced up his old walking boots. Before the sunlight had lit the canyon floor he was in the open desert. Unaccustomed to the boots, he walked slowly at first. Then he walked swiftly and then he was running. He ran east, in the direction of Paragonah. Coming to a high plateau, he observed the horizon for a long time. But there was only desert emptiness, not even a column of dust to tell him where they'd gone. The sun shone in his face and rode straight above him and turned to his back. His shadow lengthened and became a man, then a giant, then a long thin arrow pointing eastward before it vanished.

After two days of walking in a tightening spiral, he found Namer's body in a lonesome gully ten miles east of the settlement. She was stretched out peacefully across a mattress of dust, her fingers laced over her heart and dried blood like a mauve halo on the ground around her head. It was all too obvious what she'd been struck with. The stone was resting next to her, almost perfectly round, with a single sharp corner: a new rune in the alphabet, painted black.

When Ravel was a child he had fire drills at his school. From time to time, there were other drills, called shelter. A simple buzzer signaled a fire alarm but a high whine meant shelter. Hearing that whine, Ravel was to close his books, stand, and file swiftly to the far wall. There he was to sit with his head folded over his knees, eyes closed, until the whine sounded again to indicate that the drill was ended. He was not to speak and he was not under any circumstances to lift his head and look upward. The light, he was warned, would blind him.

Where he lived he had already seen that light in the west. More than once he had observed the rising firestorm of orange and white and black. He had seen it at least a dozen times and was not yet blind. His mother had seen it as well and more often than not would turn away, toward the east, and hurry into the house.

That light was the end of everything and his father walked into the heart of it. Whatever he meant by that final act, Ravel is sure that he hadn't planned on a homely woman like Namer dying in his memory.

The Er returned to the canyon and bent to work in the dry fields. At night their chanting was plaintive and sorrowful and the cycle of the Mingling was resuscitated on orders from Gazer.

Ravel rummaged through drawers for the ancient companion to stone known as flint. Finding none, he settled on matches.

He sat cross-legged on the floor in the lotus position. Then he struck a match under his nose and the smell of sulfur stung his nostrils. Taking a second match from the box, he lit it and watched the flame burn down to his fingers and then go out. He lit another and another. My days are numbered, he was thinking. And only these matches will save me.

He lit another and in its flame was his inspiration and his vision.

Closing his eyes, he could see the fireball rising from below the earth, from the canyon floor to the high heavens. He lit every match but one and watched the flame die out. He saved the final match for his leave-taking.

A NOTHER thing about that desert was the conspicuous absence of witnesses. Ravel cannot say the same about Nashua Coe's Auto Body and Salvage. The owner himself is there to greet him when he strolls in for a night's work.

"Saint Francis I don't need," Nashua says. "Sandy is one thing, but this place ain't no Best Western."

Ravel tells him he'll see to it that things are straightened up.

Nashua says he'd like to know what the hell is up with Ravel, like maybe he's been doing too much weed. "You're even more in the clouds than usual and I notice all kinds a bullshit going on in the yard."

"Like what?"

"Beer busts or whatever. Campfires left and right. And why in hell didn't you tell me you broke your window?"

Ravel says it's news to him.

"Well it's your responsibility and I'm docking the cost of new panes from your pay. Chew on that while you hunt down whoever threw that rock."

Long before he sees it he already knows that it won't be white. The office is intact, the dust still thick along the unused desktop and the calendar still turned to March 1976. Someone, probably Nashua, has swept the broken glass into a small pyramid in the corner and the moonlight shows in slivers through the remaining jagged edges of the window.

The black rock promises, if not death, at least a maiming, a subtraction of limbs or eyes or tongue. Whatever has most offended them.

Which of the Er has come for him is a question that should be important. His ass is in this sling because he led them into the business of walking into light and then burned their settlement to the ground. And the sling is firmly in the hands of some derelict from his calamitous past. Sun and moon, Vance Ravel. Moon and sun. First you are a fisherman and then you are only bait.

RUNNING
WITH
GABRIEL

I T I S B Y now a time-tested ritual, this alcoholic absolution. He learned it more than two years ago from a fellow veteran of the Plumbbob series, a Marine pilot named Danielson who on twelve occasions flew his F-84 through rising mushroom clouds and gathered samples of smoke and ash and profane gases for the Aftertest crew.

"What I do is get blind drunk six or seven hours before every shot. That way I don't get anxious about it like I used to. I can't concentrate on the dangers or think too clearly about what I'm flying into. With five hours to go, I've got time to sober up. Not so's I'm feeling chipper, understand. But at least so I can still button up my shirt and fly the bird. Then I just fight my way through the same routines, dip in and out of the mushroom, return to base, hose off, puke, and file my report with the sample canisters. By the time it's wrapped up I'm so beat that all I can do is hit the bunk and sleep it off. When I wake up the next day I can hardly believe that I've done it again."

Ravel follows. Getting up from his E-Z rocker, he grabs a bottle by the neck and heads into the kitchen for another glass and more ice. A message is waiting for him, held by a magnet against the refrigerator door. "Back at six. Gone to movies. Get out on time so Vance won't see."

See what? These rheumy eyes? Scotch stains on my dungarees? My yellowing teeth? The bald spot on the back of my head?

He cracks open a tray of ice and drops three cubes into a

tumbler. Breaks the seal on a fresh bottle and fills the tumbler to the brim, spilling a little on the Formica counter. Next to Mircea's message is a yellowed drawing, one of Vance's first ever, that he keeps meaning to toss out. But whenever he reaches to tear it from the refrigerator door, his hand stops in midair as if held by a different magnet. Mircea treats this drawing as though it were a precious postcard or a sacred image; like those holy cards with a saint on one side and a prayer on the other. Both image and prayer are on the front of Vance's drawing. Stick people with hair of straw and pumpkin grins: Mommy & Daddy. A house with crooked windows and a lawn of purple grass, a car without wheels floating in space above that house. In the background is what looks like some forsaken leafless tree to anyone who doesn't know better: a high black trunk with a blue halo at the top. The Harry shot.

Vance saw it from his window, that magnificent flash of orange and red that preceded the dawn by bare minutes and all through the morning kept rising into the sky. It rose eight miles before the winds tore it into deadly shreds and vapors and scattered it eastward, straight to St. George.

Driving home from the site, 110 miles of flat highway, Ravel had been immersed in a thick cloud of soot and ash, his car gathering new layers of dust with every mile. Beyond that cloud, the sun glowed red and the daylight was dimmed.

When Jack arrived at the ranch house, he found Mircea in the basement with Vance huddled in her arms. "Is it still falling?" she asked him.

"What?"

"The fire? There was fire falling."

"It's only ashes, Mircea. Cinders. Nothing to worry about."

"Jack, your face."

"What about it?"

She led him to a mirror and he found that his hair had been singed by a thousand flakes of ash and had turned gray; his skin was dotted with red splotches from tiny burns. Though later, after a haircut and a quick rinse, he found his familiar face again, he would never forget that moment of believing he had turned old overnight after a drive through the falling hot snow.

Harry had proved to be the dirtiest shot of all time. Someone back at Livermore blamed it on the wind.

Taking his glass and bottle to the living room, Ravel settles into a chair from where he can see the green-blank screen of his television set, white curtains pulled tight against the Utah sunlight, which nonetheless comes burning through. To his left is the wall. There are pictures of forest landscapes, mountains, the seaside, anything not desert; a reprint of some French guy's painting of pink-faced fat women on a picnic; framed military certificates and commendations; a U of Montana pennant; dried flowers between pressed glass; and a wooden crucifix. He and Mircea have been fighting over this wall ever since they've moved into the house, each of them putting up images and keepsakes of his or her choice. In four years the wall has become a real piece of art by Ravel's standards, a ten-by-twelve collage of their marriage and their argument. This is her and this is me and if the artifacts don't add up to anything harmonious, at least the man and the woman are. Were. Have been.

He tips back the tumbler and thinks to himself that an occasional advantage of the alcohol intake is the way it stills the pain in his joints. Death may be a cruise in a Chevy convertible but this dying is a barefoot tramping to a rocky uphill grave. The doctor in Cedar City has been as clear as day with each passing diagnosis. Bone cancer, cancer of the liver. Either one terminal. Do you piss blood? It's normal, you're dying. Take this for the pain and say your prayers. I won't even suggest chemical therapy or removal of that liver. You're too far gone.

"When?"

"A few weeks or a few months. As you weaken, the bone cancer will accelerate and your legs will give out. You will also develop a tolerance to the painkillers and require stronger doses. I suggest morphine on a daily basis. You'll get hooked but it doesn't matter. It depends on how you want to take this: with gritted teeth or glassy eyes."

The painkillers make him stupid and he spends his time at home in bed, easing the pain in his legs and ribs. The only alcohol he allows himself is for the preshot ritual, but Mircea doesn't know the difference. All she sees is a man who goes long weekends without getting dressed, whose eyes have turned red from watching television and staring at the ceiling, and who hasn't in months made the halting gestures and tenuous caresses that in other times bespoke his want of her. Language between them has been reduced to single words. When he opens his mouth he feels the death coming out of him, his sick spittle or decaying breath, and so he shuts up.

When I'm gone she'll say I was a drunk.

Negatives and double negatives. Overlays, images of wind, sand, and neutron buckshot making an already grainy surface even grainier. He has seen eighty-seven shots and now is just playing out the string. It's too late to take a stand on what he knows, on what they don't know, those Marine recruits out in the trenches with their film badges and their steel helmets, facing invisible bullets and taking atomic showers, inhaling and swallowing. He has only made gestures, only hinted at what he knows. Out there, friend, is the worst enemy you'll ever come up against. He has always stopped short of breaching security, of saying the words aloud; rems, rads, fallout, ionization. Once he took a reading of an incoming platoon and discovered a young man who registered well past four rems. "Am I dirty?" he'd asked Ravel, having heard others before him pose the same question.

"Filthy," Ravel had answered.

"So what do I do?"

"Take a long shower with good hot water. Shave twice. Cut

your hair until your skull shines like the moon. Clean your fingernails. Vomit if you're up to it. Shit and piss like there's no tomorrow."

"Is that all?"

"It won't help much but it *will* improve your appearance."

It is his duty and his inclination to clam up, and if ever he finds himself in the field, zoot-suited and surrounded by half-naked platoons, he does as the phantom from his past did, raising a hand and pointing to his gadgets. I'm in a suit and you're not, so blow.

He'd been in maneuvers for three years, still a sergeant, when the offer came down from Livermore: Join the Aftertest section for the Plumbbob series and when the series is complete you'll be an officer. That would make a hell of a difference in Mircea's pension but so far the series has been endless. In the beginning, he'd imagined a space of months, a year and a half at the most. That was two and a half years ago and new prototypes are still being wheeled out at regular intervals. The kilotonnage multiplies and Plumbbob has begun to look more and more like an open-ended equation: $x = \{1, 2, 3 \ldots\}$. For some time Ravel has felt himself at the mercy of pencil scratchings on clipboards, serpentine screen blips, needle readings, valences, and space/exposure algorithms. They are still waiting for the last dit and dot of the immaculate coupling of fission and fusion, Teller's promised clean bomb, something they can set off and admire from close in, without needing to wash their hands and face and genitals afterwards.

For the past year his work has been more of a circus act than anything scientific. He and another sergeant tend the dogs, an amalgam of breeds to which they give instructions—sit, stay, roll over—until each and every one is measured as to capability and alertness on a scale of 1 to 20 (margin of error ± 1.2). He and his partner no longer bother assigning names to their hounds.

Numbers suffice, particularly given their mortality rate. Prior to each shot the dogs are placed in a large wire cage at an assigned distance from ground zero. They are left fully exposed and film badges are fastened to the cage or to the dogs' collars to allow for a later measure of the gamma levels. One or two hours before each shot, Ravel and his partner put the hounds through their paces and note on clipboards the last-minute levels of reaction and comprehension. Some of the dogs have survived previous blasts and others are facing their first one. Within an hour after each shot, though preferably sooner, Ravel and his partner return to the cage but now they wear their lead-lined suits. Each time, they find that a number of the dogs are already dead, from either the impact of the shock wave, or the heat, or, in some cases they are certain, cardiac arrest. These dogs are loaded into a jeep and sent to the lab for autopsy while the survivors are once again put to the routine of tricks. If they fail to sit up or roll over or—a wrinkle in Ravel's song and dance—play dead, the failures are noted and commented upon, again with a rating from 1 to 20. These figures are later entered into some rushing river of statistical analysis and, for all Ravel knows, they are put to music. Often the dogs are drugged either before or after the shot and Ravel has to spend long hours in the observation lab with a veterinarian or an animal biologist at his elbow. They take notes, write numbers, catalog hours and minutes. Now and then he has to take on other animals as well: pigs, chickens, cats, even once an aviary filled with birds—pigeons, crows, sparrows, hawks, parakeets, geese, and blackbirds. The intention was to study varying rates of heartbeat before and after detonation, but when the blast was over every single bird was as dead as dead can be, feathers singed to ash, their hollow bones pulverized to a fine dust. Not a single heartbeat to register on the clipboard. A zero.

For a time, Ravel was privy to the results of the film badge readings. They were a part of his dossier from dog to dog. But during the past six months he hasn't seen a single digit and his access to information is increasingly restricted. Something about his attitude, he's been told.

"What about my attitude? I've been a soldier."

"No one's saying otherwise."

"Then what's the complaint?"

"You're obsessed with the dirt. You have no confidence."

"I follow the regulations. I wash. I turn over my suit. I file my report."

"You made some rash comments about the AN/PDR 27."

"It was insufficient material for the job required."

"The AN/PDR 27 is classified equipment and its utilization is beyond your experience and know-how."

"But the maximum reading—"

"Is none of your affair. You are here to record, not to analyze."

"Sixteen of my twenty-two dogs died yesterday. How do you analyze that?"

"Back to your post, Ravel. You're treading on some very thin ice."

During the week leading up to this shot there have been disquieting rumors of infiltration. One man, possibly two, has slipped the gears and chains of security and is said to be prowling the test site. A spy, perhaps. Maybe a peacenik. Or worse, as far as Livermore is concerned, a journalist. Whatever is written can be more damaging than what is said, and a single error-riddled article in even the most backwater journal can cause a public outcry that will throw a three-month glitch into the testing schedule.

Ravel doesn't have three months. He has grains of sand in an hourglass. He and the others are addressed by the Aftertest security crew. "Your safety, we remind you, is in your silence. Your country is depending upon you to keep a tight lip. This includes chitchat with wives, girlfriends, family, and military personnel not related to this mission. Your duty is not fulfilled unless it is carried out in strict silence. Even in your sleep. Is this clear?"

Crystal.

The man is preaching to the converted and this prayer, long since memorized, is the key to the promised christening of Lieutenant John Ravel. Ravel is convinced of this and has thus kept his silence longer than most, years now, while countless others have come only long enough for a limited series of maneuvers or for isolated sightings, sample takings, or conferences. Ravel is a soldier. Ravel endures.

And he clings to the dream of becoming an officer. Though there is nothing more in it for him, really, this elevation to the elite will ensure that his family will be looked after. He has already spent insomniac hours at the kitchen table, the small print spread before him, going through the calculations with finely sharpened pencils. A dead officer can leave his family in the neighborhood of 32 percent more in direct benefits than can a dead sergeant, not to mention increased medical coverage, the capping of teeth, orthopedic shoes, immunization, and the numerous boutiques where military discounts are outrageous. When my time comes, my zero hour. What he cannot do with pencil and paper is trace a chronology of his own that might have been lived far from this field of spectral battle. He has long since come to the conclusion that his lifetime has been a leaping from stone to stone across a rushing river and that any single misstep could have done him in. He remembers the unholy risks he took as a boy. Once, in the company of a loud-mouthed drunk, he'd accepted a ten-dollar wager and raced his father's car down a backcountry road. The next day, hung over, he'd driven the same road and found skid marks along a hairpin turn at the top of a gorge. Two of the marks led over the edge. He realized that for a moment the front and rear left wheels must have dangled in midair. Another time, taking up a dare, he'd walked through a nest of snakes at a reptile garden with only his wading boots to protect him from the fangs. A dozen rattlers had leapt from the dust to take his measure and one of them, grazing his hand, had nearly done the trick. He'd made fifty dollars on that stunt and spent it all the same night to impress a girl whose name he can't remember now. He'd bought flowers and a belt buckle with both their names carved into the brass. I don't remember her name. She wouldn't remember mine. She didn't want to keep the belt buckle and I probably threw it away.

In Korea, a mortar shell had once landed fifteen feet behind him as he'd lurched into a trench. The explosion had only showered him with dirt and made his heart leap to the base of his tongue. Later he had taken inventory of the variables in that near hit: the six-millimeter variance at the source of that shell's trajectory, the hundred fewer grams of weight that gave the shell its arc and pattern, his running velocity from the death point of x to the sanctuary of y, and the split-second wavering of an Oriental hand before it dropped that shell to the chamber. Hairbreadths, reflexes, and decimals to the fourth digit had spared him that night and by now had added up to these six more years of life with Mircea and the survival of a fast-swimming sperm from chamber to womb and the flowering of his son. Six years of being a sergeant in an army gone mute, an army that no longer fights against other armies but wages war against earth and sky, dog and bird, man and woman. An army that uses threats to conjure silence and fights its battles against fission and fusion, poisoned rain, microscopic bullets, and fragments of toxic light.

Who on God's green earth would intrude upon this? And for what purpose?

He remembers an ancient shot, in 1954, when Gabriel snapped. The aftershock had already passed, but the wind was still howling and the desert around them was a sea of tiny cyclones and burning sage. Fine points of flame filled the air like hordes of spiraling fireflies. When Ravel had given the signal to attack, Gabriel had climbed out of his trench and headed the other way.

Ravel had shouted to him to stop but he had just kept on going. Still running, Gabriel had peeled away his helmet and his battle gloves, tossed his film badge to the wind, unbuckled his gear, and abandoned it on the desert floor. Ravel pursued him, running with the gale at his back. He passed an incoming jeep, and a group of men, advancing in white suits, waved at him to turn around. Gabriel disappeared in the smoke and when that smoke cleared he was naked but for his boots. Ravel followed him. There were stabs of pain in his chest as he ran and tears stung his eyes. Gabriel disappeared into another cloud of smoke and Ravel pursued him. Then he knew he was no longer chasing Gabriel. He was running with him. He was running as fast as he could. We are all of us running. Running. We are still running.

Tonight's shot, scheduled for sometime after midnight, is a follow-up to the only misfire Ravel has ever witnessed. On June 27, Diablo had clicked but it hadn't ignited. The Marine divisions, poised in the distance, had been cleared out, and after hours of panicky debate a team of specialists had been sent to the tower to defuse the warhead, knowing that it might detonate at any random second. The follow-up shot, Hood, had twice been postponed owing to tricky winds. The disastrous winds of the Harry shot had not been forgotten and Livermore wanted a calm sky for Hood, which had been estimated as somewhere in the sixty-kiloton range; another prototype, of course, and far more powerful than anything Ravel had yet seen. He'd received the message while still in Las Vegas with the o + 2.2, picking up a slip at the hotel that said simply, "Yellow lights, 5 July," and had confirmed by telephone that he was on call.

Sixty kilotons. Ravel puts the cap on the bottle, then reconsiders and twirls the cap off again. He raises the bottle to his lips and tips it back. The last living nerve in his spine winks out and his paralysis is complete. Though he can barely read his watch, the luminous dial tells him he has fifteen minutes to shower and shave and get on the road. Ever since he's owned this watch, its dial has been a source of private laughter, its glow so like the glow of radium. Once he'd learned the rudiments of radioactivity and grown familiar with words such as strontium, radon, alpha and beta particles, lithium and krypton, he'd become an avid reader on the subject. He'd searched high and low for evidence of his intake and written personal Aftertest reports for his own files, including in these reports his rem readings, wind velocities, dates, times, names of shots, and kiloton estimates. He is not enough of a scientist or physicist to be capable of collating any of this information into something meaningful but he finds it comforting to have his own written version of events.

In the course of his reading, he'd come upon the story of a group of young women employed by the Radium Luminous Material Company in the 1920s. The women had been assigned to paint watch dials and instrument panels and crucifixes with the new luminous material known as radium. Radium, as in radiant, glowing, ethereal. Because the painting required a fine precision, the painters had been given thin brushes, which, after each application, they would lick to obtain a fine line. Then they would dip the brush back into the radium, apply it to the dial or control panel or crucifix, and lick again. Many of them found the luminous material so lovely that for a lark they would cover their teeth with it and go into a dark room together to laugh openmouthed at the spectacle of themselves as phantom Cheshire cats in the darkness, disembodied smiles in the black void. Others hand-painted their fingernails or toenails or, dipping a finger into the paintbox, wrote their names across their palms. They found that the glowing effect lasted even after they'd washed those hands at the end of the day.

It was a miracle, that radium. Light itself in captivity. As cheap as dirt and as lovely as the moonlight.

By 1924 so many of these women had fallen ill that a local doctor began to investigate. He found that instead of passing the radium out of their bodies, they had absorbed it into their bones, where it had emitted masses of radioactive alpha particles. The women's tongues grew swollen and black and their jaws and legs began to rot away. Some lost the use of their legs and others of their hands. Teeth turned gray and then black and in some cases continued to emit a weird ray of light. Facing death, many of the women banded together to sue the company. Eventually they settled out of court. Ever after, they were referred to as the Legion of the Doomed. Or, as Wilkins would put it, first casualties. Since learning of his own bone cancer, Ravel has been obsessed with these luminous painters. He wonders at their pain and at the shock of their premature disintegration. He can hear their laughter in the darkness of the closet, their mouths opened wide and their teeth moving up and down. And what he wonders most is whether or not, in their private caskets six feet under, they still have bones that glow, still luminous, pretty as blue crucifixes, in death.

What his own pain has become:

An itch in every vein as though the blood is carrying a cargo of thorn or thistle. A skeletal ache and stab with every breath. A perpetual tread of listless feet over broken glass. Knowing that his bodily juices are poisoned and that his bones are like rotting wood.

The painkillers leave a stink on his breath, a stench of ether and of dead animals. Mircea always asks him what he's been drinking.

Dragging himself upward, he goes into the bathroom to take a shower. He scratches at his skin as though to remove a layer or two and forestall the dying. He fills his mouth with the shower spray to rid himself of the Scotch smell. Then he dresses in battle fatigues even though he'll later have to change into his suit. He laces his boots extra tight, preparing himself for the road. He's never seen more than thirty-eight kilotons, and the idea of watching sixty still wears at him, despite the alcohol and his temporary remission of pain.

It is nearly six in the evening when he finally climbs behind the wheel of his 1953 Ford, a two-tone job with 70,000 desert miles on the dial and a needle he can put to 80 if the wind is at his back. When the engine is humming, he backs down the driveway and cruises out of Paragonah in the direction of the highway. He points his car west toward the sun, which is as white as a fireball of pure helium as it drops toward the flat horizon of Death Valley. He reaches behind the visor for his sunglasses and then remembers he has given them to Danzel. Hell. So with his pupils dilated to ten over ten by the whisky, he drives wrinkle-eyed, peering through his fingers, one hand shading his face and the other on the wheel, for two full hours. At last, near nine in the evening, the sun slips like a red dime into a pocket of desert and the sky is the color of those girls in their graves, turquoise blue with an underpainting of fire. His headache blooms like a cactus behind his eyes. When he removes his hand from his face, he rediscovers the contour of the road and puts his boot to the floor. There is no wind to help him and he argues the car up to 70 and no more. Two hours later he arrives at the Nevada Test Site and is, altogether, fifteen minutes late.

The locker room is empty. The others, having already suited up, are on their way to various checkpoints by now. Ravel heads for the lavatory, pisses long and hard to get the last of the alcohol out of his system, and washes his face and hands for the fourth time. Then he hurries back into the locker room and reaches for his padlock. The combination is the same as Vance's birthday, and he begins to spin out the numbers before realizing that the door is hanging from its hinges. Dropping the padlock, he kicks the door open and reaches into the emptiness that will be his undoing. His suit, helmet, boots, and film badge are gone.

PAINTER

L ET's face it, he didn't leave any traces lying around. Neither hair nor teeth nor shard of skull nor scrap of uniform. Not even a photographic shadow on the ground, like so many of those vanished citizens of Hiroshima.

Mircea once told Ravel that a soldier friend named Wilkins, meaning to be kind, had gathered a few handfuls of ash and dust from the site and had them sealed in a mahogany box. He drove all the way to Paragonah to offer it to her but she refused, convinced as she was that the dust and ash would be sullied by the powdered remains of snakes and scorpions. "I really didn't need that kind of souvenir around the house."

Ravel was six when they told him his father was dead, and it is rumored that he didn't cry or carry on and that he never dragged poor Mircea through the tango of Why doesn't Daddy come home? Randy says that he took it like a man, straight up. But Ravel knows he was merely confused.

When he was eleven he finally asked, Why no body? Television had taught him that the dead don't just dry up and disappear. They are waxed and polished and put into shiny boxes, so why not him?

"There wasn't any body, Vance. Nothing to speak of."

"Not even pieces?"

"Nothing."

"Then how do you know he's dead?"

In the trumpet blast of her silence, his confusion flowered

into faith. A rush of blood and a point of light in the immeasurable distance. No corpse means no death.

The dawning of faith begins with doubt. Then there are misgivings, and then stubbornness, and finally a speechless assent. Before his long fall, he knew no limits and there wasn't a leaf or twig or lump of shit in that vast spiritual garden that he didn't at least sniff or chew on to find if it was edible. After a while, he grew into a social misfit. He was that mad dog you feed five times a day, mountains of meat mess and ground guts and Gravy Train, and he still takes a bite from your passing leg.

A word to the wise. There are, in the end, only two religions. That's the long and short of it. In the first one, you learn the rules, the chants, and the mythology and then you hit other people with sharp sticks until they've learned what you have. In the other, you make up your own mythology and then sit smugly on your haunches and stare into the spaces of it, calling those spaces the mystery. Ravel's was of the second form, but then he carried that staring into the perpetual flu and disorientation that only Randy, of all people, recognized as drugs.

In the ensuing psycho-fracas, sometime before heading out to the desert with Cassie and Jered, he forgot about his father. Then he forgot entirely about light, maybe because there suddenly seemed so little of it to go around.

WHEN the flames were so high that even the most indifferent of gods couldn't miss them, he climbed up from the canyon and went to his truck before remembering that they'd cut the heart from it while heading forth to kill Namer. So he went on foot in search of the easterly door out of that desert. After nightfall, even from miles away, the canyon gave off a red glow. He found a flat space between a pair of ragged Joshua trees, stretched out on the ground, and watched that glow until sleep gathered him in. The next day he searched the western horizon for a plume of smoke and found nothing. That fire may still have been burning, may still be burning to this day. He didn't know. There were twenty more miles of desert to be crossed and then he reached Interstate 15 a few miles north of Roadside Business.

While he stood by the side of the road he was thinking that he'd take a week, maybe a month, to clear the cobwebs from his head, and then he would make a beeline into the circle of Cassie's arms. There would be hell to pay but he would build another house within the city limits of Paragonah and take up gainful employment as a solid citizen, husband, and father. But there were those cobwebs to deal with first, and all the residue of shame and regret at having gone through the motions of being a demigod for nigh on two years.

So he headed north by northeast, away from Paragonah. He rode various bus or truck routes away from the desert and as the days passed he grew smaller and more diminished. From god to priest to man to stray leaf to grain of sand. He had sore feet, a sunburned neck, and nothing in the way of sensible shoes. Worse, his odds-and-ends clothing inspired fear among the natives of the little towns he passed through. He could see in their eyes that they were unable to identify him as one of theirs. He was neither Ute nor Navajo, neither Mormon nor Methodist. And he looked nothing like the usual road bums that traveled those roads. He was hot and then he was cold and he was constantly on the lookout for something to put into his mouth. Every little thing made its impression on him: the distances from one town to the next; the smell of coffee and flapjacks in a roadside diner; the ripe forearms of truckdrivers and the rhythmic bounce of the road; the welcome sush of air brakes when the grade of the downhill slope was too much for a sixteen-wheeler. In Provo he bought a pair of jeans, two T-shirts, socks, and a cowboy shirt with mother-of-pearl snaps and threw the old robes in the trash. Then he took a chance and looked in the mirror. The relief of seeing just another Joe was indescribable.

He spent cold nights in doorways or in the windbreaks of cornfields. He found that he wasn't alone on the planet. In the western states, there are transient tribes one never reads about, tribes that are never mentioned. One night he was invited to share pork and beans with a family of illegal Mexicans camped in the weeds behind a Conoco station. Dispersed Hopi, up from the reservation, wandered the streets of Denver, their eyes on their shoes to hide their disbelief. On the main street of Lusk, Wyoming, Ravel watched an old woman circle a half-eaten sugar doughnut that was lying on the sidewalk. Two steps to the left and two steps to the right, it took her a full five minutes until she was standing over that mass of dry bread. There was no one watching but Ravel, and she stared into his eyes as she knelt and recovered the doughnut and put it straight into her mouth.

In the towns between Salt Lake City and the Dakotas were children of mixed race: ocher, walnut, auburn, ebony. East of Rapid City he stopped by the side of the highway to eat his last apple. In the window of a slow-moving bus he saw the face of a boy. The boy was watching him as if he was something special and as he passed he reached his arm out the window as though to snatch the apple. In the sunlight, his skin was the color of wine.

In Sioux Falls, Ravel stumbled over an Indian woman who was sleeping on the stairway of the rattrap hotel where he was staying. Her eyes were swollen shut and when Ravel asked a man nearby what had happened to her, he was told, "Sterno." Pursuing the matter, Ravel learned that, short on funds, she'd bought a thirty-seven-cent can of Sterno and drained away the alcohol. It can do that to your eyes. He tried it the next night just to see, and after two cans' worth, his eyes were swollen and he was as blind as the night.

A man he couldn't see found him in the street and led him through the darkness to a room. He could hear others around him, coughing, scraping chairs, and speaking a language he didn't know. When he heard laughter he assumed that he was the joke. The man led him to a cot and bade him to sit. Then the man spooned soup into his mouth and said, "You're not Sioux."

"No."

"Christian?"

"In a manner of speaking. Where am I?"

The man didn't know Ravel's name but seemed to feel that he didn't belong there. "You can stay the night. I'll be round to see you in the morning."

When the soup was gone, Ravel reclined on the cot, meaning only to rest. He fought to open his eyes but the swelling was too great. He could only manage to get one eye open long enough to see a bare light bulb overhead. Voices rose and drifted around his head and he heard glass breaking on the other side of a wall. The only words he could understand were spoken not ten feet from him: "White guy." A headache grew from a seed of stone in the center of his head and threw branches of pain to behind his eyes. He made sounds that he didn't mean to make: moaning or calling out. Someone came by to wash his eyes but when he thanked him there was no answer.

He slept and when he awakened the voices were gone. He could hear snoring from nearby and assumed that it was late at night. He fell back to sleep and when he awakened much later his eyelids opened as if they were wood. Looking around, he found that he was in a garage. Twenty cots were scattered across the concrete surface and against one wall was a gas stove, a coffeepot, a sink, and a broken refrigerator. The walls were covered with worn posters: a black-light Janis Joplin, Chief Joseph, a watercolor Jesus, Red Cloud. Only two of the other cots were occupied and in a far corner of the garage three men and a woman were camped in a semicircle around a television.

Ravel helped himself to some coffee and went over to them. "Mornin'," he said. Only one of them, a teenager with his hair tied in a ponytail, looked in his direction. The boy's eyes accused Ravel that he was white but he nodded all the same. The others were older and had no expressions on their faces. Without looking at Ravel, the woman said, "Morning's over." He looked closely at her face, thinking for a moment she was the one he'd found with the shut eyes. He couldn't swear yes or no.

They were watching the television but the picture was bad and the colors tended to orange and green and nothing else. It was a soap opera and on the screen were pea-green faces with laughable amounts of makeup. Ravel chose a seat off to one side and joined them. The picture grew worse, as though the antenna was badly connected. Snow filled the screen in waves and then dispersed. It took Ravel a while to realize that there was no sound. The story unfolded as lip-moving and gestures. A commercial swept by, a smiling child in diapers, and then the story gathered them back in. Then it was over and another story began. They all watched the television wordlessly. Ravel rose and poured more coffee. "Anyone else?" he asked, but no one answered him. Just as he was sitting down, they all got up and walked away, leaving the television on. They went back to various cots to gather suitcases or tote bags and then they filed out the door. After a moment's hesitation, Ravel stood up and followed them. They were climbing into an old school bus that was already half full of other Indians. At the wheel was a priest with long hair. He was wearing jeans and a Hawaiian shirt, with his white collar fastened loosely around his neck.

"So," he said to Ravel. "Looking better today."

Ravel recognized the voice. "Just a little dizzy, thanks."

The priest said, "That's the price you pay."

The others were already on the bus. Instinctively, Ravel lifted his feet to climb in, but the priest turned to him and shook his head. "This is the reservation bus," he said.

Ravel watched the doors close and then the bus rumbled out of the lot and down the street. He went back into the garage, gathered his pack, and filled his canteen at the sink. Stepping out onto the street, he put a finger to his mouth and then lifted it high in the air to see which way the wind blew. No surprise; west to east. He fixed his aching eyes on the highway and headed that way.

Eastward, veering south.

Between Des Moines and Ottumwa, he found work hand-picking corn for a truck farmer. It was easy work compared to what he'd known in the canyon. In Iowa, the soil is jet black and without stones and the water runs fast and deep between the rows. As the summer progressed, the stalks outgrew him and he saw the sky through a mosaic of green leaf; the ears were fat and the kernels the color of the rising sun. When Ravel told the farmer that his land was blessed, the old man just looked at him as if he had holes for eyes.

He carried four spoons, three forks, a working can opener, and a pair of telescoping cups. Though he didn't smoke, he developed a habit of gathering butts for those who might and learned to roll the tobacco remains into cheap papers. He could trade these cigarettes for food or hand them out in exchange for goodwill.

He never stayed anywhere longer than a week or two. He was led ever eastward and had the impression that he was fulfilling the route that Namer might have chosen had her exodus not been so tragically interrupted. He was learning a new language, something more eloquent than the coloring of stones, and when a year had passed and he arrived in New York, he felt he had mastered the rudiments of street jive or whatever. Arriving at the Port Authority after a long bus ride from Pittsburgh, he ran into a short black man who offered to sell him a ring for twenty dollars. "Gole," he told Ravel. "Gole and dammons."

"How much?"

"Twenny dolla."

"Sounds like a steal."

"Say what?"

"A deal. Sounds like a deal. Just let me scratch it on this marble over here."

"Wha you wanna do that fo?"

"See if the diamonds are real."

"Who talkin' real?"

W I T H the general intention of continuing the long row homeward, he kicks his way out of bed after only four hours of sleep and heads for Cassie's to get to work on that neglected lawn. The midmorning sun is gunpowder white in a blue sky and he is the only human stirring on Cimarron Street. First with his hands and then with a rake, he compiles an impressive mound of Paragonah artifacts, few of which could be construed as obviously religious. Pop bottles, beer cans, tire tread, bits of pencil and crayon, plastic kneeling soldiers with bazookas or M-1s, a comb, uncounted bottle caps, and, to his momentary heartbreak, what he thinks he recognizes as the wing from an airplane. All but that wing go into the trash can and before the dust can settle he's back with a spade and fork to overturn the weeds.

The earth is sealed and comes away in yellow plates like baked ceramic. He shatters these plates to dust with his shovel, working until the whole front yard has been churned at least once. Then he rakes over the clumps to extract as many weeds as possible; but this is the desert, where weeds grow either in a downward reach to China or into horizontal baskets and webs that can never be traced. He knows that whatever he does he will end up with rope ends, snags, and buds galore, and the weeds will grow back in no time. Then he will be on hands and knees to pluck them out.

At around three in the afternoon he hikes to the Rexall in the center of town. Behind the drugstore, in an otherwise empty lot, is a plant stand where a woman is selling potted geraniums and marigolds, baby fir trees, alyssum, springrei, dusty miller, and devil's ivy. It is the end of the season and several cartons contain dried-out petunias going for five cents each. Ravel orders a twenty-pound bag of fertilizer and the last six two-pound bags of grass seed. The woman at the register tells him that for the same price he could get a thirty-pound sack at the seed-and-feed in Parowan. "These bags're for filler. Thickening."

He tells her he's in a rush.

"Won't make the grass grow no faster."

Walking to Cimarron Street with the bags on his shoulder, he turns this over in his mind and decides that it's fair. The trouble with most offhand advice is that it's been honed and readied for use. He's come full circle now and prefers that kind of slack-jawed it's-no-skin-off-my-nose type of commentary: disinterested wisdom.

Back at the house, he lightly hoses the soil and spreads the fertilizer directly from the bag. Then he rakes over the surface to let the fertilizer sink in and hoses again. The soil turns from tan to pink and he is satisfied. At long last he starts flinging seed around until half the sacks are empty and the topsoil has already begun to dry. He is just ripping open a fourth sack of seed when a minibus stops in front of the house and drops off Jered.

He is dressed in jeans and the first thing Ravel notices is the big hole over his right knee. The second thing he notices is that Jered isn't wearing socks. For the longest time, the boy just stands there as though he isn't any longer certain he is at his own house.

Ravel tells him he's just in time to help finish. "Got three more bags of seed and I need a sower."

"Does Mom know you're here?"

"It's a surprise."

"That you tore up our lawn?"

Ravel shows him an open bag. "It's grass seed. We're growing a new lawn and you can help. Hold out your hand."

When he does, Ravel fills the palm with seed and tells him to spread his fingers.

"Like this?"

"Wider. Now swing your arm this way and the seeds will fall through your fingers."

"What's the trick?"

"That way they don't spread in clusters. Can you handle that?"

Jered nods and Ravel fills his other hand. Then the boy heads into the mud and begins to spread the seed. When his hands are empty, he stops and turns, saying, "More," so Ravel pours again. Jered reverently continues, measuring his steps and mindful of his gestures. They continue this way, Ravel filling his palms and Jered scattering the seed until the bag is empty and Ravel is sorry he hadn't thought of waiting for Jered to spread all of the seed.

"So what now?"

"We're finished."

"But there's two more bags."

"Let's save them for the backyard."

"Tomorrow?"

"Right now if you want to. But first we have to dig it up."

They are almost finished digging and raking at five-thirty when Cassie comes home. She steps out of a car that is driven by a man Ravel doesn't recognize and in her eyes is what Ravel takes to be a royal flush in spades.

"Cassie, if it's about the lawn . . ."

"Don't look at me like that."

"Like what?"

"My car wouldn't start and he gave me a ride home from work."

"Who?"

"Don."

The car pulls away and Ravel doesn't get a good look at his face. "Nice of him."

"Just don't start anything, Vance."

Jered comes by to give his mother a quick howdy and to exchange the rake for the shovel. Then he hurries back to the muck they've dug up out back.

"Well, *he* looks happy," Cassie remarks, and right there Ravel figures he's earned his universal keep for the day.

"We're, uh, putting in a new lawn."

"What on earth for?"

"Oh, ah, picnics, baseball, nude sunbathing. Homage to the color green."

And like that she touches his arm. Just a touch. "Don't try so hard, Vance. It's as though you're shouting when I'm in the same room with you."

Then she goes into the house and he is standing there with a rake in his hands and a dumb grin on his face and Jered says, "Hey, Dad, there's no more weeds."

He's invited to dinner but he'll need the night, or part of it, off work, so he dials Nashua Coe's number. As the phone is ringing he invents and rejects fourteen lame excuses, but Nashua beats him to the punch.

"Don't say it, Vance. Not a word. I don't need any ring-around-the-rosy out a you just now. You ain't got the flu and I seen your mother yesterday in the pink of health. You don't play the dogs in Nevada and no one at the Two Guns has ever seen you around. My guess is you're with your wife."

"Right on the money, Nashua. My wife."

"Well, that plain fits and I'm not gonna be the one to stand in your way. Mend your fences and face the music. And don't forget: When everyone else in this town gave you up for a hopeless spook, Nashua Coe gave you a job. You got till midnight."

"I've got till midnight."

"Dinner's almost ready. Where's Jered?"

"Watching television."

They are alone in the kitchen and Ravel notices his picture has been removed. His place on the refrigerator door is vacant.

"I took it down last week. Jered says you're better-looking than he was."

"What does his mother say?"

"His mother has no opinion whatsoever." She is peeling potatoes and for a moment there is only the shick-shick of blade against peel to fill the silence. Then she adds, "But she could be made to be inclined to consider to agree."

Taking this sleight of mouth for encouragement, he is right. She slips into his arms and stays there, and both of them are slightly unhinged by the manner in which they've clapped together for no apparent reason. Then she leans backward to look at him. She tells him he looks too worn out and too burdened. "Can't you be somehow stupid or at least carefree?"

"I've already tried stupid and look where it got us."

"I love you, Vance, but I can't save your soul. You burned our house."

"It wasn't ours. They'd taken it."

"You gave it to them when you drove me away."

"It was how I left them, burning that house. Walking away wouldn't have gotten the message across. I didn't want to picture them sleeping in those rooms. What do you think?"

She shakes her head and only then does he notice they are no longer embracing. The Er are still among them. Turning her back on him, she takes up her knife and resumes peeling the potatoes. "If you want to do something," she says, the tone of her voice gone dry, "Jered will help you set the table. Whatever."

. . .

After an almost silent dinner, they settle in the living room, where Cassie hides behind a magazine and Jered is riveted to a taped film, a gore flick. Kids at a summer camp are getting slaughtered by a hulking man with gardening shears. In one scene blood splatters onto a mirror and in another various children are massacred on a river raft. Jered's eyes are lit up like the foyer at Caesars Palace and Ravel feels an itch in an unscratchable place.

"Who chose this movie?" he asks Cassie.

"Jered."

"You let him?"

"He's his own man."

"Don got it for me."

Man, Ravel is thinking. Whatever happened to the simple precision of words? "Boy," he says too loudly to Cassie. "He's a little boy."

Jered turns around and tells him to pipe down. "I can't hear the music."

Ravel leaves the couch to lean down and listen with him. "When you hear that sound," Jered explains, "it means he's coming to get them." On the screen, a young girl in shorts and a halter top searches the forest for a lost softball and the blades of a pair of garden shears flash in the sunlight. The sound is an organic hum that layers an electric, labored breathing. This is it, bloody curtains. Then suddenly the girl has found the ball, the electric hum ceases, and the girl races merrily back to her friends, unscathed. While Ravel is relieved, Jered is unperturbed. "He'll get her later, Dad. Keep watching."

When the movie is over and every single child actor mercilessly slaughtered for home entertainment, Jered is ready for bed. Tucking him in, Ravel asks him if he still speaks his language.

"What language?"

"The one you made up."

Jered says he doesn't remember.

. . .

The cheapest advice around is the advice you give yourself. It is so cheap that you tend to ignore it and place your fog-ridden trust in the amateur wisdom of strangers. Ravel's advice to himself is to make with the feet music, the very tune that Cassie seems to be waiting for at the end of a long day of slow healing. But he just sits there, having more than once heard that other bit of offhand advice: He who waits long enough gets what he wants.

Cassie goes to the bathroom and seems to be making an intentional racket, drumbeats or Morse code to unseen neighbors. Then she is in the kitchen washing dishes that he's convinced he has already washed and dried. A man appears on the television to make an appeal for America's poor and Ravel turns his eyes to inventory the room around him. It is the only part of the house in which Cassie's touch is evident. The floorboards are warped but freshly stained with what he recognizes by hue and scent as one of her homemade oils. What look like authentic Navajo rugs are in fact discarded rags that have been cut and stuffed and sewn into a passable design, then stitched onto bamboo mats so that they won't curl or shred. Above the television is a high bookcase filled with cookbooks, sewing patterns, geological texts, and photo albums. In place of bookends are stone and clay pots filled with bright beads. The couch, beneath its gold polyester throw cover, is a ruin of spring and stuffing, a sure candidate for the Dunes, but it serves its purpose, as does the smooth stone slab propped on four thick legs to provide a coffee table. The walls have been painted a faded blue, making the room breathe with imagined space, and the few pictures she's hung are abstracts, simple watercolor swirls of mingled blue and green and yellow. He is looking at these with wonder when she finally comes in from her kitchen hideout.

"Who did these?"

"Jered."

"My Jered?"

"No, mine. He was four and a half and I wouldn't buy him a coloring book. Just paintbrushes and paper and a little cup for water. That ruins kids, you know, learning to color between the lines."

"Imagistic fascism."

"Cartoons and distorted anatomy. So he did these watercolors and I couldn't help falling in love with them. But he's lost it, whatever he had. The teachers have gotten to him but good. At his school they teach some things all wrong, like art. I couldn't undo their corruption of his sense of color. He keeps bringing home stick men in color-coordinated purple-pink space suits."

"He told me he's forgotten his language. The one he made up."

"He gave it up the day we moved back to Paragonah. When I asked him why, he said, 'There isn't anyone to be afraid of anymore.' " She looks at Ravel with eyes he remembers, a sincere gazing into his own face. "Vance, do you believe in the innocence of children?"

"Not for a second."

"I've always wanted to. I used to see them as victims of growing up and having to leave the garden for the desert. As if just by getting to know the world around them they lose their innate magic. Like Jered forgetting his own language."

Ravel tells her he has a different picture. "At a playground, those circles of tiny savages plunder, insult, and indulge in the occasional torture of lizards and insects. Like Attila's Huns, only with far less muscle."

"So we haven't got a chance? As we grow older?"

"No. We only have vague hopes of being treated with courtesy."

There is a pause. Her bottom lip is between her teeth and she is looking at Jered's watercolors. "That's dismal," she says. Then she turns to face him. "You're depressing me again. First time all night, but there you are with your bleak landscapes. Why don't you take a powder?"

"It's only nine-thirty and there's something I've been wanting to ask."

"I've already forgiven you almost everything. What now?"

"Sanctuary? Resuscitation?"

She smiles. "What is it with this flashy speech, when I know all you want is a roll in the hay?"

Within seconds he's standing at the back door with his hands on her shoulders to hold her upright. "If you kiss me I'll swoon," she says. "No lie."

So he leans into her, touching his lips to hers and then exploring the cathedral of her mouth with his tongue. When he releases her and is on the other side of the door, she does a mock swan dive in slo mo to the kitchen floor. The fall of bliss.

He's out of her doghouse now and the years of frantic barking are coming to an end. "I'll be back tomorrow," he tells her, "to water the grass."

"That's as good an excuse as any," she says, looking up from the floor. "You're welcome."

With time to spare and surrounded by the protective aura of Cassie's good graces, Ravel stops into the Two Guns for a fast beer. Utah law says no selling over the counter. It's a law that holds about as much water as a tennis racket. The Two Guns gets around it with the simple gymnastic implied by the name. On paper, there are two legal establishments, one a restaurant and the other a liquor store. The premises are demarcated by a yellow line painted on the floor. On one side of the line is the liquor store, where you buy whatever you want to drink and it is put into a brown paper bag. Then you cross that yellow line to the restaurant, pick out a table that suits you, remove your firewater from its bag, and open it with your own two hands.

The night is still young but the Two Guns is half full. A dozen cowpokes and truckers wearing baseball caps play pool or pinball or just prop the counter of the bar with their heavy haunches. Country music is playing on a Rock-ola, one of those lo-lo-lonesome numbers with a high-flying fiddle in the background. Randy is nowhere in sight but Sandy is seated at a table in the back, where she is making fast time with what Ravel can only describe as a galoot. Ravel steps up to the bar as though he means business.

"So?" says the bartender.

"So, a beer."

"Tap or bottle?"

Ravel knows little about bars. The terminology eludes him. "Bottle," he answers.

"Light?"

A word he can never refuse. "Sure."

"Coors or Bud or Schlitz?"

This is getting elaborate, he is thinking. He chooses Coors. The bartender brings a bottle and pops the cap. Then he puts the open bottle into a small brown bag. "Glass?" he asks.

"You bet."

The yellow line is at his heels and he crosses it to a bar that's been set up on the other side. A man settles in next to Ravel and watches his profile. Ravel remembers he used to be afraid of this man. He digs for his name but all he can conjure are isolated syllables: Si, Saw, Say.

Ravel pours his beer from the bottle to the glass; too quickly, and there is more foam than beer.

"Pussy beer," the man says to him.

Ravel asks what he means.

"Coors Light. I ain't never seen a *man* drink it is what. Allus womens. Or mostly."

Ravel says there's a first time for everything. "To your mental health," he adds, and drinks up.

The man is still watching Ravel as though his face were a television screen. After a long time he says he knows the face. "You're in movies, right?"

Ravel tells him he's got the wrong man.

"Like hell I do. I know that mug. Cop stories, maybe."

"Sorry, sir."

"Take that back!"

"Huh?"

"The sir part."

"Sure. Right."

When Ravel was in his most outrageous stage of high holiness, years before the Er, he would wander Paragonah in an orange robe and clink finger bells to the rhythm of the wheeling heavens. He would chant and pray and om. It was no surprise when the locals started heaving their guts at the mere sight of him. The abuse was a source of joy to Ravel, a surefire sign that he was onto something. Little steps for little feet. He didn't have the good sense in those days just to do his number in the shadows and then lie low.

Seth! That's his name. He will never forget it again. Seth once caught him on the edge of town, where he was sitting lotus over a constellation of grouped stones. The cowboy had stopped his car by the side of the road, clomped over to Ravel and made some crack about how he should get his skinny ass out of the dirt and make tracks. When Ravel hadn't moved, Seth had yanked down his zipper and laid a slow stream across the rocks, up Ravel's lap to his shoulders, and onto his face. Despite the discomfort, Ravel had barely stirred from his trance. Lifting a finger to his wetted face, he'd touched a drop of it to his tongue. "Sweet," he'd said. Seth's face had turned every color of the kaleidoscope and he'd shuffled his feet to get in a good boot to the ribs. But he'd been too knotted up and sweaty and he finally had turned on his heel and done a half-dozen fishtails down the road and away.

Standing in the Two Guns, Ravel can't remember whether they've run into each other since. It isn't probable and that makes ten years of dust.

Seth says he never forgets a face. "Buy you a beer?"

Then the strangest thing happens. He falls to the floor. Not in stages of buckled knees, a faint, and a tumbling, but all at once, like a felled tree. Ravel is staring down at him openmouthed and the bartender says, "Christ, here we go again." He comes from behind the bar and gestures to a couple of others to help him. Together they haul the body to a back room and leave it on the floor.

"Too much to drink?" Ravel asks.

"Naw, hell. He does that all the time. Says he's got something in his brain."

"Aneurysm," says a man at the bar.

"That's just a word!"

"Yeah, but it's the right one."

"You say."

"He pissed on me once," Ravel tells them.

The bartender is unimpressed. "He does that to everybody."

"All the time," says the other man. "Drunk or sober."

"What for?"

"He says it makes him feel better. Gets the poison out."

"What poison?"

"The pain of living," says the bartender. And a grin spreads across his face like spilled beer. "Knowing that he's a numskull and he's ugly and is gonna die all by his lonesome."

Ravel looks for a pay phone and dials Randy's number. When the old man answers, he starts telling him about what he's seen. "His name's Seth. He a friend of yours?"

"What is it with you, Ravel? Always going on about these things. If I weren't here you'd just tell someone else. And if they weren't there you'd tell it to your shoes."

He hangs up.

Arriving at the yard before midnight, Ravel heads straight out for a tour of the yard. The Caddies are empty and Limbo is peaceful, so he swings up to the Heap where he can see smoke rising over one of the alleys. Crouching low, he edges forward and peers around the bumper of a tangled wreck. A man sits wrapped in a blanket before a small fire. He pokes a stick at a can that is resting on a bed of glowing embers.

Sol. I've found him.

When he steps from behind the car, Sol leaps in fright and heads for the alley but Ravel chases him down easily enough and clutches at the blanket.

"It's all right, Sollie. I'm unarmed."

"It's you, Ravel? I thought it was the spook."

This doesn't make much sense to Ravel and he says, "Come on back and eat your beans."

"It's soup," Sol corrects him. "Cream a broccoli."

"You need a spoon?"

"Got one right here."

They sit by the fire and Ravel watches Sol eat the soup until it's gone. Then he licks the spoon and puts it back in his bag before rubbing his finger around the rim of the can to get the last drops. "Sure was good," he says.

"I'm glad, Sol."

"I been a good tenant, Ravel. I hope you been noticing."

Ravel assures him that he has.

"When I gotta shit or pee I do it way out there where it don't matter." He means the Dunes but Ravel is the only one who knows the name.

"Bet you never been hungry like I get."

"You'd be surprised, Sollie."

The old man just looks at him for a long time. "No, Ravel. No, I wouldn't."

The fire burns low and Sol tosses on a few twigs to give it life. "I been moving around a lot," he says. "Maybe that's why you ain't seen me. First I was hiding from you but now there's that spook."

"What spook?"

"You ain't seen him? Guy in jeans and a white shirt all frilly and torned to pieces. He don't talk to nobody, not me and not them rail bums coming through. Just walks around the yard all spooky like, humming to hisself."

"Humming what?"

"Who knows? Just these funny noises that make my hairs stand up. Once I stayed on his tail for a while just to see what he was up to. Middle of the night and he's walking around picking up rocks."

Ravel already knows. The only question left is which of them.

"Then he takes these rocks back to this car he's shacked in and gets out a box. I can't see so good what he's doing so I move a little closer. Then he gets shook and just lights out a there. When I'm sure he's not coming back I walk over and take a look at those rocks and damned if there isn't black paint all over them."

Painter, then. The angel of devotion.

"What's it mean, Ravel? I can't figure it."

Sol shows Ravel where Painter did his work but there isn't anything to see except random drops of dried paint on the ground.

"Maybe he's gone."

Ravel says he doesn't think so.

"What's he gonna do, Ravel?"

"He's harmless, Sol. A real sweet kid if you get to know him."

"Be a cold day in hell."

"All the same, stick close to the front gate. Is that Indian family still camped in the Dunes?"

"What're the Dunes?"

Ravel points. "Out that way. The old parts."

Sol nods. "They're set up pretty permanent by the looks of it."

"Give them the word to keep their eyes peeled. And if they want to come closer in it's OK by me. There're plenty of places in the Heap that'll do just fine."

"Where you going?"

"For a walk, Sollie. See what I can see."

"Don't forget your tire iron."

But there isn't a trace of him. Neither campfire nor painted stone nor print of bare feet in the dust. Ravel can't even find the Navajo family in the wilds of the Dunes, though the coals of a recent fire tell him that they're still in the neighborhood. Heading back to his office, he sees a light in the direction of the Caddies. It could be Sandy or it could be John Q. Public.

He flashes his light into various windows and passes from car to car until he sees her sitting in the white Lincoln Continental. She is wearing a blue blouse tied into a knot at the navel and when she sees him she strikes a bunny pose on the passenger side of the front seat.

"Cassie?"

She opens the door and gestures for him to get in. "After you left I had these second thoughts. I couldn't sleep so I walked out here. It seemed like the thing to do."

"How'd you get in?"

"Like everyone else. I climbed the fence."

He decides that it's only right after all the obstacles she's thrown in his path. "It's not that you're unwelcome," he tells her. "But this isn't the time for it. You've got to go."

"You're not serious. I'll overheat."

"It's not safe here, Cassie. Yesterday's shit is hitting the fan."

"Translation, please."

"Painter's here."

She considers this for a moment and then shrugs. "I'm not enchanted by the news. I thought we'd seen the last of these people."

"He's come to kill me."

She rolls her eyes. "You're imagining things. Painter dotes on you."

She doesn't know about what they did to Namer or any of

the weirdness that went down after he'd completed the Mingling; his perpetual shadows and the cries he heard when his house and chicken coop went up in flames. He considers putting her wise to the evil, here and now, but doesn't have the heart. His list of regrets is already embarrassingly lengthy.

"Take my word for it," he says. "My days are numbered on painted rocks."

"Well, he won't find you here."

"No," he admits. "This isn't his taste in surface transportation."

"Then we can drink this." She's brought along a bottle of red wine and a pair of stemmed glasses. "Only trouble is I didn't think to bring a corkscrew."

"Then we'll go without."

"No we won't, Vance. Be a man. Think of something."

He wanders the Heap until he finds a long, pointy, twisted piece of steel. Wrapping a rag around his hand, he pierces the cork with the metal, turns it twice, and yanks. Burgundy, like black blood in the darkness, spills across his lap. This I don't need, he says to the moon. He takes the bottle back to the Lincoln, where he pours, they clink glasses, drink. The ensuing silence is the wool he's pulling over his eyes. He and Cassie alone.

"One of us will now say something foolish and romantic," she suggests.

But he doesn't answer her. He tosses down the wine and pours himself another.

She says she's been expecting something more out of her visit. "That fence was no piece of cake. I had to balance the bottle and the glasses in one hand and climb with the other. And I thought you'd be jumping my bones by now instead of going all gooey on me. Got another girl? Is that it?"

"Me? I'm a model of male restraint."

"How sad. But what about the kindness of passing strangers?"

"You mean Sandy?"

"Uh huh. Did you ever?"

"No, I never."

"I thought you might," she tells him. "I thought at least you wouldn't be all alone here. I wouldn't have minded if you had." There is a silence, and then she suggests a switch to the backseat. "Look at all that wasted space. We can push the front seats forward and stretch out our legs."

When they are settled hip to hip and the conversation is as empty as the wine bottle, he tells her maybe he should go make another round of the premises.

"Still fretting over Painter?"

"More or less."

"Then try concentrating on the business at hand. This isn't an auto salvage, Vance. We're on the open road and a discreet someone up front is driving us to the sea. You're a poor hitchhiker I've picked up on the road and I'm a kindly slut in need of your affection. What do you say to that?"

"Sounds danceable."

His hand moves up her blouse to where her breasts are cool to the touch. Her nipple stiffens like a smooth stone in the center of his spiraling palm. She pushes him away long enough to untie the knot of her blouse and then she shimmies out of her jeans. "Ta da." His field of vision narrows until he is blind to all but the fuzziest periphery. This time he's not groping for her in a bedroom darkness; they are in collusion rather than collision. Think of it: she wants me back. And when he leans over her she draws him down and they start off slowly at first, as if they are unsure of each other and this backseat scene they've been making up out of loneliness and regrets and wisecracks. All of her sharp edges, her broken glass, her fine needles of rage, are no longer there for him while she is telling him to do this and then more of this and then this again, her language coming to him as if from under water. They both come, seconds apart, and he props himself on his elbows to look at her face. He is thinking of how good she is, how fine, when he notices in her eyes a soundless terror. Following her gaze, he looks over his shoulder and there outside the car, grinning stupidly, a basket of colored rocks in his hand, stands Painter.

WALKING over dead grass and cigarette butts, high and low, he combs the grounds. In the northeast corner of the Heap he comes across the remains of a recent fire that could have belonged to anyone, local or transient. There are no telltale signs of Painter. Passing through Limbo, Ravel cuts his hand on a jagged strip of Chevy bumper. He stops to suck the blood through his teeth and his throat goes dry.

The rising sun glitters through shattered windshields as if through stained glass and the high weeds sway like Baptist choirs in the morning breeze. There is nothing to be found in Limbo or in the south end of the Heap so he crosses into the Dunes, the tundra of ancient cars piled into pyramids, the Edsels and Packards and Oldsmobiles, eyeless and engineless and stained with a blood-red rust. This is where Painter will be. Where the weeds have long since ceased to grow and the rats, gnawing on metal, die in bloody packs in the middle of the alleys.

Ravel moves deeper into the thicket and steps over the refuse from a previous dumping ground: ashen mattresses, gaping iceboxes, loose springs like haywire plant life, rusted pipe fittings, and bits of metal jingling and chiming underfoot. Farther on he comes to a mass of old tires gone gray from the sun. The towers into which they'd once been stacked have long since collapsed, and this part of the Dunes is particularly windblown and melancholy, like a deserted city. Just over a high hill of tires is a wisp of rising smoke, a black tentacle reaching up and dissolving in the sky. Ravel scales the rubber hill; he slips and sways on burst tubes, truck tires, bicycle tires in shreds like black snakes, and heaped shards of tread. When he reaches the top he can see down into an arena-like space, a clearing in the ruin he had never known was there. Painter is on his haunches staring into a small fire of twigs and trash. The flame is surrounded by painted stones. Ravel is relieved to see that they are white.

He knows I'm up here. He knows but won't look up at me. My presence will undo his prayer.

Ravel waits a long while and then screws up the courage to descend into the clearing. When he is standing over the fire he says simply, "Why you, Painter?"

Now Painter looks up from the fire and Ravel sees how his face has changed. He had remembered him as a taller version of Jered, wild and dirty and wide-eyed. Now the boyishness is gone. His eyes are narrowed and gray and his skin is weathered and cracked like the desert floor.

"Me," Painter answers, "because of allbody I wanted you most."

His language is still askew. Only his gaze is altered. Ravel senses that he won't try anything now, not while the fire continues to burn in that circle of white stones. The sun is finally risen and seems to have no color at all. Painter reaches to his side for more twigs and drops them into the flames along with the torn bits of a yellowed milk carton. "How long," he asks, "will you stay away?"

"From the Er?"

"From us."

Ravel doesn't hesitate. "Forever," he answers. "And then some."

He is relieved to see a smile come over Painter's face. His lips move but there are no words and Ravel realizes he is forming them silently before speaking aloud. "Damn," Painter says. "I thought so."

"I'm retired, Painter. Or whatever your real name is. I'm not what I was. Or what I never was."

Again Painter's lips move before he speaks aloud. The effect is unsettling, like seeing a poorly dubbed foreign film. "We fucking loved you. All of us. You did us shit."

Ravel just shakes his head. It's like talking to a black hole. You throw down a few words to see how deep it goes and you never hear anything hit the bottom. "I told Namer it was a free country. Before you killed her, that's what I had to say. Don't you feel anything about *that*, Painter? After the way she took care of you and taught you how to write?"

He says he hasn't forgotten. "I can write my name good as gold."

"Are you the one who killed her, Painter?"

He shakes his head, but there is pain in his eyes.

"Then who did?"

"I don't fucking know."

"Was it Gazer?"

Painter goes silent for a while and tends his fire. It occurs to Ravel that he may not have known about Namer. It's a wild enough thought but that's his mood. All of his ideas are screams and howling for the moment. Fear burns like a fuse all the way to his next question. "Did you kill anyone else?"

Painter reaches into the fire, extracts a burning stick, waves it a few times, and puts it back. "After you left," he says. "After, the goats left too. Then nothing happened all the time. Weaver cried and Gazer went to town to get drugs. I was hungry and we never saw any rain. You took it with you and you didn't come back. Gazer told us we should find you and punish you but you weren't in Paragonah, you weren't nowhere. Rainer said you must a walked into light but nobody believed her."

"Are those tears, Painter?"

He wipes his nose on his bare forearm. "Tears, yeah. It was a long time ago."

"How long ago?"

"I don't know. I don't count. We were just lost as fuck and then there was no more food or water. No more Mingling either.

I lost my prayer sticks in the fire and couldn't find no feathers to make me more of."

"So it's over."

"Nothing's over but except you and me."

"Then you didn't kill anyone else?"

"You. We killed you in all our prayers. You died every night."

Ravel ponders this for a moment. "So how long have you been looking for me?"

"All times since."

It takes Ravel five full seconds to understand what he means. "Three years?"

Painter's eyes are angry and he is no longer weeping. "I had to live in the world again because of you. I had it made and then you had to fuck it all up. Time gets on top of time and I been every damn where but then I came back here 'cause I knew you'd come. I learn things. I'm not so dumb." His lips go on working as though he has something else to say which won't metamorphose into speech. Ravel decides it's time to get down to the business at hand.

"Painter, it's about those rocks."

"What about them?"

"The black ones. I never taught you black."

He smiles again and for once doesn't form the words in his mouth before saying them. "Why ask me? *You* already know."

"Because time has passed and I don't trust my memory. Are you fixing to kill me, Painter?"

"If the rocks say so."

"What cheap theology does that come from?"

"From you." He is still smiling. "Vance." The smile widens damn near to a jack-o'-lantern grin. "I can say your name, see."

"Christ, Painter, it's only one syllable." Ravel is doing what he can to hide his annoyance but it's too much like old times again. "And I suppose if the rock says for you to do me in, then it has its reasons."

"You burned the shelter and the"—his lips twitch silently—
"and the food and all."

"You've been misinformed, Painter. Think back. I burned
my house, *my* chicken coop, and *my* part of the garden. I didn't
touch your tents or shelters."

"But we all *shared.*"

Ravel is exasperated. "So what do you want? A property
settlement?"

No answer but the pursing of lips, a slight whistle from between Painter's teeth. The fire is burning out and he doesn't
make an effort to stoke it back to life. Ravel takes this as a sign
that Painter has nothing more to say to him. But there remains
a single, thorny fact to be cleared up.

"If you've been out in the world for three years, how do you
know the Er are still there?"

It's as though Painter's been shot through the heart and for
the first time Ravel has the impression that he's home free. Or
at least holding the tickets. He continues: "My guess is that they've
scattered for good while you've been hunting me down. My guess
is Gazer didn't wait for you. Three years is a long time. What
do you think?"

Those dry lips move and his eyes dart from right to left. The
last tiny flame of the fire winks out; a snuff of smoke rises near
to his face. "They're there," Painter answers. But his voice is dry
from hunger and thirst and the words are covered with the rustle
of dead leaves.

Standing alongside Interstate 15, Ravel sticks out his thumb and
reels in a station wagon driven by a woman with four kids. She
won't let him in unless he agrees to give her a dollar for gas.

"Got two," he tells her.

"My lucky day."

Back in Roadside Business he decides to try Randy's for a gun or a word of advice on the art of self-defense. Ravel raps a two-four riff on the aluminum door but gets no response. So he goes around the side to look in the porthole that passes for a window. Randy is sprawled facedown on the trailer floor, naked as sin and snoring like a lumberjack on Sunday morning. Ravel scans the room for the ivory-handled Colt but it is nowhere to be seen.

So he can't save me either.

He stomps over to the souvenir shop with the vague intention of buying something for Jered, a pacifist toy of some kind, something to take his mind off the cinema of mayhem. On the children's wall are bows and arrows, silver six-guns, rubber-bladed tomahawks, cap pistols, and a plastic burp gun with removable shell case. Indian headdress, cowboy hats, plastic GI helmets with camouflage netting.

He confronts Mircea, who is behind the counter filling out an inventory slip. "Don't you have any Tonka trucks in this place?"

She looks up from her list and gazes across the counter at him. "What is it, Vance?"

He asks again about Tonka trucks. "Or something that doesn't have carnage and bloodletting as a base motif?"

"How about a Bowie knife?"

"Mircea, it's for Jered."

"They're made of rubber, Vance."

"No dice."

"How about a Tommy tank? They're batterized."

"Don't you have a truck? An earth mover? A road grader? A single fucking *dump* truck?"

"Your language, Vance."

"Jesus suffering Christ."

"Your father used to say that."

"What else did he say?"

She doesn't answer this. She tells him only that he looks like death warmed over. In response Ravel offers her his bleakest of smiles.

. . .

Swimming upward from merciful sleep, he surfaces to a ringing telephone.

"Now that you've had some time to mull over my offer . . ."

It's Don, Cassie's hovering drink of water. "I thought we settled this already."

"We settled nothing. I made you a heartfelt offer and you talked gibberish."

"I thought I was clear as day. Save your quarters and don't call back."

There is a pause. "Would violence convince you, Ravel? I'm an ex-Marine and could give you some pointers. A little visit from some locals who remember my good works? Is that what would make you less hard of hearing?"

Ravel tells him he's talking to a man who was once peed on for sitting peacefully in a desert flat.

"Everyone in this town is so sick of you, Ravel."

"Like I told a girl who died, it's a free country."

Another pause. "What'd she die of?"

"Of exposure, Don. Exposure to me. You say your prayers now, hear."

The receiver hits home with a click, a detonation. Before Ravel falls back to sleep he considers how light, as a word, has multiple meanings. He must be translucent, then. Why else would it be that everyone sees right through him?

Everyone on God's green earth has something to tell him. A story, a confession, cheap advice, a gag. He's convinced that it all started with that man in the bar, Seth, who ten years ago thought to water him like a plant. But he may be mistaken.

He's propped up in bed after four hours' sleep, sunlight prying at his eyes, while Randy, looking suddenly fit, pours him coffee.

"So what's the mating call of a Provo belle?"

"I give up, Randy."

" 'I'm so drunk.' "

Ravel smiles but he doesn't laugh.

"Where's the sugar?"

"Third cupboard from the left."

"Whose left? Yours or mine?"

"Ours."

"Just the sugar."

Randy rummages through Mircea's orderly cupboards but can't find the canister. "Tough luck," he says.

"Tell me something else."

"Sure. This out-a-work Asiatic reads in the *L.A. Times*, 'Mexican Wanted for Rape.' Says, 'Shit, these wetbacks get all the good jobs.' "

"No more Two Guns humor, Randy."

He says it's his way of making people feel better.

"Why? Am I sick?"

"That's a definite maybe. Now suppose you tell me what you want with my Colt?"

"There's someone who needs the fear of God put to him."

"Anyone I know?"

"Just another one of those ghosts of my own making."

Randy says he'd like to oblige but he has these nagging doubts. "You and a gun, Ravel? And my gun at that? Guns can kill people, you know."

"That's not what they say at the National Rifle Association."

"You'd do better off to point this guy out to me and let me get it over with."

Ravel answers that he'd prefer to handle it himself.

"So what's he want you for? You kill somebody?"

Ravel is facing the window and the sun is full on his face. He closes his eyes and reads crimson through his lids. When he opens his eyes Randy is still there and by the look on his face it is obvious no one has to say anything more.

Randy has an errand to run and they cross the flat together to his trailer. Beneath the trailer are a half-dozen shopping bags filled with empty beer bottles.

"For the major," Randy explains. "I prefer cans myself but he likes the sound of breaking glass. It takes all kinds."

Together they haul four of the bags across the shallow ravine to the ranch house. It's been twenty years since Ravel was last inside and Randy says not to count on it today. "You think maybe you're the only loony tune in town? Get a load a the major."

After three rounds of furious knocking, the major finally appears at the door. He's wearing blue pajamas with white-stitched monograms. His eyes are red and his graying hair is in electric disarray. He ignores Ravel, nods to Randy, and peers down at the bags of empty bottles.

"Brown," he says. "What happened to green?"

Randy tells him he's changed brands. "It's all glass, Major. Same shape and size."

The major shrugs.

"So how's the target practice coming along?"

"Smooth as silk," the major says. "Just look at this." He extends a hand outward to exhibit its steadiness. "She'll be home in no time. I made her bed up just this morning."

"Need any shells?"

"Nope. And I did the laundry, too. All her things is decked out like for a night on the town. She's a dancer and I can still move a leg when I'm so inclined. How much I owe you?"

"Fifty bottles there, give or take double vision. Call it five dollars."

The major recedes into the house and comes back with a fold

of ones. While paying Randy he notices Ravel for the first time. "This your son?"

Randy is speechless for a moment and Ravel senses he is about to say yes. Then he says, "No, just a drifter."

"World's full of them," says the major, and he closes the door.

"You see, don't you, that everyone has got his own handmade cross to bear?"

Ravel admits that he hasn't understood a blessed thing.

"That major there, living all by his lonesome. Good pension, nice house. He must be eighty if he's a day and he's still got all his real teeth. You might remember his wife from when you were a kid. Her name was Audrey and she used to give you toys you couldn't break. Made out a wood."

Ravel remembers only vaguely.

"Well, the major shot her. Don't look at me like that—I'm telling it to you straight. They were playing William Tell or some such nonsense. Him in his uniform and her standing there with an apple on her pretty head and smiling peaches and cream at him, saying, 'Go to it, honey, split us that there apple.' The way I heard it, he didn't miss by much."

"Is this more talk from the Two Guns, Randy?"

"No, Ravel, it is not. It is the gospel truth about a man who fucked up with a single stupid shot and has been trying to perfect his aim ever since."

Trash is making hunger noises so they head back to Randy's trailer to feed him. While the hound goes to it, they stretch out on folding chairs in front of the trailer. It is midafternoon, the end of the summer, and the sky is high and white. From across the flat they can both see Mircea in the garden. She is on her knees with her back to them, digging under the rosebushes. Ravel together or with a group of boys from Cedar City, but no matter where they headed at sundown Jack was home before sunup; that was Mircea's rule. "A good-looking man with eyes like yours, all soft around the edges. The kind of man men could love without feeling queer about it. He loved your mother and I'd swear he never once stepped out on her except when it came to God. He couldn't do that, not that church business of hers. Made him unhappy, he said, thinking about sin and redemption."

They had watched a few bombs together, during a brief period in which Randy had served in Jack Ravel's platoon. They had shared the same stirred dust and frayed nerves.

"He's been dead for a hell of a long time now and all the funny stories I can tell you won't add a jot to what you think you want to know."

"The same thing," Ravel tells him. "Why he took that walk."

Randy tosses his empty bottle into a new brown bag reserved for the major. "Is that a mystery or something? You go on and on, don't you? Like a radio I can't unplug." He steps into the trailer for another beer and when he comes back out he moves his chair a foot farther from Ravel's. "The reason," he says, "you never seen me work is what I got out a watching them two bombs. I nailed those Marine bastards to the wall over what they made us do. Told them they could take their shut-up rules and stuff them sideways. I made them pony up and let me out of the service with a bankroll. Damn. I saw two of those hydrogen mothers and it shook the cold sweat out a me for years to come. And your old man saw eighty-eight of them. Count that to yourself, Vance. Count it real slow: one, two, three, four, all the way to eighty-eight. And with each number think hard on what you're seeing and feeling. That's what I did the day I got the news. I just counted from one to eighty-eight."

Ravel feels himself getting hot and knows it for a bad sign. More and more he's allergic to omens.

Randy's still talking. "Who knows what his instincts were? You're asking about a man who folded kings and eights for no observes Randy watching and senses an intensity in his gaze. Randy catches Ravel's glance. "I can hear you thinking from here, Vance. I watch her all the time. She's part of my landscape, your mother. I keep an eye on her. She's always there and I'm always here. You want to get nasty about it?"

When Ravel doesn't answer, Randy pops the caps off a pair of bottles and hands one of them to Ravel. "Don't you ever wonder," he asks, "why you never seen me work?"

"You got a pension from the Marines," Ravel answers. "Just like Mircea. And by now you must be on social security, Medicare, the works."

"Serves me right," Randy says. "I make a little homespun conversation and I get insults about my income. And just as I was about to invite you to a barbecue or something on that order."

"It's been a long time since you talked to me about my father."

"Not that again. I thought you was scarred over by now. I thought you was clean."

"I am, but I'm still his son. Tell me."

"Wait till bedtime."

When Ravel was younger it was Randy, not Mircea, who told him stories about his father. He filled in the blanks of Mircea's silences. Jack and he had been pals, according to Randy, not blood brothers. Went to the Paunsaugunt Range to hunt or fish. Cooked barbecue and watched the sun go down over bottles of Southern Comfort. Pitched horseshoes, watched rodeos, played eight-ball, straight pool, and stud poker. Jack Ravel had a fair bluff but a tendency to fold a strong hand at the wrong time. And it wasn't a question of nerve; it was bad calculations. He couldn't count the cards like the others. They were all just colors and numbers getting played left and right. Sometimes his own hand brought him into some money, sometimes not. He was a fair shot with a rifle but an impatient fisherman whose lines had a way of snagging on tree limbs or rocks downstream. He never got the hang of casting, and his best catches were usually accidents, gifts from God. Sometimes the two of them would drink reason at all but would take a pair of jacks through hell and high water. He'd cast his fly into the sand and drag it back toward the water like he knew what he was up to. And he used to dream about being an officer but even that idea was less than half-baked. The war game was rigged out there long before he even showed up."

"And he took that walk."

Randy gives Ravel a look that reminds him of a gunshot in the night, a flash of fire and smoke. Then he says, "I hear it was suicide. Now go ahead and tell me something different."

Ravel wishes back the day. To start it over again with a different measure of equanimity and another brace of Randy's jokes. He wishes he had a joke of his own to tell. He realizes that he wants Randy's esteem almost as much as he wants news of his father. "I don't know the words, Randy. I'm just casting too."

"Yakkety yak." Randy finishes his second beer and throws the bottle into the bag with the other. "Major's gonna have a field day if we keep this up." He stands and surveys the horizon, then turns toward the door of his trailer. When Ravel asks him where he's going he says to shower and shave. "Then I might take a nap, Vance. God knows, after talking to you I always feel about ten years older. Like yellowed linoleum with scuff marks from Thom McAns. Gonna go find the original luster while you disappear."

With his heart set on seeing Cassie and one way or another staving off the anxiety of impending death, Ravel makes that walk into Paragonah. The white stones along the way have been replaced with black ones, and he can only consider how Painter must be a very tired boy, going through all this ritualistic rigmarole just for his sake.

Jered is waiting for him at the house and Ravel shows him how to hook up the sprinkler so they can give first the front yard and then the back a thorough soaking. Jered says this part of the job is pretty damn dull and Ravel concedes the point. "Most of the fun's in the digging and the raking, watching the earth turn. But when the grass grows, that's all right too."

Cassie comes home in her secretary garb, a white blouse and a blue skirt with Navajo stitching at the hem. She has the worried look of a woman who's forgotten her keys and is hoping the front door is still unlocked. She tells Jered to go into the house. "I want to speak to your father alone."

When the boy kicks up a fuss, Ravel says his name aloud and to the surprise of everyone he obeys, but not without giving the screen door a medium slam.

Cassie says she hears that Don's been calling him. "You've got to understand, Vance. It wasn't my idea. I'm not seeing him anymore. Not in weeks now."

Ravel says he wasn't asking. "I'm minding my own business and for the moment my business is this lawn."

"He wasn't the only one I went with, Vance. He's just the most persistent. There were others. Things got messy for a while and I'm not going to say just who the father might be. Can we leave that much unsaid?"

Ravel reaches to turn off the water. He realizes he is standing in mud. "I'm not asking anything, Cassie. I just came to water the lawn."

"He says he wants to marry me."

"Tell him to wait his turn."

"I already have."

This is news and Ravel reads it as though it were small print. A point of light in her brown eyes. "Say it again."

"I want to count on you, Vance. I have a feeling that I can. What do you think?"

"You can," he answers. "Anything is possible. The grass will grow."

Her laughter hits home and he whirls her in his arms. She

says this time she wants a church wedding. "Nothing fancy, though. Your mother, some friends, a few flowers strewn around."

"Leave it to me."

"We'll buy things. We'll finish this house."

"That's it, Cassie. We'll shop."

"Sheets and pillowcases for a double bed. A new sofa. Silverware, trinkets. Whatever. But, Vance, there's this one more thing."

"Shoot."

"Painter. You said he came to kill you."

It sounds stupid, put just so. They both laugh and Ravel says, "Oh, that. I'll persuade him otherwise."

But her face is mapped with lines he's read before. This way to consternation and that way to heartache. "I have this idea," she says, "of growing old with you. And now this baby. Do you mind all that much?"

"I love the baby. You?"

"I don't feel anything but hungry. When you were gone I felt as down as I've ever felt, including the bad times when we did drugs. I stayed home and fell asleep to the television. I never ate unless it was to help Jered finish his meals. When I went with men I felt windy-headed and stupid. I didn't understand the jokes or the things I was being told. I didn't know how to dance or make small talk. I didn't want to be alone. I kept my diaphragm in my purse but I never had the nerve to use it. It seemed silly to put something like that inside of me. I already felt empty and barren. Then when I knew I was pregnant, I had kind thoughts about myself again. I spent a lot of time in front of the mirror just looking at my body. I hadn't really looked at myself in months. I decided to grow my hair long and I spent more time cleaning the house. Then I knew I didn't need you. I didn't even want you to come back anymore. I had what I needed. And ever since you've come home, I wake up at night for no reason and

I walk around the house with no clothes on and think of you out there in the yard. In the day all I want to do is sleep. Is that being pregnant, Vance, or is that a bad conscience?"

"It's insomnia," he tells her. "It's rage stored up in my name." He circles his arms around her and presses against the small of her back until their bones touch. "Don't worry so much. We'll be right as rain."

"Rain," she says, looking over his shoulder. "Now there's a thought. Rain."

As if expected, Painter is waiting like a bad check in the office of the yard. He is wearing the same filthy white shirt and worn jeans and his long hair is tied into a natty braid in back.

"You do that yourself?" Ravel asks.

"No. The harlot helped me."

"Sandy?"

"I don't know her name."

His speech is fluid tonight, only slightly preconceived. If there's electricity in the air it would barely register on a graph.

Ravel says it's time he made his rounds. "Care to trail along?"

They wander the yard together and Ravel teaches his mythologies of various wrecks, of numberless transients and their abandoned campsites.

"This minibus, for example, once housed a family of Vietnamese. Three generations. You remember the boat people? There were eight of them here, including the grandfather, who must have been ninety. He was a muckamuck of some import back in the French colonial times. They stayed three weeks and I didn't hear a peep out of them. Steamed their rice and whatnot and laid low. They were Buddhists, Painter. Nice folks."

"What about this car?" Painter wants to know. He is pointing to a squashed Austin-Healey, almost unrecognizable in the gloom.

Ravel admits that he doesn't know. "It's from before my time."

"Your time? What time is that?"

"The here and now, Painter. Which reminds me. How's it supposed to happen, this last ritual?"

"Knife, maybe. Maybe arrow. I don't know yet."

"No bullets?"

His lips move again before the words arrive. "Don't you remember?"

"Remember what?"

"Stone, Vance. Only stone can make you die."

Ravel sighs. "How long do you plan on keeping this up, Painter?"

"The time it takes."

They arrive at the chain-link fence that borders the row of Cadillacs. Sandy is in the pink one and she is not alone.

Painter wants to know if she lives there.

"No. You might say it's her place of employment."

"She said to me ten dollars. That's almost free."

Ravel says she's a generous kid. "For everyone else it's twenty. She's a true heart, Painter. You'd be surprised."

"No I wouldn't. I found ten dollars."

While Ravel ponders this they approach the Dunes. And all at once he has a feeling that his time has come. If ever there was a place of spiritual reckoning it would be the Dunes. He glances again at Painter to assure himself that he is unarmed, and he doubts that Painter could kill him with his bare hands. They pass over a field of strewn spark plugs and head into a thicket of stacked metal. A pair of rats scatter as they approach.

"This could be hell," Painter offers. "You could be a demon here."

"I could also be a scared young man with a wife and child to worry after."

They come to the tire mounds and skirt around the stacks to the last remaining hint of alleyway. Beyond is a mass of ancient waste, primordial plumbing, nuts, bolts, glass, and scrap iron of every hue. Any and all of it, Ravel is thinking, could be made into a Neanderthal weapon, but none of it is stone. Painter is thinking the same thing. "Not tonight," he says. "Tonight I'm not ready for you."

When they have circled back to the office and are sharing a thermos of coffee that Cassie sent along, Ravel asks him what grudge he is bearing.

"You created me," he says, his gaze cool and even.

"All I ever did, you cretin, was to give you a place to sleep in and food to eat."

"And you taught me words. The walking into light was what you had for me."

"Words?" As if to settle the matter once and for all, Ravel rummages through the garbage for a week-old *L.A. Times* and begins to read the news aloud. A man accused of rape took a knife to his private self, cutting off what offends thee, but a surgeon sewed it right back on, good as new, if forever awry. Twin babies discovered in a plastic bag on the side of the San Bernardino Freeway. One of them survived and the other one went to paradise. "Remind you of anything?"

Painter remains still, staring at Ravel.

"Three dead in a six-car *mishap*. You've got to love the words, Painter."

"Why?"

"Because they're written, that's all. News of the republic. Chitchat. These things we make up for reading in barber-shops."

"I don't understand."

"Because you're not listening, Painter. Because you're still tuned in to Gazer's sick frequency. Listen to this. Lottery winner plunges to death. News too good for reality. Test tube baby wins Christmas canned ham. Do you follow? There's good news here, Painter. Want to read for yourself?"

Painter is hot. "You know I can't read."

"That's what I mean. You sit here listening to me and I made it all up."

There is a silence. Then Painter rises and heads for the door, as if to leave. He stops, as if changing his mind, and says, "I don't understand a goddamn thing you're saying."

"I've got another idea," Ravel tells him. "We can go dig up the bones."

"What bones?"

"Paiute bones, maybe even some stray Anasazi. Did you know this car salvage is built over an ancient burial ground?"

"No."

"But you believe me?"

After a pause, Painter nods.

"As a matter of faith?"

"You just said so."

"I did. And I lied."

"About the bones?"

"About everything, Painter. Including my father."

So now Painter is smiling but there is terror in his smile. I've gone too far, Ravel is thinking. Now Painter is at that fabled edge, the perimeter of sanity. He turns away from Ravel and offers his right profile in the yellow lamplight. For an instant he resembles the orphan he once admitted to being, left to the elements in a plastic bag. Ever since his twin expired he's been wandering around in search of someone inclined to hold his hand or to smooth the hair away from his eyes with gentle fingers. But then the wind blows, it just does, and it makes him crazy. If he weren't here, Ravel knows, he'd be locked up somewhere, taking his dinner through a straw and learning the patient art of basket weaving.

"Give yourself a break, Painter, and take what I say at face value."

His voice is a whisper. "Your father . . ."

"Was run over by a stray bus."

Painter goes pale around the eyes. His lips move but there are no more sounds. And then Ravel can see he is choking and he leaps from his chair to his side. He reaches a hand to Painter's face and begins to apologize, but suddenly a blade is at his throat, Painter's whittling knife.

"There are things to believe in, Painter. But my father isn't one of them. Now put that knife away before one of us bleeds to death."

A wind is coming from between Painter's teeth, a whistling of life and death. Then, after a long hesitation, he drops the knife and Ravel kicks it into a corner of the room.

Painter hits the floor on his knees. "My other name is Tom," he says.

Only then does Ravel's fear dissolve.

ROENTGEN
EQUIVALENT
MAN

TWO NIGHTS before the last bomb drop he will ever witness, he lies in bed and can hear Mircea in the next room playing music on the RCA Victor he bought for her two Christmases back. The records all date from when they met, the Swing Era, and she doesn't, can't, know how it hurts him to hear those old songs. She can't know his grief at being unable to rise from bed and go to her and take her in his arms in a dance.

I'm not blind, not by a long shot. I know that's all she's waiting for, even as she sings along. She hasn't forgotten the words to any of those songs and is just waiting for me to be the man she fell in love with, to get up and fold her head onto my shoulder and press my hand against her back. I'm supposed to say it's over, all this loneliness, forgive me, babe, it's over now.

He has always been sentimental but has spent a lifetime hiding that sentiment under a uniform or beneath words he learned from TV westerns, doing what had to be done. He is aware that he is not an original, that the brunt of his every viewpoint has been culled from cowboys, friends, simple soldiers, fishing talk, and the like. Calling a spade a spade and playing it where it lays. His master's voice plays back the music of yesteryear and his wife is waiting for him to get up. But he stays in bed and runs through his own past like flash cards and the memories go a long way toward stilling the rising pain. He was too young for the Second World War but was ready and willing for the Korean conflict, where he first learned what it meant to stand alone in the dark of a foreign night with a rifle in his hands and say aloud to any passing sound, *Who goes there?* This is what occurs to him as he lies abed and the pain swells and his head is filled with the racket of voices from overseas, Oriental babble that seems to signify that the end is at hand. Footfalls in the brush and whispered threats. *Who goes there? Who?*

He had awakened once before dawn on a remote Pacific island. Six miles across the water was another island. For seven weeks he had awakened to the sight of that island. He had often wished to take a boat there but the brass had refused his requests. They had assigned him to Eniwetok atoll for an operation that had been going on for some time. He was to lend a hand for a limited period, testing animal and bird behavior before and after blasts. It was a long way from Nevada and the detonations were more numerous. At the Nevada Test Site there was a detonation, on average, every two weeks. At Eniwetok there were sometimes two a day. Butternut, Elm, Tobacco, Rose, Magnolia, Linden, Elder, Oak, Sequoia, Dogwood. He'd been convinced that the blasts would end only when they ran out of names for trees. Koa, he learned, had been the first megaton shot in the area. A million tons of TNT that had outshone the sun.

He had stayed drunk most of the time, even during working hours, briefings, and archiving. After the third week he was plastered even during blast observations, and no one bothered to take him to task. He had seen early on that there was no discipline on the island. Most of the soldiers had been there for months and the tropical charms of the Pacific had long since worn away. All that remained was a tense and malicious boredom. Chaos in the barracks followed every series of shots, and Ravel had wondered if perhaps someone among them was taking laboratory notes for the eggheads back at Livermore; like his own notations of the behavior patterns of dogs and birds and cats and white rats. There were card games that ended in overturned tables and smashed chairs, insubordination of every stripe, constant fistfights; the base was vandalized daily. One afternoon, walking deep into the jungle with a new bottle, he'd come upon a man screwing one of the dogs that the fleeing population had left behind. To his own surprise, he felt neither disgust nor pity. He just wanted out. They gave him a three-day pass to Guam, and while there he bought a prostitute and gave her triple time, thinking of that man and that dog and of what might be in the air when he got back to the island. There once were people on these islands. Families and tribes. Fishermen, shell gatherers, boat makers, and dancers. But the islands were part of the Marshall chain, American territory, and the civilians had been relocated to islands that hadn't yet been targeted. Every morning he awoke and saw the island across the water and he thought of taking a boat there and not coming back.

And one morning he was awakened before dawn and ordered to the beach. In the distance he could see only the black water and a blue streak of the moon setting down in the horizon. The countdown was chanted over a loudspeaker, and then another of those fireballs rose into the sky. Half an hour later, when the sun rose in the same direction, the island was gone.

From the next room he can hear the record skipping and if it isn't Morse code it is nevertheless another language to enrage him. But when he calls out to Mircea to fix it for the love of Christ he knows immediately that his shouting is a reflex from pain, that he's flown off the handle again, and then there are those needles of regret pressing deep around his heart.

Morphine or alcohol? He reaches across the pillow to his hollowed-out copy of *Webster's* and opens to the space where he's removed the words from *D* to *V*, the pages like severed tongues. He settles on a single pill from the bottle inside that book; one, so he won't later slur when he speaks, so he won't say *sorrow* when he means to say *sorry*.

Counting to himself, he closes his eyes and then opens them. Mircea changes the record and he hears clarinets, trumpets, rachatta-cha-cha. Those shuffling sounds *could* be Mircea dancing all by her lonesome; he doesn't know but, God, how sad. She has guessed at everything, the way women do, assuming any and all explanations for what's gotten into him. But she has never guessed at death. Too obvious or too unbelievable? His drunkenness, of course. Other women, gambling debts, drug addiction. Sin is no stranger to the desert, that's a fact. But all she really comprehends is a payoff of diminishing returns on her affection for him. She doesn't know that his bones have gone dry and that he can barely walk. She knows only that he is lurching and feeble and spent. When there's no one else around, he relies on his cane, whipping it from its hiding place and pulling its telescope ends to full length so that he can move around with his sagging weight bent to the merciful wood handle and cheat gravity out of those slapstick falls.

Alone in his bed he feels the miracle of an erection, a lazy-warm stirring of want. But when he touches himself there the blood recedes, or was never truly there. Reaching for him in the night, Mircea will sometimes frisk him as if in search of a weapon or evidence, bloodstains or lipstick, the salt smell of another woman, and all he has to offer her is an empty sack of skin and his dry breath on her hair. It's been forever since she cried about it. She just goes on with her life in imitation of the saints and he knows only that her silence is more terrible than her wailing.

A letter has come from Wilkins. He has left the service and taken up with a Mexican woman in a village in Baja California. "She wants a green card and I want a nurse so the wedding is tomorrow. This should be the last time you hear from me. Time is getting short. Like a midget if you get my drift."

For weeks on end he had cussed out God, calling Him every name in the book, but the cursing stopped weeks ago, after that incident with his asbestos suit. Ever since, he's settled into his oblivion and he rolls and roils in its current like a rudderless boat. Images of his life are overlaid, past upon present, and the trick is to distinguish one from the other without prompts or the aid of photographs. After his suit was stolen and the unidentified thief wore it all the way to his personal destiny at ground zero, Ravel had been confined to base for an agonizing week without hope of medication. He was questioned, fed, taken for walks, and then left for hours at a time in a secure isolation. Had he known the man? Had there been previous contact? No, nothing, never. Then why *his* suit? And why had he been late for the day's shot? Chance, bad luck, car trouble. Write these things down.

Weren't you in some sort of ad hoc club?

Yes, the Zero Plus Two Point Two.

Which was what exactly?

Old soldiers getting laid and drunk once a year.

That's all?

And, uh, commemorating what we've seen. You know, as witnesses.

And what is it you've seen?

Can I talk about this?

Just answer the question.

The bombs. The flash of light. Our bones through our arms. Theories of quantum physics made manifest.

Do you really want this in your report?

No sir. Listen, you got anything for a headache?

There are aspirin in that cabinet.

Nothing stronger?

I'm a shrink, Sergeant, not a pharmacist.

Never mind.

He wasn't tested for alcohol content until it had been too late and his tests bore the stain of innocence. All the same, he was told, the time had come for him to fold up the tent and let the circus die. This was a neat way to signal the end of the dog show and good riddance to Sgt. J. A. Ravel. He would have one last look-see at a sixty-five-kiloton bomb and that would be the final curtain on a lifelong dream of becoming an officer.

In the darkness of his bedroom he reasons that it is not the squarest of deals. In agreeing to participate in Plumbbob, he had signed his military name in disappearing ink and would die without any title other than mister. And anyway, to feel those bars on his shoulder, even now, so late in the game, might only lead him to laugh his fool head off, or to cry, to make some kind of scene. His upbringing has been to do otherwise. He's from the west and is not much for scenes. All his life he's taken pride in shutting up, in standing tall and dry-eyed, in being at least one quiet example of an otherwise raucous and complaining species.

The next night, in a last-ditch effort to mask the truth of his dying, he builds up the courage to take Mircea all the way to Cedar City for dinner in one of those restaurants she's always going on about. He wears the blue suit she bought him years back in San Diego, the one that went clean out of fashion and then came back in without his ever noticing. Mircea wears a beige dress and dancing shoes that he realizes are as old as Vance. When the baby-sitter arrives she tells the girl that they'll be home before midnight and adds something about how Mr. Ravel is feeling under the weather and won't be up to dancing till the cows come home.

To preserve his wits he has laid off the medication and has allowed himself a single pill over a twenty-hour haul. On the way to Cedar City he grips a double wad of peppermint gum between his teeth while every crack and bump on that highway turns the knob of pain to full. To camouflage the silence, he tunes the radio to a Las Vegas station and even snaps his fingers to an irregular beat, showing Mircea that tonight, *tonight*, he is all there for her. She gives him an odd look once or twice, but is otherwise ensconced on a cloud of marital satisfaction. She reaches a hand across to his knee and leaves it there all the way to Cedar City.

Dining Dancing Steaks Live Band.

After you, Mircea.

Jack, there's no door there.

They order steaks and red wine, baked potatoes with sour cream, and two desserts. He fills the napkin at his lap with whatever he's pretending to swallow and in the men's room he tosses it all into the bin. At table, Mircea tells him that Vance is doing well in school but has these problems with math and with history. Jack says he better get his ass in gear and Mircea says, But Jack he's only seven years old. Later she says, My God winter already, I wonder why we haven't had any rain, and Jack says, There's time enough, there's all the time in the world. And he smiles and she says, Why are you smiling like that, did you tell a joke? No joke, Mircea. I meant to tell you how nice you look tonight. The dress and all. Her eyes are sad and she casts him a searching glance before saying, It's been a long time since you've said so, Jack.

Then the music starts up again, a full eight-piece band for the Friday-night crowd, and he knows he doesn't have a chance in hell of getting out of it. There are times in your life when you can't not dance, and when he extends a pale hand toward Mircea she nearly lifts him bodily from his chair and holds him fast in her shaking arms. Later, lying in bed and dizzied by a handful of those pills, all that he will remember of that dance is that it was a simple two-four, almost a waltz, and the way he leaned on his wife to keep from falling over.

There was nothing to find of that man who'd stolen his suit, nothing to compare to dental records or lists of the Ten Most Wanted or the files on suspected commies who were said to be in the area. Whoever he was, he'd slipped the bonds of security and headed straight for the bomb, and there would be only a lone smudged fingerprint from Ravel's locker to go on. Tented arch, probably the ring finger of the right hand. Someone asked aloud what the odds of survival were that close to ground zero and the answer had something to do with a highway of zeros. At the same time, a joke made the rounds at the test site, something witty about how the intruder hadn't even gotten his combat pay. For a long time the joke had been over Ravel's head and he began to realize that a perpetual fog had long since set in and that he would have no more God-sent breezes of clarity. One curtain always followed another and the light was leaving in layers instead of all at once.

One morning when he comes out of the bathroom, Mircea asks why he's wearing makeup. Am I? he says, and goes into the kitchen to look at his face in the darkened window. Corn-silk dust covers the blackness under his eyes and his cheeks have the color of rotting peaches.

I didn't think she'd notice. I must be losing it. Going gaga now, for crying out loud.

Sitting at the kitchen table, he spreads the papers in front of him and with the aid of a magnifying glass he reads and rereads the fine print. It is clear to him now; he has read the same lines every night for a week and is satisfied that he hasn't misled himself. He knows that if he were to perish in a bomb test the effect would be the same as if he'd perished in combat. The punch line is there on page three. The telltale loophole, the nub of his contract. Death in combat is an uppercase Death and there are degrees to these things, footnotes and appendixes to asterisks in the updates. For one thing, death in combat suggests heroism. For another, *there is considerably more pension for the next of kin.* Ravel's italics.

I was never much of a dancer, Mircea.

But I never minded, Jack. Really.

THE
BOOK
OF
TOM

AFTER wandering the western world, lonesome and abused by time, you are invited into the Vatican and given food and shelter. Health is restored to you and you become devout, of easy faith and obedience. Time passes and your instructions come full circle. You are baptized.

And one day the Holy Father comes to waken you in the night. You rise from your bed and follow him. Taking you by the hand, he leads you down a winding stairway into the cellar of St. Peter's. The light is dim and you can feel the cobwebs brush your face as you pass.

From under his robe the Holy Father produces a key which he inserts into a lock. An ancient oak door opens into a room of scant light. The air is chill and you are afraid.

There, on a table, is the unrisen corpse of Jesus Christ.

"But, Holy Father," you say, the tears streaming down your face. "I was taught that Jesus had risen from the dead."

"Just kidding," is the reply.

Nobody ices the pope. And Painter, getting the word from Ravel, took the news even harder than expected.

"My other name is Tom," he said. And then he disappeared into Limbo.

A few years after Jack Ravel's vanishing act, the Japanese made a monster movie called *Godzilla*. A prehistoric beast, struck by lightning, emerges from a deep slumber to raze Tokyo with his fiery breath. Toppled buildings, toasted citizens, stomped babies. A horror story from the fifties.

Ravel saw that movie when he was nine and had pointless, unexplained nightmares over it for the next ten years. Not only of the terrible beast but of those Oriental eyes witnessing the unchained mayhem of a city turning to flame and rubble.

His nightmares didn't end altogether but they eased up noticeably after he read that the Japanese had made the movie as a metaphor for Hiroshima. Godzilla was nuclear terror and the film, as corny as it was, became an underground classic.

Imitating, perhaps, the phantom of the opera, or any shady character from the B-movie netherworld, Tom appears and disappears, crossing Ravel's nocturnal path at odd times to beg a glass of water or to ask some gibberish question about can openers, rust cycles, or the state of the Union. He has gathered up all of the painted stones and thrown them like obsolete toys into a Dune ravine, but he persists in wearing his hunter getup, knife in sheath at his hip, the bow slung round his shoulder, and a single arrow clutched in his hand. While making his rounds, Ravel comes upon his spent fires, empty cans of fruit cocktail or peaches, various debris of his rotating stakeouts. Ever since their showdown in the shack Ravel senses that he's no longer a target, that there is no target whatsoever, only those disquieting blanks of estrangement to be filled in like a connect-the-dots. The suspense is killing him, but for now the word *killing* is only a figure of speech. When three nights pass without any sign of Painter, Ravel begins to breathe easier, until Sol sets him straight.

"I seen him at the cemetery down the road sitting in the Jansen plot where there's no grass."

"What was he doing?"

"Reading a newspaper."

"He can't read, Sol. He's illiterate."

Sol scratches his neck. "That explains it."

"Explains what?"

"It was dark as hell, so how could he see? And he was making funny noises again."

"Singing? Chanting?"

"More like barking. Woof woof. Gave me the willies."

Ravel tells Sol that if he sees him again to give the high sign.

"There's a word for a guy like that," Sol says.

"What word is that?"

"Rabid."

Two days later Randy comes to kick on the trailer door with a stiff boot. Still shivering with sleep and the hangover of a dream, Ravel answers to his pounding.

"There's a dog out here I'd like you to take a look at."

"No more dogs, Randy. I already told you, the barking upsets me, and even worse, their groveling."

Randy's eyes are filled with something like mercury and Ravel is made to understand that he means business. "It's Trash," he says. "Lonesome old Trash. I don't have the nerve to bury him all by myself."

Ravel puts on his pants and follows Randy across the flat toward the trailer. Trash is lying facedown in the dirt with his forelegs crossed at an unlikely angle, his lips ringed with foam. The arrow slants from throat to rib, its point emerging from a rent below the heart. Ravel searches wildly for the signature of stone, but there are only patches of mesquite.

Randy stands stock-still, his hands limp. Grief has exhausted him and Ravel can see dried tear tracks below his eyes. "I already dug a hole," he says, "but I don't feel the what-for to pick him up and put him in it."

Ravel nods like an idiot, paralyzed as usual before genuine heartache. He realizes that he never loved anything that died, not even his father, who was gone long before his son had placed a foot within the age of reason. Now, standing over the hound's grave, he considers muttering a few words of condolence, but decides against it. It would be like dropping loose pennies into a beggar's hat, a useless hedge against a wager of extremely long odds: is there a paradise or isn't there?

Randy says, "Tell me all is right with the nation, Ravel. Go on, tell me."

Ravel admits to recognizing the arrow.

"One a your God freaks again?"

Ravel nods. "The last of them."

"And I suppose," Randy says between his teeth, "that there's some kind a meaning to this slaughter."

Ravel can't say. "Events have passed me by. I've been gone a long time."

"But you recognize the handwriting, I bet."

"There's no getting around it. That's Tom's arrow for sure. He only had one."

"Well, suppose you locate this Tom and tell him his ass is grass."

"He's got troubles, Randy. Social fallout of the worst kind. He's illiterate and crazy and a little short on memory. Let me handle this."

"You first and then my Colt. Where I come from they call this murder."

When you hold that conch to your ear there is a sound of artificial or remembered wind. It is something conjured, a trick, and not entirely the real thing. Like this desert, one has-been of an ocean, resting on its ancient laurels. There were fish in these parts, but now there is only the imprint of their bones and slim hopes of successful carbon dating. After that, there were Indians to kick off the trade in souvenirs and to inspire paperback tales that you can buy in any drugstore. Nowadays the place is dotted and dashed with uneducated white men who persist in thinking they can believe in anything they feel like just because there's no one around to tell them otherwise.

Tom's trauma, Ravel is convinced, has something to do with a colossal disappointment. Somewhere along the line he must have pictured himself ascending fully clothed into a heaven on earth. Ever since Ravel fled the Er, Tom has been asking himself where that promised host of angels has gone to. The settlement of the Er must have looked something like a modified Disneyland to Painter/Tom's eyes. And then the prophet had to go and spoil the fun.

Now Ravel's got Cassie and Jered and Mircea and Randy to help him pass the time. And Tom's got only his fruit cocktail and newspapers that look like ants on a yellow matrix. Which shitty unfairness makes Ravel rack his brains over the equation that sorts men into haves and have-nots. The wild card in that equation eludes him. God's will is a simple enough answer, but it is also the kind of simpleton reasoning to which Ravel turns a deaf ear. And calling it the devil's work is just another lazy gesture, comparable to rolling over and falling back to sleep. Ravel wants to think that he's slipped that leash by now and he's settled on the fact that Tom will need some tending to according to the Golden Rule, or any creed that isn't too obtuse to allow for simple human kindness.

He spends the afternoon debating drunkenness but opts for anxious sobriety. Then, near sundown, he heads into Paragonah assuming the worst, a long climb through hill and dale in desperate search of a pea-brained dog-killer who claims *he* created him. But when he arrives back at the shack Tom is waiting for him, Miss March 1976 in his hot lap.

Giving him the once-over, Ravel is satisfied that the knife is in its sheath, so he comes straight to the point. "Who killed Namer?"

"All of us."

"Together?"

"I was there. I painted the stones."

"Did you kill anyone else?"

"No."

"Are you going to kill me?"

"No."

There is a long moment of silence during which Tom runs his fingers over the yellowed nude. Ravel asks him where he's been lately and he shrugs. "Don't you remember?"

"Sure I do. I've been here. The harlot wants money and I don't have any."

"OK, Tom. Whatever you say." Reaching to the wall, Ravel takes down his flashlight, considers the tire iron, and decides against it. "I'll have to put you up somewhere," he says.

Tom wants to know where.

"Not far. We'll find a car. You must be hungry."

"Hungry," he says. "Yes." He pins the calendar back to the wall and says he ate yesterday. "Or the day before. It was a long time ago. I lost my arrow, too."

"What arrow is that, Tom?"

"The only one I had."

Ravel spends the night keeping watch over him while Tom sleeps fitfully in a Honda close to the shack, his shoeless feet dangling from the back window. The night is cool, summer gone for good, and Ravel considers lighting a fire but Nashua would see the ashes this close to the gate and there'd be hell to pay. Sometime during the night Sol wanders by to ask if that might be the spook in question. Ravel nods.

"I'll sleep better knowing the cat's in the bag."

Ravel suggests he try the Olds Cutlass down the way. "Got a backseat like a Motel 6."

"I know my way around," Sol answers. "Can you keep this goofball under wraps?"

Ravel says it's his job. "Sweet dreams, Sol."

"No dreams at all might be a better idea."

. . .

At dawn Ravel locks the gate behind him and leads Tom out of the salvage. They look too ragged and dangerous to attract any drivers and have to walk the full distance into Roadside Business. After several deep breaths, Ravel bangs on the trailer door and Randy comes stark naked to answer it. "Shit," he says, and slams the door. Seconds later that door flies open again and there's Randy in jeans and bare feet, his Colt at the ready. "This him?"

"Yes and no."

"I didn't ask for double talk, Ravel. Just a straight answer."

Ravel points to Tom and explains that what they're looking at is a group portrait. "One of him is named Tom and another one Painter. If we ask enough questions we might get to know the whole tribe."

Randy's gaze is as level as the desert floor. "I get it. You're gonna nitpick his nuts right out a the fire, is that it?"

Ravel is looking down the barrel of Randy's gun and all he can see is a black hole, a clear enough vision of oblivion. But the thing about pistols is the way the bullets show; there are four of them in plain sight. Ravel decides to try some song and dance. "I had hopes," he says lamely, "of borrowing the keys to your pickup."

"There's an idea," Randy considers. "We can dump the body in the desert. I know just the place."

Ravel says that Tom would be sorry if he could remember. "Let's say it was lightning that killed Trash, not an arrow. Let's say it was an act of God."

"That word again."

Ravel apologizes. "Mercy, then. He didn't have to come here. He could have crossed that desert in those bare feet and you'd have never been the wiser."

There is at last that hesitation he's been counting on. The Colt lags a few crucial notches toward the dirt.

"I had my heart set on kingdom come," Randy says. "What more can you ask of an old man?"

"The keys, Randy. We've got an errand to run."

"To where?"

"I'll tell you when I get back."

Casting a look at Tom like at the one that got away, Randy goes back into the trailer and emerges moments later with a rabbit's-foot key chain. "Is he really like you say he is? Or is this just some soft-shoe for my sake?"

Ravel glances toward Tom, who is looking more and more like a cigar store Indian, his eyes full of sky and not much more. "He has the best of intentions," Ravel answers. "But he's from the wrong side of the social tracks. I could tell you stories."

"I'm sure you could."

When they get to the pickup Tom sits ramrod straight in the passenger seat and reminds Ravel not to go faster than sixty-five, some crack about being safe instead of sorry. The truck is on its last legs anyway and so Ravel complies, staying in the right lane and holding the needle at fifty all the way to Cedar City. Then he drives in narrowing circles until he comes to the place he's looking for. There is a spacious parking lot only a quarter full and, beyond it, a lawn the size of a par-five fairway. Tom follows Ravel to the front door and at the desk a woman in white remarks what a glorious day it is.

"I'm bringing you a very tired boy," Ravel tells her. "So put your kid gloves on and keep them on."

She frowns at Tom and then at Ravel. Only then does Ravel realize how awful Tom must look. He is barefoot and his jeans are torn in a dozen places, including the crotch, where a distressing patch of flesh is clearly visible. His white shirt hasn't been washed in weeks and seems to bear the signature of all sorts of flora and fauna. He hasn't shaved but doesn't much need to, and his hair is waving to the four winds all at once. Taking a deep breath, the woman says, "We'll see. Are you a relative?"

"He says he's my brother. Why don't we humor him?"

She has a comeback to this, of course. She explains to Ravel that he is standing in a state-run organization, not a house of charity. Only a court order or a relative's consent can consign this . . . this boy into their care.

"But what if he commits himself? Tom, do you feel up to that?" Tom just shivers and it's like watching the last hope sink with the sun. "He needs attention," Ravel argues. "Food and a bed. *Care.*"

The woman wears a fixed smile, somewhere between happy face and jack-o'-lantern, and in serious need of erasing. "So," she says, and the rest is no surprise, "so take care of him."

He realizes that it's pointless to admit that he has his hands full taking care of his own ragged self, and even more pointless to explain the short and tragic history of the Er. Like explaining acid trips to teetotalers or astronomy to earthworms. Such is his frustration but the only thing he breaks is her appointments pencil. Unless that slammed door leaves a wake of miscellaneous destruction. Ravel's not watching where he's been; he is already driving north.

Tom asks where they're headed and Ravel says in the general direction of a notion called home.

"Fine," Tom says. Then he gestures to the fuel gauge and wonders aloud how much gas they'll need.

When Mircea arrives home from her cashier job at the Outpost, Tom is sitting at the kitchen table mooning over a bowl of uneaten Cheerios.

"Mircea, this is Tom."

She approaches to shake his hand but then gets wise and stops short. "Always glad to meet a friend of my son's," she says.

"Tom will be staying with us for a while if that's OK."

"Oh."

"Just until a few things get straightened out."

"What things, Vance? Or is it wrong of me to ask?"

"Spiritual things. Tom's an old friend. From out there."
She takes a moment to soak this in. "Out there?"
Ravel nods. In a low voice he adds that he suspects Tom is his penance for sins that, out of respect to her, will not be detailed.

Mircea rummages through her purse for her glasses and puts them on. Gazing toward Tom, she examines him from head to toe. "He's only a kid," she says. Then she puts the glasses back in their case and snaps the purse shut. "So where's his dirty laundry?"

When Ravel answers that there isn't any, just that shirt rotting on his bent back, she becomes, for the first time, worried.

To the long list of his earthly blunders, he may soon have to add that he left his own mother in the company of a madman. That Randy is nearby is of no consequence whatsoever, his grief over Trash having sent him to the heart-numbing bottom of a green bottle for the day. So Ravel is running on faith again, a conviction that Tom has long since shot his wad of rage and will act the puppy for a time; long enough for Ravel to let the dust settle over Roadside Business and then get him set up somewhere where he won't hurt himself. These are his thoughts as he hitches a ride into Paragonah and makes that circular walk to Cimarron Street.

Cassie and Jered are waiting for him on the front step, and it's like one of those scenes from a camera ad, minus the aunts and uncles. There is even a pitcher of fresh lemonade and three glasses. Coming up the walk, he merits a kiss from Cassie and big how-do wave from Jered.

"I was meaning to wait," Cassie says, "but it was just too much for me. Come." She takes him by the hand and leads him into the bedroom. New curtains, clean bedspread, and the walk-in closet has been emptied on one side. "Drawers too," Cassie says. "But you don't move in until after the wedding. Fair enough?"

"Fair's fair." He is tempted to withhold what he's come to

To Ravel she says, "You attract these people, Vance. It's always the same. The sick ones find you. You seek them out to make yourself look sane."

"These things happen, Cassie."

"They happen to *you*, Vance. Not to me or to Mircea or to anyone else I know." She is crying and for a moment he thinks he might be out of the woods. But then she is up and shouting at him. "You liar! Messianic creep! Who could trust you with a baby in your hands? No, don't touch me. This time you've gone too far."

Another face appears at the door.

"Shoo, Don. We've got family business here."

Cassie is screaming, "*What family?* You goddamned spook! Demon! You're not anyone's idea of a father!"

Don is already in the kitchen and has Ravel by the arm. Ravel shakes him off and reaches for his wife but then finds himself pinned facedown against the kitchen table. These ex-Marines have a way of doing him in.

"Is this what you want?" Don asks Cassie, and she gives Ravel a look that suggests hog-tying, razor blades, and irretrievable loss.

"Yes," she says.

TIME PASSES. That's all there is of hope in times of grief. Misery weakens with advancing age, and as the desert autumn settles into winter, the arc of the sun shifts a few crucial notches and at noon Ravel has this shadow at his side.

The first few weeks with Tom, Ravel keeps him close at hand, even going so far as to haul him along to the salvage, where he can keep an eye on him. Together, they wander the Heap in search of interlopers or sites damaged by roving nomads. From time to time Ravel trusts Tom to make a round all by himself, tell her, to keep a tight mouth over news that he expects she will take the wrong way. He will announce scattered clouds and she will say rip-roaring hurricane. Eggshells would feel like terra firma compared to what he's walking on.

"Did Jered tell you? No, I guess I didn't give him a chance. The first blades of grass are showing through. When he saw that, he was beside himself."

Ravel suggests they go into the kitchen for some of that lemonade. Cassie takes his hand and leads him inside, then sits across from him at the table, her elbows resting on a book of wallpaper samples. Ravel drinks the lemonade and clears his throat.

"It's about Painter, Cassie. His real name is Tom."

"That strange boy," she says. "Is he gone?"

"Painter is but Tom isn't. There's a new wrinkle in the fabric of events."

"And?" The word itself, isolated, is tinged with suspicion and sounds like the first warning shot of anger.

"And I've brought him home for a while. Just till he can get his head straight."

There is a pause, at the end of which Cassie asks him to say it again. "Though I can't be that hard of hearing."

He says again that he's taken Tom under his wing. "The state hospital won't accept him and I can't just cut him loose."

He can see in her eyes that approaching hurricane. It's not the kind of threat he can wave a hand at and say please no. The lemonade is on the floor and he has to listen through the sounds of breaking glass. "It's the Er all over again!"

"It is not."

"Riffraff on the doorstep and burnouts at the dinner table."

"You're wrong, Cassie. This time it's human kindness in all its brightest colors."

Jered comes to the back door to see what's what and Cassie tells him to run away and to hurry. "Daddy's done it again."

"Done what?" Seeing the broken glass, he thinks he understands.

the flashlight in one hand, his other hand empty. No need to give him the tire iron. Ravel figures that disaster has already been courted, wooed, and bedded to everyone's infinite satisfaction.

Cleaned up and with new clothes and haircut, Tom looks less frightening, more his age, and his eyes have lost some of that worrying glow. It's been more than five years since he first arrived at the settlement of the Er and Tom thinks he will be twenty soon. All he remembers is December. "From the article in the paper, when they found me and my brother. It was Christmas and I was a just born."

Sol is still welcome in the salvage. He has mastered the etiquette of living in the environs, burying his spent fires and doing his toiletry in the Dunes, where no one cares. He has even gotten used to Tom, whom he recognizes as "just another of the me's." Once, Ravel comes upon the two of them together in a nearby Limbo alley, where they are sharing Sol's soup. Between swallows, Sol is revealing to Tom his secrets for panhandling in a town as small as Paragonah: to disappear from time to time so as not to be viewed as an eyesore.

"I make it a point to hold down a job a few months a year," Sol says. "Nothing fancy, a course. I'm worlds away from a diploma, but I get by with day-labor stuff that usually has to do with a shovel."

When Ravel hears Tom ask if maybe he might find a job too, something in him fairly melts.

Each daybreak they make that five-mile walk together, all the way back to Roadside Business, where they sleep once Mircea heads out to work, Ravel in her bed and Tom in Ravel's. Ravel listens carefully for Mircea's meaningful sighs or tip-off looks of exasperation, but she seems to have taken to Tom without the least fuss. One day she remarks that Tom isn't, after all, what she'd thought him to be.

"What was that?"

"I wasn't sure, but the word *pervert* sprang to mind."

"That so?"

"I can't tell you how many Acts of Contrition went into *that* basket. All because of the clothes he was wearing and that dirty hair."

Ravel assures her that she merits forgiveness.

"And what convinced me was the day he spread that manure. You remember? Randy brought over another wheelbarrow of puppy droppings. Nice of him, I thought, but as usual I didn't have the heart. So Tom did it for me. I watched the whole time, the way he spread in the dead leaves and mixed it all with his bare hands, and not once did he so much as make a face. Humility of that kind is rare enough. And he helps with the dishes, too."

After a few weeks of barely letting Tom out of his sight, Ravel eases up a little and cuts him a bit of slack. Going alone to the salvage, he reminds Tom to stick close to Roadside Business. "That way and that way there's only the same desert you know by heart. That way is Paragonah and that way are the hills. Sit tight and stay clear of Randy. He's holding a grudge that can't do you any good."

Mircea takes care of Tom's lunch and leaves him in front of the television or with magazines he can scan. Whenever Ravel has the time he takes him for hikes into the eastern hills, and while they walk he teaches him words he wants to know. As far as Tom is concerned, vocabulary is kindness and he is soothed when he knows the words for things he's seen or felt all his life. Sometimes he asks about words he's heard but doesn't know the meaning of.

"Tepid," he says.

"Neither warm nor cool but closer to warm."

"Envy."

"To begrudge someone else's good fortune."

"Threshold."

"Where you're standing."

"I'm standing on the ground."

"It's a figure of speech, Tom, but believe me, you're there."

.   .   .

One desperate afternoon, unable to stay away any longer, Ravel bisects Cassie's path with his own. Sidling up to her on the main street of Paragonah, he offers to carry her groceries.

"One step nearer and I'll scream for help."

"Cassie, I'm—"

"Go away!"

The groceries are already in the street. Oranges roll like orbitless planets in a galaxy of spilled wine.

"Let me help you."

"I'd rather you didn't."

He leaves her there alone, but the next day stops by to inspect the yard. Weeds have sprung up in the midst of new grass and he and Jered bend to the task. Half a bushelful has been gathered when her car pulls in.

"You have rights," she tells him, "when it comes to Jered. All the same, I'd rather you called first."

"I tried," he answers. "You hung up."

"Is that man still there?"

"Tom? Yes, he's convalescing nicely."

"In that case, fly."

"Not just now."

"And stop writing. I haven't read your letters anyway. Not since the first one, with all the pleading in it."

"What happens when Tom's gone?"

"Don't even think about it. When one disciple leaves you'll always find another. These no-minds are *your* version of the other woman and I wouldn't trust you in a monastery."

Later he calls from a pay phone on the edge of the highway and she answers on the sixth ring.

"You're embarrassing me," she says.

"Then I won't say a word. I will listen to you breathing and decode what I can from the rhythms."

She is crying before she hangs up and that lifts his spirits somewhat. Her rage is something he can never get his arms around but her sorrow is as familiar to him as his own face. He refuses to stare down the irony of being the source of that sorrow. Irony is the sneaky Pete of those who turn their lives into literature and forever observe in themselves a guiltless third person to whom these terrible things just keep happening. All the same, after she hangs up on him he feels as though that trigger has been pulled and he's surprised, for a miraculous instant, that he's not yet dead. Back in Roadside Business for his weekly night off, he finds Tom and Mircea together on the couch. A book is held between them and Tom is reciting aloud a tale of Dick and Jane and look and look and see see see.

IN MID-NOVEMBER, the desert heat is rescinded and the nights bring on a bone-chilling cold. Ravel rises before dawn and dresses up in his old gear: Dad's green fatigues, walking boots, baseball cap, and wide belt to which is fastened a water bottle, food pouch, compass, and hunting knife. Randy offers a light-weight pack, sleeping bag, and his loaded Colt, and doesn't bother asking why Ravel doesn't take his pickup. Times like these require footsteps and not the leap and spark of a rasping V-8.

"If you find them," Randy advises, "keep your distance. That's my Colt you're packing and, as you've so pointedly reminded me, it's meant for snakes and such, not crazy men. Besides, you might get hurt and that'd be a damn shame now that you're finally home."

The sun is rising as he heads out of Roadside Business and faces the desert he once thought of as Elsewhere. In the first hour he cuts south of Little Salt Lake and then he crosses into the emptiness. From horizon to horizon the land is flat and almost devoid of reliable points of reference. Walking in the desert, you have the illusion that you are not moving. A bluff in the distance seems to remain in the distance although you have taken a thousand steps in its direction. There is nothing to be passed by and the shift of scenery is so gradual as to go unnoticed. Some people call it monotonous but Ravel persists in thinking of it as tranquil.

Toward the end of the afternoon, he stops to rest in the middle of nowhere. He drinks from the water bottle and chews raisins to soothe his throat. An irritating wind is blowing up from the south and so he fills his ears with paper wads to muffle the howling. A tiny tornado, a dust devil, blows by. To the north are the mines, sulfur and copper and surface coal. A century ago, whiskered free-lancers passed through in search of diamonds, a hopeless enterprise, then headed back west in a state of desert shock. Ravel is thankful that the wind is blowing from the south and not the north. Any other time he'd be breathing in that mine debris, painting his lungs a livid yellow and having visions that defy description. Not to mention a tom-tommed skull-splitting headache.

He crosses Dry Coal Creek and hits his evening stride and continues to make tracks until night has fallen. Then he makes camp on a high mound of sandy soil. He's been gathering bits of cactus wood along the way and in another half hour of scavenging he has enough for a night fire that will ensure his survival against the roving wildlife. He fashions a wide oval with the wood, puts his belt and pack in the center, and douses the twigs and lumps of dead cactus with Randy's fluid. Striking a match, he lights it up. The flame lasts mere seconds before settling into a smoky red coal. He tosses dry grasses onto these coals and fans the new flames until the entire oval burns red and white embers. Then he leaves it be, not wanting the embers to burn out too quickly. Stepping into the center of that oval, he eats two apples, a handful of raisins, and some soggy bread and allows himself a long pull from the water bottle.

The cold has set in, so he doesn't waste any time before unrolling the sleeping bag. It is new and smells of nylon and plastic and whatever chemicals have been used to waterproof it. He strips off his khakis and crawls into its sleeve and when he rests his head on the backpack, he is face-to-face with a field of stars. It is one of those moments that cancel all heartache and unravel every knot in the yarn of possibility. Watching those stars, he realizes that he's forgotten the connections, the geometry, that will fit them into sky gods: the Bowman, the Bear, the Scorpion, the Crab. They are all nameless and without category and though he wishes to lie this way for long hours, the day's walking catches up with him and he falls asleep with a sudden leap into darkness and spends a dreamless night in his ring of protective fire.

The next morning comes up blue and white and he looks around himself, to find a circle of gray ash that the winds are already dispersing. Breakfast is a handful of bread and instant coffee with a lone lump of sugar, and once he's dressed and geared up for another haul, he considers that he's already past halfway. That rise in the distance is familiar, and he expects that somewhere beyond there he will begin to see the painted rocks. He starts out slowly, feeling a tenderness in his legs. Five months of living in a trailer have taken their toll and he's not as fit as he once was.

Walking alone, he's got world and time enough for an A to Z inventory, from birth to this last step over a prickly pear and back again. That's what happens to autobiography in the silence of the desert; it takes on all the aspects of some well-fingered object to be examined for chips and scrapes and damages that can't be repaired with spit and glue. Whoever says the desert is empty is lacking in imagination. These kinds of people want snow-capped mountains, timberlines, lakes and streams and wild-flowers to occupy their eyes and distract them from the landscapes of their own lives. Nature as television. In the desert, you rely on your own devices and the inevitable shrieking evidence of your own soul. If that's not yourself you're speaking to, then who is it? And if prayer can be reduced to a conversation with yourself, you may be God. In which case, beware the disciples.

If he finds them, the Er, he will have to come clean. Though he cannot produce a corpse, he will testify that his father is dead. Whether he died fighting Indians or walking into an unholy fusion or simply expired at the end of a long flight is of no consequence. Ravel has ridden the pale horse of the Er into the image of his brightest hopes and most clinging of dreams: that his father did not die. Now he will have to tell another story and it will have to resemble the truth.

In the afternoon he comes to the spot where Namer was killed. Her body, or skeleton by now, is no longer there, and all traces of her murder have been removed by man or by nature, even the painted rocks that had circled her head. Still moving westward, he traverses remembered gullies and mounds, places where in the past he prayed or wandered in search of round stones or firewood. Farther on, he comes upon the first of those stones, blue, and as he continues he sees more and more of them and so knows that he is not far. When he stops to rest, he measures his water and finds that less than half the bottle remains. The constant wind has dried his lips, and he is tempted to drink but reminds himself that this is no time to be foolish. Survival, to a Christian, connotes such self-denial: evidence, perhaps, that the religion was formed in the Sinai Desert, where there is never enough of anything except space and time and sand. He is tired by now, his feet worn and hot, and the light pack seems to be filled with the stones of fatigue, one for every mile he's walked. He compares himself to his shadow and estimates two more hours of sunlight and so continues on, knowing the way by heart, down a steep hillside and through a ravine of sudden vegetation. He moves swiftly for fear of being trapped by darkness and then he comes upon another rise and finds a plethora of painted stones, green, white, blue, and red, all arranged into various circles that intersect. Their language is beyond him and his heartbeat quickens. Running now, he crosses a last flat and follows a rough trail through thick patches of cacti, scattering birds as he goes. He arrives at a hole in the earth he has forever remembered as his starting point and gazes down upon the settlement.

They are gone.

From the look of it, they have been gone a long time.

He climbs downward and comes to a stone wall, beyond which is a wood shack where potatoes were stored belowground. Snakes are now nested inside. Lower down is the foundation of his house. Glass and plaster are mixed with the ashes, and weeds and mesquite have sprung up amid the ruin. The site is encircled by a ring of black stones, which he gathers up and tosses into the canyon. Then he stops for a moment and sweeps the horizon to see if he is being watched. But there is no one to watch him; he is alone. He descends to the bottom of the canyon and finds that everything has been burned: lean-tos, sheds, garden fences, and tents. Though the mud-brick houses are standing, the rooms inside are empty. A bubble of water still rises from the center of the canyon and sinks across a collapsed garden. A few stray stalks of corn are growing wild near the spring but the rest is husk and powder. If only Cassie could see this, he reasons, that shaft of light called forgiveness might be shining over him this minute.

He takes a seat on a nearby stone and permits himself a long drink of water from his canteen. It is warm but sweet and seems to wash away a taste of loathing that's been stuck in his throat for too long. They are scattered now, dust to dust, and he can only imagine that, like himself, they have all regained their senses and are soothed by the end of it all. Weaver, Harper, Gazer, and the others, all of them rediscovering old names for themselves. The sun begins to set in the west, and in no time it is like a hot red eye looking askance on the scene of a civilization's ruin. Ravel sets about gathering wood for the night and makes his camp within the remains of his destroyed house, picking a spot where he imagines his bed had been located before the

Mingling put an end to things. He hasn't had the last word, he's thinking. There is still time enough for encyclopedias of the myth and mystery of whatever it is that took place here. But he's already said enough. And done enough.

Paleontologists, to your shovels.

ABSOLUTE
LIGHT

TWO MILES away, in the middle of Yucca Flat, the bomb canister hangs from a floodlit balloon. Already the night's half-moon has set behind the rocks and the sky is wet with starlight. The last of the clouds have fled the desert and Ravel wends his way down the steep back of a gully, then stops to check his wristwatch for the seventh time. There is only one hour left and he still hasn't found a spot to camp in.

To his right, two or three miles off, a Marine division is already in place and the trucks have been pulled back to a safer distance. Up ahead, a series of painted rocks points the way to ground zero and Ravel skirts around them, keeping low to the ground so as not to be spotted. The night is warm and he is sweating in his heavy suit. He is tempted to remove the helmet but doesn't want to show his face. He has already come across other men in the same white suits and no one has taken any notice of him. Behind his mask he is as anonymous as they are, and if anyone stops to ask him what's up he can always flash his badge for identification.

Farther ahead, he comes upon a maze of trenches dug deep into the yellow earth. The maze is no longer used. It is too close to ground zero now that the kilotonnage has passed fifty. Ravel slides into a trench and makes his way around the periphery of the site to a spot where the floodlighting can't reach. Ahead of him is a row of wooden stakes with red ribbons, which he knows to be a delimiter for the point of no return. On the other side of the stakes is his dog cage. The animals are already inside and his partner, alone, is running them through their paces. In the stillness, Ravel can hear the man giving orders. Sit up, Twenty-seven. Sit. Good boy, don't die. Two-oh-one, roll over. Roll over, boy. Damn it, Two-oh-one, you're losing it fast. Hang tight, boy. Don't die.

When the man says Speak, they all begin to howl.

Ravel waits for a moment and then moves on to where the network of trenches ends. He finds himself in unfamiliar territory, near a high rise of rock and earth where the fill from the trenches has been deposited. He climbs a mound and looks out over the flat, where he can see a dark table of land covered by a bowl of deep sky and the illuminated balloon in the distance. In his waist pouch is a box of salt tablets, a compass, a new film badge, and a few dog biscuits. A water flask is clipped to his belt, but when he spins the cap open he can smell traces of whisky and he tosses it to the ground. Then he tears the film badge from his pocket and throws it to the wind. His thoughts drift to Mircea and Vance and for a moment he is very, very tired. He sits on the mound to catch his breath. Then there is nothing more to inventory except his own self and he knows that at that moment he is a whitened figure against the earth's darkness, nothing more or less, and a sweet and longed-for tranquility comes over him. Stretching out, he reclines at a forty-five-degree angle and can see through his visor the ebb and flow of the Nevada starlight, points of unreachable light, which, intersected with lines, might take on the aspect of an encephalogram, the visage of a deity, the contour of a far country, or the tracings of the map of a lifetime leading to this same spot.

The loudspeaker crackles and the warnings become louder and more insistent. The last trucks drive away from the floodlit circle and for long minutes the only sound he can hear is that of the barking dogs. Then the countdown begins at sixty and the last minute sounds out like a slow drumroll. Ravel slips off his helmet and breathes deeply of the night air, which seems sweet and clean after the hours he's spent inhaling the remnants of his own heavy breathing. He is finally aware of how alone he is. Out here, there is nothing but the machinery of night, the silent wheeling of the moon, and transparent overlays of sky moving soundlessly around the inert flats. In the distance at his back, a siren wails and the count reaches thirty. For a second or two he is shaking and so he stands to face the floodlit balloon. As the count reaches twenty, he is painfully aware of having learned no prayers, of being functionally ignorant of omniscience, the afterlife, hymnody, psalmody, libations or oblations, evensong, vespers, the refuge of ritual, catechism, unction. What he has in mind is combat pay and Mircea's nest egg. A painless death.

I've had time to think it over and this is the best I can come up with.

With only seconds remaining, he emerges from behind his rock. He has brought along his cane, but he decides he won't need it where he's going. Wherever he's headed, he can get there under his own steam.

When the count hits ten and he knows that nothing more can stop the detonation, neither hell nor high water, he limps into the floodlit arc and merges with the circle of light and then with the color white and then with no color at all.

WALKING
INTO
LIGHT

A F T E R New Year's, Randy pulls a few strings in the cowboy network and wangles a job for Ravel as an apprentice carpenter in Parowan. The pay is not much better than at the salvage, but the hours are daytime and Ravel is all for working with his hands. When he gets to Nashua Coe's office to break the news to him, he adds that he's already got his replacement lined up.

"What's his name?"

"Tom."

"Tom what?"

"Tom, uh, Thompson. He's been around a few times to keep me company and he already knows the ropes."

Nashua is suspicious. "I don't want no more college types like you. It's a job for an idiot or a reliable drunk."

Ravel assures him that Tom's just the man. "He doesn't drink but otherwise he fits the bill."

Pretending that he's doing Ravel a favor, Nashua tries to screw the salary down a notch, but Ravel holds fast. "Same job, same pay."

"So what're you, his lawyer?"

"In a manner of speaking."

"Bring him in tonight for a look-see. If he passes muster I won't hold you to that two weeks' notice we talked about."

. . .

His last night at the car salvage, Sandy tells him she's thinking of retiring from the business. "I was waiting for an offer to work Vegas, but I can't see myself in rhinestones. I'm more the home-spun type, don't you think?"

He nods, though he has his own opinions. For weeks now he's considered wandering into the shade of her tree for an hour of female mercy, anything to ease the heartache. But hired af-fection has always seemed like no affection at all and he's held off. Tom, she tells him, has no such reservations.

"I've been giving him credit for weeks now and he keeps telling me he'll come up with the cash. He's cute but he's not very bright. I don't think he gets the message."

"What message, Sandy?"

"I'm not interested in his money. And since he's been coming around I'm not interested in money, period. I keep turning down old regulars 'cause my heart's not in it. Just with Tom."

He tells her it sounds like love.

"Don't throw any more words like that in my face. Even the sloppiest old goat I take on in that backseat has mentioned the word at least once to get on my good side. I think I'm immune to it by now."

"What does Tom say?"

"Not much. He spends a lot of time just looking at me. At my *face*. It takes a while to get used to having a face but I'm getting the hang of it."

Through the remainder of the winter he sees Cassie at the be-ginnings and ends of his Sunday visits to Jered. Jered is used to him by now and the two of them spend more and more time just lazing around the new yard. The grass has grown in all too sparsely and they labor a long weekend reseeding with bags of filler while Cassie is off somewhere, staying out of sight. Don is still in and out of the woodwork and although Ravel worries over him Cassie has made it clear that he's not what she's after.

One February night he calls and she says not now. He is made to understand that she's not alone. Deep in the night she calls him back to congratulate him on the new job. "Are they treating you well?"

"With all due respect. I'm a novice but I'm giving it an honest effort. I'm told I pound a straight nail."

"Is that important?"

"To them it's the be-all and end-all."

"Then I'm glad."

When he mentions how time is running him down, she changes her tone. He's always there, she says, sanding at her to get to some layer he assumes she's reserved for him and him alone. "I want a man who will stick up for me when I'm slandered. A man who won't insult my hopes for a simple marriage. A quiet type who likes hunting and fishing and agrees that the starlight makes a fine decoration for the nighttime. Someone who won't drag stray animals in the door and keep them as pets. A man like that, or any reasonable facsimile."

He considers proposing a lamebrained carpenter with immaculate intentions but is afraid of another long-winded chain of called-up IOUs.

"So how's Tom?" she asks, and he can imagine it isn't just to break the silence.

"Just fine," he answers. "Reading third grade level already and happy as a clam."

"He's still one of them."

"One of whom?"

"Your inhuman crowd."

"Now which of us," he queries, "is being small in a world of midgets? We're talking about a man who was left in a plastic bag at the side of the freeway. This was in infancy. His twin never even made it to the charity ward. Time passed. Now you fill in the blanks."

There is a silence that neither of them knows how to break. Then Cassie says maybe it isn't Tom who frightens her but the Er.

Ravel tells her again that they are gone, dispersed. "I told you, I walked out there and there's nothing left. Everyone's gone, even the goats."

"It's a pastime for you, isn't it? Saying things you know I'd like to believe?"

"I'm minding my manners, Cassie. What more can you ask?"

"Impress me. Stay simple. Don't do *anything* out of the ordinary."

Life with Tom and Mircea is blessedly uneventful. Mircea feeds Tom, houses him, and teaches him to read, putting her lifetime of Christianity on the line of his education. As the words are imprinted like wood-burns into his memory, the man emerges from the bewildered skin of the boy and no one in the household is in the least surprised. For two thousand years the predominant theory of the Western world has been to treat the malicious with kindness and the moon will shine on bright and blue thereafter. Bathed in this same moonlight, Ravel takes a walk one night and, as requested by Tom, ends up at the salvage. Tom answers Ravel's tapping by opening the gate to let him in. None of this climbing the fence for old hands. "You got my message," he says.

Ravel nods. "You wrote it yourself?"

"Mircea helped."

"Well, I'm here. What's up?"

Tom calls down the alley for Sol, who's hiding behind a wrecked Fairlane in case Ravel turned out to be Nashua. "We got something to tell you," Tom says.

Heading with them toward the shack, Ravel comes across a pile of Tom's handiwork, a collection of hood ornaments, ancient chrome cones of winged women, naked women, circles filled with triangles, stars, and arrows pointing the way to the road or to heaven or to ground zero.

"That was my idea," Tom says. "To pick up all them statues.

I clean them and polish them myself. And Nashua's doing big business. Made five dollars for Nashua this week already."

Sol wants to know if Ravel is thirsty after the long walk. "I got apple juice," he says.

"What happened to the moonshine?"

"We're a bit short on cash. Besides, I'm cutting down."

Tom says Sol hasn't had much to drink in a week now. "He's behaved."

"That's a new word, Tom."

"Learned it yesterday."

Ravel declines the apple juice but is nonetheless led down the alley to the shack. All of Tom's possessions are there on the table. Shirts that Mircea's found at the Salvation Army, shoes, books, comb, pencil and pad, soap, towel, jeans. Turning to Ravel, Tom makes his lips move for words that won't come. It's like old times but he snaps out of it quickly. "I'm better now," he says. "I can read and I can write more than my own name. I still have blank spots in my head, but Sol fills them in for me."

Before Ravel can respond, Sol says he's found a place to hole up, a rent-free shack with two rooms south of town. "There's electricity but no plumbing and it needs paint real bad."

Ravel is slow in understanding but not eternally so. Somewhere in all of this lurks the word *home*; he doesn't even have to read lips to gather that much. Like a dope he asks if they need any money.

"Hell no," Sol answers. "I got me some work sweeping up at the Two Guns and Tom here is doing a sweet job on the night shift. We'll be fine."

"I'm wearing shoes," Tom says.

Looking at his feet, Ravel sees that it's true.

"And I can cook. And Nashua likes my work. He says the yard's never been so quiet."

It has taken Ravel up till now to realize that he's been asked here so that he can give his consent to the deal. There is ample fuel for optimism: the shoes on Tom's feet, the culinary skills, the shack, and talk of fresh paint. Ravel tells Tom that his permission isn't needed, but if it makes him feel better the answer is yes.

Then, no matter what Ravel says, Sol is intent on breaking out the apple juice, so they drink from Campbell's soup cans and smile at each other across the yellow light. Sol says aloud, "We could kill ourselves trying," and Ravel doesn't know what he means.

"It's the life," Tom tells him as an answer.

And in this flush of success, Ravel is smiling too. Then he tells them where to find a couch that could be reconditioned in his workshop.

"In the Heap," Tom says.

"Tucked inside a VW minibus," Ravel adds.

Sol says he thought he knew the yard inside out. "I never seen that couch."

Tom tells him it's where the Buddhists lived. "In Ravel's time."

Desert spring arrives early and the few saguaro in Roadside Business are topped with enormous blossoms that Mircea wishes would last year round. Randy has a new pup, courtesy of Tom, and spends a lot of his time teaching him old tricks, sitting and rolling over and speaking, all the tricks that Trash could never do. At sundown, the major takes his rifle into the backyard and guns down a dozen innocent bottles before retiring for the night. But the shooting doesn't last as long as it once did and Randy tells Ravel that the old man's heart has gone out of it. "He's figured out he'll never be perfect. The way he's carrying on, my guess is one of these days there'll be a bullet left for himself."

Ravel learns sanding and staining, how to prime a notch for a screw, how to slice an eighth of an inch from a board with a hand saw, and how to glue Formica sheeting to plywood planks. At his own insistence and expense, he masters the V-joint, and just for practice he tears down Mircea's old porch and puts up a new one in the space of a weekend. With Tom gone, Mircea casts around for new company, and for the first time Ravel can remember she even crosses the flat to have a sit with Randy while the pup rolls in the dirt at their feet.

One late-March morning Ravel is hard at work on a mahogany bookcase when a phone call from Mircea tells him to come quick. He doesn't have to ask twice where or why.

As he arrives at the clinic, Don is already coming out the door, his face flushed with disappointment.

"So?" Ravel asks him.

"So he's not mine. I got eyes."

"I thought it didn't make any difference. I thought you had a heart."

"It makes a difference," Don says. "You figure it out."

When Ravel gets to Cassie's room he finds that there are already flowers in his name, Mircea's doing no doubt. The card is blank and Cassie, smiling up from her bed, tells him he's free to fill it in anytime.

"It's a boy," she says, "and I'm naming him Michael."

"Like the archangel?"

"Like in row the boat ashore."

When he reaches for her hand she doesn't say no and they remain like that for a long time, just holding hands and grinning. Then she tells him that Don has been and gone. "I think I've seen the last of him."

"Does it matter?"

"No," she says. "It never really did. I had these notions of a man whose face I knew. Thinking of Jered and how I'd rather not be alone all my life. Fitting in with my own nature."

Ravel catches himself doing like Tom, just moving his lips in search of the words, but then Cassie smiles and that is the original sunburst he will remember for weeks on end. She says he doesn't have to worry so much.

"About what?"

"Me, Jered, Michael. I have something to confess."

He says he's listening.

"A few weeks ago I went out to visit Tom."

All Ravel can do is nod. Again he's reduced to sign language.

"He remembers me. I thought he would have forgotten by now. And Vance, he's just a nice man now. Not at all what I expected I'd find."

There is in him that sensation of a cloud moving away from the sun, a lightening of his burden, that Papago swirl of wandering closing in on itself once again. For a moment he imagines tears in her eyes and then, looking closely, sees they are for real. Bending low, he kisses her forehead and then her lips.

"Vance, will we forever be trading apologies like this?"

"Not if we're fast on our feet."

"Then let's be fast on our feet, Vance. For once and for all."

In Randy's borrowed pickup he drives straight to the main street and buys all he knows to buy. First a fire engine for Jered, who's been making siren noises of late, and then diapers, skin creams, Q-tips, cotton swabs, nose drops, cough syrup, pajamas, and whatever infant whatnot the store has to offer. Next he throws in a book of fables, kid stuff, with bears and witches and enchanted forests and wizards with long white beards. Someone is going to have to read these things aloud to them and, all things considered, he prefers that it be himself.

He drives back into Paragonah and puts everything in Cassie's bedroom and arranges the baby things just so. Later, looking out the kitchen window over a sinkful of dirty dishes, he is surprised to see rain. It is a broken rain and there are almost no clouds in sight. It is as though the rain is falling from nowhere.

He takes a can of beer from the refrigerator and sits on the back step to wait for Jered to get home from school. Before the world comes to its coda and time runs out on men walking into light for no apparent reason, he will read to him the story of

Beauty and the Beast. Or he will read to him whatever story he likes. Or if Jered doesn't want to hear a story but to tell one of his own, then Ravel will listen to him. When the rain falls in the desert, everything seems possible.

Later he will go in and wash the dishes and after that he might take a look around the house to see what it wants in the way of paint. He will choose a color the way others choose words. But for now he just sits on the stoop and sips from his dwindling can of beer and watches the rain that's falling on the Escalante Desert at the end of March: the rain that is falling on his house and on his eyelids and on the grass that grows green over his father's long-sought grave.

A NOTE ON THE TYPE

The text of this book was set in a digitized version of Electra, a typeface designed by W(illiam) A(ddison) Dwiggins for the Mergenthaler Linotype company and first made available in 1935. Electra cannot be classified as either "modern" or "old-style." It is not based on any historical model, and hence does not echo any particular period or style of type design. It avoids the extreme contrast between thick and thin elements that marks most modern faces, and is without eccentricities that interfere with reading. In general, Electra is a simple, readable typeface that attempts to give a feeling of fluidity, power, and speed.

Composed by PennSet, Inc., Bloomsburg, Pennsylvania

Printed and bound by The Haddon Craftsmen, Inc., Scranton, Pennsylvania

Typography and binding design by Dorothy S. Baker